Be Still My Heart

Jo James

PublishAmerica
Baltimore

© 2007 by Jo James.
All rights reserved. No part of this book may be reproduced, stored in a retrieval system or transmitted in any form or by any means without the prior written permission of the publishers, except by a reviewer who may quote brief passages in a review to be printed in a newspaper, magazine or journal.

First printing

All characters appearing in this work are fictitious. Any resemblance to real persons, living or dead, is purely coincidental.

ISBN: 1-4241-7715-4
PUBLISHED BY PUBLISHAMERICA, LLLP
www.publishamerica.com
Baltimore

Printed in the United States of America

Acknowledgments

My first debt of gratitude is to my husband Kirk. Without him this book would not have been written. When I told him I had written a book in my head and needed to write it down before I forgot it, and that I needed a typewriter ribbon, he laughed. He then said I needed to get checked out on the computer. I didn't even know how to turn one on. He not only gave me technical support, but gave me love and encouragement through the whole process.

To my children, Kelly Weir, Scott and Brad James. My heartfelt thanks for your love and interest. To my granddaughters, Lindsay Fetters and Kristin Weir, thanks for your help.

My sincere thanks to Nancy Sluis, who read the first draft of the book, then encouraged me to continue.

To Barbara Riegel, who first edited the story and made great suggestions. I joined her writing class after the manuscript was written, but I will be forever grateful to Barbara and to those in the class, Denise Terry, Elisabeth Boaz, and Suzie Massey for their help, suggestions and encouragement. As a first time author, I needed all the help I could get.

To Arlene Elkins and Caryl Herman, who helped with names, places and information in Kansas that I grew up with, but had since forgotten.

To my Aunt Helen Van Der Stelt for her corrections, constant encouragement, interest and believing in me.

To our dear friends Johnny and Anne Edmundson, and Leaky and Joyce Thornal, who came for a visit and all read the book. Thanks for your help editing and your encouragement.

And to all those who spurred me on with their enthusiastic support and help; Pat and Don Kunard, Chris Green, Sharon Latour, Elizabeth Young, Chris and Alissa Seiple, Pat O'Brien, Mary Perkins, Carole Lawrence, Aunt Mary Lippert and Donna Eisenbarth.

And finally, thanks to all those at PublishAmerica for their help in giving this story the light of day.

Chapter One

When Annie left her farmhouse in eastern Kansas it was a bitterly cold, clear, moonlit morning. Many hours later, she was in western Kansas where all she could see was an occasional farmhouse or barn dotting the flat landscape. A winter storm loomed ominously on the horizon as her lone car sped down the highway to Colorado Springs. Little did Annie know that she was embarking on a journey that would impact the rest of her life.

It was December 1963, the weekend between Christmas and New Year's. Annie and three of her college friends were on their way to Sarah's wedding at the Air Force Academy. Annie and Sarah had met their freshman year, and had become dear friends in a short while. They shared the same schedule and had spent many hours studying together. The entire time she had been Sarah's roommate Annie listened to her friend talk about how wonderful Steve was, and how much she loved him. The couple had met at a wedding two and a half years before; a long distance romance had been in progress ever since. Annie believed this was a match made in Heaven.

Light snow began to fall and the wind started howling. However, this did not diminish the spirits of the four young women. Their conversation was lively, interrupted with occasional outbursts of laughter.

When the snow started coming down in huge flakes, they still had a long way to go. The temperature was dropping and a sheet of ice was forming on the road. This forced Annie to slow down, and she could see a huge truck following them. Within minutes, the snow changed to sleet that sounded like pellets hitting the car. Now, the four women were quiet. Annie was thankful it wasn't dark yet. As they were coming down a hill, they suddenly spun out of control and then the car stopped abruptly, spanning a ditch. Annie opened the door, got out, lost her footing, and slid under the car. The ditch was solid ice. Martha opened her door, stepped out, slipped and quickly joined Annie in the ditch. Jenny and Nancy peered out of the window and Annie told them, "Please do *not* get out of the car!" The sleet was covering Annie and Martha. They shivered as neither one had a coat. Each one attempted to stand up and try to put a hand on to the car to steady herself. The result was the same each time; they were both in the slippery ditch, laughing.

By the time the truck driver came to their rescue, Annie and Martha were giggling like two young school girls. It was so slick the two women fell every time they tried to stand up. When he peered down to see if they were okay, the driver asked if he could help. Annie said, "Oh, I certainly hope so! Can you please pull my car out of this ditch?"

She and Martha tried again to stand up, but back down they went, laughing hysterically. The amused trucker went back to his rig to get a chain. Annie and Martha crawled on their hands and knees out of the ditch and then held onto the car to get back to their doors. Jenny helped pull Annie back in the driver's seat and Annie pulled in Martha. They both were exhausted from their ordeal, but thankful to be back in the car. They were still laughing as the trucker fastened the chain to the bumper and pulled them back onto the road. Annie thanked him profusely, and he kindly offered to follow them to Colorado Springs. She looked at the car and there wasn't a scratch on it. She was so thankful that everyone was okay. *I do believe Someone is watching over us.*

As they drove on, she was holding on so tight that she felt as if she was leaving her fingerprints in the steering wheel. Martha kept trying to figure out how many miles they had to go. Annie's adrenalin was still soaring from the mishap, and she was taking deep breaths trying to calm down. She knew she needed to relax, but under the circumstances, this was difficult. However, it was comforting to know their newfound guardian angel was following them.

After what seemed like an eternity, Nancy cried out, "I think I can see the lights of the city!"

When at last they came into Colorado Springs, the trucker flashed his lights and the girls waved a grateful goodbye.

Martha's map reading proved unnecessary as Sarah's directions were perfect. Relieved to be at their hotel, they rushed up to their rooms to change. Soon they would meet the groom they'd heard so much about. Eager to put a face to his reputation, they were back in the lobby in thirty minutes, surely a record breaking turnaround. Sarah and Steve awaited the foursome; Annie gave Sarah a hug, then whispered in her ear that she looked gorgeous. Steve, a handsome young man, could hardly take his eyes off Sarah. She was so lovely in her green dress; it was perfect with her red hair.

In the fall, Annie had helped Sarah do some of her shopping and it had been such a fun time. Sarah had lost her mom to colon cancer when she was ten. Her older sister, Sally, who had helped raise her, was now married and living in California with a new baby, so Annie was happy to assist. Their first find was the Kelly green dress for the rehearsal dinner. It was perfect, and spurred them on to look for a going away dress. The wedding dress had been purchased the previous year, just a week after Steve proposed. Looking for a nightgown was a hilarious shopping trip. Being extremely modest, Sarah wasn't sure she wanted to wear anything that was "see through." They laughed and giggled as they spent hours looking through the rack of lovely, but very sheer nightgowns. When she finally selected one, it was a lovely satiny gown; that was alluring, but opaque.

Sarah had planned every detail of the wedding; Annie wondered would it all get done with both Christmas and the wedding in one short period. However, not to worry, Sarah had a wonderful way of putting everything together and making it special.

That evening the wedding party gathered in the lobby of the hotel while waiting for a bus to take them to the chapel for the rehearsal, then on to a restaurant for the rehearsal dinner. Annie had never seen such well mannered young men, so clean cut and full of "Yes, ma'am," and "No, ma'am." She was amazed. When one of them asked if they had been caught in the storm, they related their slippery tale as "sliding all the way to Colorado Springs," but each took a turn telling a bit of the story. Conveniently, the bus arrived as the story ended. It was snowing again and the pavement was slick. Each of the cadets offered to take a lady's arm and help them to the bus. What chivalry!

Martha whispered to Annie, "I've never seen so many cute guys. Do they have to be cute to get into the Air Force Academy?"

At the Cadet Chapel, Annie was captivated by the tall spires that looked like they were extending into the sky. Once inside the Protestant chapel she stood staring. It was unique and impressive. At the end of each pew there was a propeller and on the backs of the pews were strips of metal. She had never seen anything like it.

Chaplain Farley explained where to stand and what to do. Annie was preoccupied by thoughts of which young man she would be walking down the aisle with, as she was five foot ten inches tall and hoped she wouldn't tower over a groomsman. A bit of a comic, the chaplain told the girls not to walk like birds when they came down the aisle, bobbing their heads and jerking to the music. He demonstrated what not to do as Martha played the organ. If there had been any tension before the rehearsal Chaplain Farley had made it disappear. He had everyone laughing.

Martha started playing the music and Nancy went down the aisle first, followed by Jenny, Annie, then Sally, Sarah's older sister, and then Sarah with her dad. Annie watched Sarah and her dad just before they started down the aisle. Sarah smiled at her dad with a look of pride; he was looking down at her with adoring eyes. In the tenderness of the moment, Annie felt a twinge of sadness, knowing this would never happen to her. When the music marked the end of the ceremony, everyone in the wedding party started walking back down the aisle with a groomsman. Annie took Brian's arm, relieved that he was so tall. Glancing up, she remembered what Martha had said about so many cute guys. She thought, *Wow, this young man is not only cute, he is handsome!*

Back on the bus, Brian sat down beside her. Martha smiled when she saw them. Annie knew what she was thinking and returned her smile.

"Brian, tell me about the chapel, it is most unusual."

"Well, it's made of steel, aluminum and glass and the seventeen spires extend one hundred fifty feet upward. Inside there are three separate chapels; a Protestant, a Catholic and a Jewish one, and they can all be used at the same time. There is also an all-faith room for people to have meetings. The pews in the Protestant chapel were made so that the end of each pew resembles a World War I airplane propeller. The backs of the pews are capped by a strip of aluminum similar to the leading edge of a fighter aircraft wing. It was just finished this year. We feel very fortunate to have it."

They exchanged the usual "getting to know you" routine of where do you live, what are you studying in school. Annie said she was a junior at Kansas State. When Brian asked why she chose Kansas State, she told him she had grown up not far from Manhattan, Kansas, and she had decided as a young girl that is where she would go to college. She had cheered for their football and basketball teams for years before she had actually thought of college.

Brian seemed amused at this, so she continued, "I'm from a very small town and we only had six man football; that is all the other small surrounding towns had. The first time I attended a college game, I couldn't believe there were so many men on the field. Six man football was very straightforward and easy to follow. College football was mass confusion for me at first." Brian was grinning at her through the story. He shook his head and said he had never even heard of six man football. She wondered if perhaps he didn't think she was a "country come to town" girl.

Arriving at the restaurant they were escorted to a large private room where the rehearsal dinner was to be held. Steve's mother had placed beautiful holly, ivy and red rose centerpieces on each table. They looked to see where they were to be seated and Brian was disappointed that he was not at the same table with Annie. They stood and talked for a few minutes, then went to their separate tables.

Martha could barely contain herself once Brian was out of earshot. "Well, a really cute one found you, didn't he?"

"He did indeed," she nodded, smiling. Brian was two tables away. Every time Annie checked Brian was staring at her.

The dinner was delicious, starting with an antipasto, then on to veal scallopini and ending with Amaretto cheesecake and coffee. There were numerous speeches and toasts and many, many laughs. Sarah's dad gave a very moving speech about Sarah. He said she had always been a "daddy's girl" and that they had gone fishing and horseback riding since she was a little girl. Annie felt a longing, as she had done these same things with her dad. He ended by saying that he was proud to welcome Steve into their family.

Brian came over to the table after dessert, sat down and asked what Annie was doing before the wedding. She told him she had a bridesmaid brunch at 9:30 in the morning. When she said her hairdresser appointment wasn't until late in the afternoon, they agreed he could pick her up after the bridesmaid brunch to show her around. She could barely control her excitement.

On the bus, Brian sat beside her, again, this time taking her hand as Annie asked about his family and his years at the academy. She had never met anyone quite like this young man that was showing her so much attention. He was kind, confident, considerate, and the most polite young man she had ever met. They said their goodnight in the lobby before she went up to her room.

Martha was waiting. "I want to hear all about him."

"Oh Martha, he is a 'be still my heart' young man for me. He brings new meaning to the phrase 'tall, dark and handsome.' He's asked me to go out with him tomorrow after brunch. I said I would. He's from Des Moines, Iowa. His dad is a doctor. His mother is a nurse. He has two brothers and a sister. This is his third year at the academy. He is so nice, and I really do like him." She hadn't taken a breath as the words flew out of her.

She remained breathless as she and Martha talked in the dark for what seemed like hours, yet she felt like she hadn't said it all. They finally decided to get some sleep. It had been a very long day. Annie closed her eyes and felt as if she were still moving down the road.

Sarah's Aunt Polly was the hostess for the brunch the next morning. She had reserved a private room for the festive occasion. Large round tables were set with green tablecloths; in the center of each one was a hurricane lamp with a white candle, surrounded with a cone wreath. Sunlight was streaming in, and through the windows one could see a blanket of snow covering the evergreen trees and the ground below. Sarah looked lovely surrounded by her family and bridesmaids. She couldn't believe that everything was going according to her plan. The bridesmaids had the pleasure of meeting Sarah's grandmothers, who beamed with pride. Grandma Newton was a tall, elegant woman with her hair in a French twist, while Grandma Emerson was a smaller gray-haired lady and overtly warm and charming. Both wanted to meet Sarah's friends. The bridesmaids received silver picture frames and would receive a wedding picture at a later date. When the brunch was over, Annie went up to her room and changed into a navy-blue pair of slacks and a new navy and white sweater she had received for Christmas. She brushed her teeth, combed her hair, pinched her cheeks and put on lipstick, then smiled into the mirror and tried to calm her racing heart before going down to the lobby where Brian was waiting for her.

Annie got into his bright red Ford Mustang as Brian held the door. She was overjoyed to be treated with such respect, and was impressed with his thoughtfulness. He had picked up deli sandwiches, chips, pickles and sodas for their drive up into the mountains. The view from the first lookout spot was breathtaking. She was glad to eat in the car and enjoy the vista of the majestic mountains. Brian asked if she would like to go for a short walk. Annie was really cold when they returned to the car fifteen minutes later. She took off her coat and turned around to put it in the back seat so it wouldn't get wrinkled. When she did this, her sweater came up and exposed her bare back. Brian couldn't resist the temptation and put his cold hands on her back. Annie yelled, and as she did, Brian pulled her into his arms and kissed her.

Holding her in his arms, he looked down at her smiling, and asked, "Why did you let me do that?"

"Because, I wanted you to."

"You have the most beautiful blue eyes I've ever seen, Annie."

"Thank you. I love your dimples, Brian; I always wanted dimples when I was a little girl. I would take hair pins and push them into my cheeks hoping I would make dimples, but, as you can see, it didn't work." He flashed another smile and showed his dimples again, much to her delight.

"Is there someone special in your life now, Annie?"

"Not at the moment, but let me ask you the same question. Do you have a girlfriend?"

He casually answered that he had been dating someone named Amy for over two years. Annie sat upright in the seat, looked at him, and said, "What are you doing up here kissing me if you have a serious girlfriend?"

He thought for a moment. "Annie, I haven't been able to take my eyes off of you since you walked into the hotel yesterday." He kissed her again and his hand slipped under her sweater and onto her bare back.

She shook her head and murmured, "Uh, Uh," then pulled away from him.

"What's the matter?"

Annie turned around in the seat and snapped, "What part of 'no' do you not understand?" Then she added, "I think you need to take me back to the hotel."

Brian took her hand and said softly, "I'm really sorry if I upset you, Annie."

Neither one spoke on the way back to the hotel. There was a chilly atmosphere in the car as well as outside as they drove through a winter wonderland. The evergreen trees were laden with snow and the branches were sagging under the load.

When they arrived, Brian turned to Annie and said, "Please forgive me, Annie. That will not happen again."

She squeezed his hand.

In her room, she felt dismayed about Brian. He had apologized and seemed genuinely concerned that he had upset her. She had been so impressed with everything else about him. *Do I want to get to know him better? Why would he do something like that? Enough of that, it's time to get back in the wedding mode.*

She showered and went to her hair appointment. The hairdresser did a great job, and she thought the final result was quite stunning. Her long blonde hair was pulled up in a bun with curls hanging from the center with a few soft curls around her face. They'd done her makeup more dramatically than she'd have been able to do herself.

The entourage of ladies, garment bags in hand, gathered once again in the lobby awaiting the arrival of the bus. Annie was amazed that everyone looked so glamorous. The hairdresser had also done a marvelous job with all of her friends. Typically, they only went to a hairdresser to get a hair cut or a permanent, so having their hair styled was a special treat. They all had on more makeup than usual and they all were dazzling. The ladies were bubbly, commenting on how pretty they all looked. They left promptly at 5:30, as scheduled. They would change clothes at the chapel. The gentlemen would leave at 6:00. This would prevent the bride and groom from seeing each other before the wedding.

The bridesmaids wore forest green gowns with green embossed ivy, an empire waist and tapered long sleeves. The bow tied high at the back had an elegant effect. They all had green shoes to match. Each woman carried a bouquet of red roses with holly and ivy.

Standing at the back of the chapel, Annie felt a shiver run through her as she gazed at the beautiful flowers. Long-stemmed roses with holly and ivy were on the altar and hung at the end of each pew. Martha came in and began playing Sarah and Steve's favorite songs; "Because God Made You Mine" and "Pachelbel's Canon in D." The photographer began taking pictures of the bride and the ladies in the wedding party. Annie thought Sarah was prettier than any bride she'd ever seen. Her gown had a wide décolleté neckline with hand clipped Chantilly lace and tapered long lace sleeves. The sweeping train was a mass of ruffles. She looked regal with her hair pulled back from her face, veil set perfectly into her hair. A small lace inset was around the tiara, and the silk illusion fell below her waist. She carried a bouquet of white roses, with ivy cascading down past her knees.

When Sarah's dad opened the dressing room door, music filled the room. Calmly, Sarah hugged Annie before they all lined up to go into the chapel. When it was Annie's turn to start down the aisle and face the altar, she was nearly overcome when she saw all the handsome young men in their dress blue uniforms standing at the front of the chapel. What a sight to behold! It made her weak in the knees. She made eye contact with Brian as she got closer. When he winked at her, she couldn't help but smile back at him. At the altar, all the bridesmaids turned around and watched Sally coming down the aisle. Finally, the wedding march began. Sarah and her dad made their way down the aisle. The ceremony was beautiful, with the bride and groom exchanging their vows, some of which they had written.

Annie was so touched by the ceremony that she was at the point of tears. When the recessional started, she had to take a deep breath before taking Brian's arm to return down the aisle. At the back of the chapel, Brian asked if she were okay, and she confessed she was more than a bit emotional. "Weddings always do this to me."

The wedding reception was held at the Antlers Adams Mark Hotel where they were staying. As they walked into the ballroom, the long buffet caught their eye. In the center of the buffet table was an enormous ice sculpture of an F-100 fighter jet. At one end was roast beef being carved by a waiter. At the other end were shrimp, oysters and salmon, waiting to be devoured. The table was filled with an assortment of salads, vegetables and fresh fruit.

Annie and Brian were seated together for dinner. When the band played, they waited until the traditional dances were finished before Brian asked her to dance. He held her close, and when the band played "September Song," which had always been a favorite of Annie's, he hugged her tight. They danced almost every dance together. When "Memories Are Made of This," a Dean Martin hit song was played, Annie thought, *How true this is!*

Drum rolls from the band announced it was time to cut the cake. The five layer lemon cake was covered with icing roses. The top layer of the cake had fragrant lemon leaves topped with fresh white roses and a miniature bride and groom.

After finishing with cake and coffee, Sarah walked up the steps to the stage and threw her garter to a lucky groomsman. The ladies in the wedding party gathered around twittering like hungry birds, hoping to catch the bridal bouquet. When the bouquet flew into Annie's hands, she couldn't believe it. This gave her a rush of excitement. *Maybe I will be the next bride?* Annie didn't want the evening to end. She enjoyed talking to Brian and loved his gentleness. He had an amusing sense of humor that was very appealing. Annie and Brian danced until the band played "Goodnight Sweetheart."

Brian walked Annie up to her room and she told him what a wonderful weekend it had been and how much she had enjoyed being with him. He started to kiss her goodnight when the elevator bell rang. He smiled with his darling dimples showing and Annie could hardly control her laughter. They waited until the people got into their room, then he started to kiss her again; a door opened and several people came toward the elevator. The elevator door closed and he started to kiss her again when the bell rang on the other elevator.

They were both trying to contain their laughter when Brian whispered to her, "Would you like to go kiss in the car?" She was too amused to answer, but shook her head. He finally kissed her goodnight and they agreed to meet for breakfast at 7:00. They had to get up early as Annie and her friends had more than five hundred miles to drive the next day.

BE STILL MY HEART

In the hotel dining room, Brian and Annie exchanged addresses and phone numbers after they finished breakfast. They said their goodbyes in the parking lot of the hotel. She didn't want to leave, but knew that she had no other choice.

The drive back through Kansas was uneventful, but lively, with excited talk about the wedding and their special memories. They let Jenny off in Hayes and Martha in Smith Center. After leaving Nancy in Salina, Annie began the last leg of the trip alone. Her thoughts were immediately of Brian and all they had talked about. She was impressed with his impeccable manners. She realized she was really impressed with everything about him, with the exception of his fast hands. There were fleeting thoughts of Amy, but she just wanted to enjoy the moment and the wonderful feeling that soared through her. With all his attention throughout the weekend, Annie found it hard to imagine that he could also have a serious relationship elsewhere.

She was a weary traveler as she drove down the lane to the house after a fourteen hour drive. Smiling to herself when she saw the light in the window, she hurried into the house and bounded up the stairs to see her mom. Dressed in a flannel nightgown, with brush rollers in her hair, her mom gave her a hug. "You must be exhausted, Annie. Tell me all about the wedding."

Sitting on the bed, Annie told her about the wonderful young man she couldn't get out of her mind. She described Brian in greater detail than the wedding itself.

"Brian did tell me he had a girlfriend at home in Iowa, that he had been dating for two years. This gives me an uneasy feeling. I'm just assuming, but dating someone for two years sounds pretty serious to me." Her mom listened intently to everything she said. Finally, Annie stood up and stretched. "I absolutely loved being with him this weekend." She yawned, then smiled at her mom, and said, "I'll leave you with that. Goodnight." As she started to walk out of her room, she looked back, saying, "Thanks for listening, I know you have to get up early to go to work. I'm going to sleep in."

As soon as Annie opened her eyes at 10:00, she thought of Brian. She got up and decided to call Julie and tell her about the "be still my heart" young man she had met. She and Julie had been close friends since kindergarten and had shared many of their thoughts and feelings with each other. She really missed not having Julie at college, but they were still very close and Annie always looked forward to spending time with her when she was at home. They talked for a while and decided that Julie should come for lunch. After lunch, they had a fun afternoon and talked non-stop for hours. Julie left, and, as soon as Annie closed the door, the phone rang. She hurried to answer the wall phone in the kitchen. As soon as she heard Brian's voice, she had to sit down; he could make her heart race just hearing his voice.

"Annie, I'm missing you. I just wanted to let you know what a wonderful weekend I had with you. How was your trip home?"

"It was a long day, but everything went well. I was exhausted when I got home, and then I stayed up until after midnight talking to my mom, but I did get to sleep in this morning. What did you do today?"

"I got up this morning and went for a run, then tried to study, but fell asleep over my books. I think I'm still recovering from the weekend. What did you do?"

"I called my best friend Julie this morning to report on the weekend. She came out and we ate lunch together and I was just walking back in the door after telling her goodbye when you called. I did help my brother Tom for a few minutes this morning. He needed me to open and close gates to move some cows. I wasn't out there very long because it was freezing."

"Annie, I wanted to let you know that I did call Amy this afternoon to tell her that I no longer wanted to see her. She was very upset and hung up in tears."

"Thanks for letting me know that, Brian. I'll be honest with you; it worried me that you had been going with her for two years and seemed to dismiss her so casually."

"I miss you, Annie; I'll be looking for a letter from you."

After he said goodbye, Annie felt her heart soar. She already missed him.

Chapter Two

January arrived with a major snowstorm that shut down the roads for several days. Soon after, Annie drove to Manhattan to prepare for finals. The Kansas State sidewalks were narrow, one-way trenches snaking through the campus. What few paths that existed were icy and snow was piled everywhere.

One evening, Annie and her friend Gwen, a Home Ec. major from Great Bend, Kansas, went to the library to do some research for papers they were writing. Rules required co-ed's to have a partner in order to go to the library in the evening so no one would have to walk home alone. Unfortunately for Annie, Gwen met her heart-throb Phillip at the library. She had had a crush on Phillip for months before he finally asked her for a date. When it came time to go back to the dorm, she came to tell Annie that she was going with Philip. When Annie went downstairs, she couldn't see anyone she knew from the dorm, and curfew was at ten o'clock. Walking alone, in the shadow of the science building, she heard footsteps crunching in the snow behind her. She started walking faster; the footsteps were getting closer and closer. Passing a street light, she looked back to see a tall man with a turban on his head just yards behind her. Then Annie's heart raced even more. She had her snow boots on and running fast was almost impossible. The dark wooded area between the science building and her dorm loomed in front of her. She remembered there were still icy patches near the creek. Panic stricken, she started running, and so did the man behind her. She could still hear him closing in, but didn't know how far away he was. Fear propelled her faster than she thought possible; her boots skidded on the ice. She didn't look back, she just ran as fast as she could. She could see her breath as she gasped for air. She arrived safely and ran up the steps, taking them two at a time. Inside the dorm, she was breathing so hard that the girl at the desk asked if she was okay. She could only nod her head. Heart still pounding, Annie went immediately to Gwen's room and after explaining what had happened, told her, "Don't ever do that to me again. The next time you want to come home with Philip, I'm coming with you!"

Annie was surprised to see the photograph envelope in her mailbox at the beginning of the new semester. Sarah was just too efficient for words. She knew she would save the newlywed portrait forever. The formal shot of the bridesmaids at the altar was a classic, too, a keepsake for her scrapbook. The last photo showed Annie and Brian dancing. Happy memories flooded back. Annie would keep this one on her desk.

The next time Brian called, she told him she had a picture of them on her desk, and described it to him. He asked her if she would go home with him when school was out and meet his parents, and she said she would be happy to go. Annie was excited just thinking about being with Brian for days at a time.

They wrote letters to each other several times a week and Brian called her almost every weekend, which was a joy. He surprised her with roses on Valentine's Day, which she loved. No one had ever sent her a dozen long stemmed roses! She thought of him every morning when she opened her eyes and said a prayer for him every night before she went to sleep. She was sure this was the man of her dreams. She had dated lots of guys, but she had never felt like this about anyone. Annie looked forward to the end of May when the semester was finished, and she would go with Brian to meet his family in Iowa. How was she ever going to be able to concentrate for an entire semester with her head in the clouds?

Once home, she was so excited about seeing Brian and going home with him she could hardly think. She had never gone home with a guy before and was a bit nervous about the whole thing. As she unpacked her belongings, a feeling of contentment filled her. Just being in her room again in familiar surroundings was comforting. Standing at the window, she looked out over the pasture and smiled at the beauty before her. The lush green grass, and everywhere she looked the cows were grazing and tending to their calves.

Annie ran out to help when she saw her mom coming up the walk carrying bags of groceries. Her mother looked so pretty in her suit. Although she was tall and beginning to get gray hair in a few places, she looked young for her age. Elizabeth had started working in the bank a year after Annie's dad was killed.

"What are we having for supper? I'm starving! I can't wait to have some of your cooking. We have been having what we call 'mystery meat' at school; no one knows what it is, and we're afraid to ask."

Her mom gave her a loving hug. Annie loved the fragrance of Channel No. 5 that her mom wore. "I have a chicken casserole in the refrigerator and fresh spinach from the garden. I thought I would do a fresh spinach salad with bacon, and I've baked 'dilly bread' for you."

"Oh, Mom, that sounds yummy."

The next afternoon, Annie was out weeding the vegetable garden when she heard a car coming in the lane. She ran to see if it was Brian. When he got out of his Mustang, he held his arms out as she ran toward him. How wonderful it was to be in his arms again and have him kiss her. She didn't want him to let her go. They took his things into the house and she showed him to the guest bedroom down the hall from hers. It had a carved walnut four poster bed that had belonged to her dad's parents. There was a lovely Goose Track quilt in red and yellow on the bed that Grandma Stewart had made many years ago.

Annie had been cooking and cleaning all day. She was preparing oven-fried chicken, potato salad, peas from the garden, a salad of watercress from the spring in the pasture, and strawberry-rhubarb pie. She loved to cook and had learned at her mother's side since she was so little she had to stand on a stool to reach the counter.

Annie's mom came in the kitchen door just as they were coming downstairs. "Mom, come and meet Brian. Brian, this is my mom." Elizabeth shook his hand.

"I'm pleased to meet you, ma'am."

"How was your trip?"

"It was good, thank you. I usually drive north through Colorado and then go straight east until I get to Des Moines. I've never driven through Kansas just before the wheat harvest. There are miles and miles of wheat fields in western Kansas."

After Annie made the introductions, she could tell her mom was impressed with Brian when she asked him to call her Elizabeth. Relieved, she left them talking in the living room while she went to the kitchen to get supper on the table. She filled the serving bowls and took everything to the table. Brian pulled out a chair for Elizabeth, and another for Annie before he sat down. Looking at the spread before him, he asked "Annie, did you fix all of this?"

Proudly, she said, "Yes, I did."

During dinner, Brian talked about his routine at the academy, how rigorous it was. He was looking forward to a few weeks of rest. He was obviously enjoying the meal as he had second helpings of almost everything.

"Annie, you are a great cook. I've never had strawberry-rhubarb pie before. It was delicious."

After dinner, Brian helped Annie with the dishes. Elizabeth went to sit down with her cup of tea and read the *Topeka Daily*

Capital. It was a lovely evening, and Annie told him she wanted to show him her favorite place on the farm where she had loved to play from the time she was a little girl. They climbed the fence and walked down to the creek in the pasture. She cautioned Brian to be careful where he stepped as "cow pies" were everywhere. His eyes were on the ground from this moment on. Annie smiled to herself and was sure Brian had never before had to navigate through a pasture of "cow pies." A soft breeze was blowing and just barely moving the leaves on the cottonwood trees that lined the creek. There was a large flat rock near the water that was her special spot to sit and listen to the creek.

Brian sat down beside her on the warm limestone. He took her in his arms. They sat, sharing the warmth of the spot and each other. Gently, he kissed her neck. "Annie, I'm in love with you."

She smiled and said, "Oh, Brian, I love you, too. You make me so happy."

They stayed there until it was almost dark, then walked back to the house holding hands. Annie had never been happier.

The next morning, Annie came downstairs before Brian. Her mom was cooking breakfast dressed for work, but wearing the Sunbonnet Sue apron that Annie had made in high school Home Economics. Elizabeth's eyes sparkled when she smiled.

Annie whispered, "What do you think?" Her mom nodded without breaking the smile.

Just then, Brian appeared in the doorway. "Something sure smells good."

"Mom made biscuits for us this morning, and this is a special treat. Biscuits are usually reserved for weekends."

Elizabeth asked, "Did you sleep well, Brain?"

"Yes, ma'am, I did. Just being able to sleep past 5:00 is a treat for me."

They gathered around the table and enjoyed a hearty

breakfast. Brian devoured the remainder of the biscuits and homemade strawberry jam.

As Brian loaded the car, Annie's brother Tom drove in the driveway. Tom was tall and blond like Annie, but had a rugged outdoor look about him. He got out of his pickup, walked over to Brian and introduced himself. They shook hands. Looking Brian straight in the eyes he said, "I wish I had more time to talk to you about my sister. I'm assuming you're serious about her or you wouldn't have asked her to go home with you." He had not meant to sound threatening, but it came out harsher than either guy had anticipated.

"I'm serious about Annie. The first time I saw her, I was attracted to her and that has only increased with time. She is a beautiful young woman, but she has inner beauty as well."

"Brian, she is very special to me. I expect you to treat her with respect at all times."

Out of earshot, Annie came to the car carrying her overnight case and purse. She smiled at her older brother. She could just imagine what Tom had been saying. His face was warm, but serious. After quick hugs and goodbyes to Tom and Elizabeth, they were on their way. Annie looked back to see her mom, so attractive and stately as she stood by the gate and waved to them as they drove down the lane.

It took them seven hours to get to Des Moines. They talked all the way, sharing their thoughts and dreams. Brian wanted to be a fighter pilot more than anything. After graduation, he hoped to go to pilot training for a year, followed by lead-in training to a fighter assignment. Annie was studying "foods and nutrition." She had serious goals, too. Her dream was to work in a hospital as a nutritional counselor. She still had a year of college, plus an internship year at a teaching hospital. She also hoped to be a mom one day, as she absolutely adored children. When her nephew Paul was born, Annie could hardly stay away from him.

Brian's house was a big red brick home set back from the street with a circle drive lined with trees. It was certainly more formal than the farmhouse where Tom and Annie grew up, but this house and the surroundings exuded their own warm welcome.

Brian had just finished giving her a grand house tour when his dad arrived. Jon was a handsome older version of Brian. He was so happy to see them that he gave them both a hug. They each got a glass of iced tea and went out and sat on the patio. There were large white pots of red geraniums with blue lobelia trailing from them, looking very patriotic. Easy talk ensued on the patio.

When Sue, Brian's mom, came home with groceries, Annie went into the kitchen to help her. She still wore her nurse's uniform and looked tired to Annie. A pleasant woman with short dark hair, she excused herself as she took off her shoes; she'd been on her feet all day long. They talked all the time they worked, putting the meal together. Annie was pleased when Sue asked her to get some glasses out of the cabinet, as she was too short to reach them.

While they were working in the kitchen, the men were cooking steaks on the patio grill. It wasn't long before Sue and Annie carried the rest of the fixings outdoors. They enjoyed a delicious meal and sat around the table until it was dark, watching the moon rise and move through the trees. The stars twinkled in the sky. Conversation never lagged. It seemed they'd known one another for ages. Both Jon and Sue were gracious hosts. Brian offered to do dishes with Annie. He wanted to give his parents a break since they had to get up early for work.

When they finished in the kitchen, Brian took her in his arms and they kissed. He smiled down at her and said, "I could get used to this."

"Get used to what, doing dishes or kissing?" They both laughed.

"As long as it's with you, I could get used to both."

The next morning, Brian brought coffee to her in her room. She ran her fingers through her hair, sat up in bed and put her pillow behind her. "You are such a dear to bring me coffee in bed, but you could have given me a minute to put on my robe." She was embarrassed in her batiste nightgown, thankful that it had tiny tucks in the front. She pulled up the bed linen modestly. He didn't say a word. Annie found him absolutely irresistible. Those dimples would be her undoing. He seemed to be enjoying himself and was in no hurry to leave, so she finally had to say, "If you'll go downstairs, I'll get dressed and fix us some breakfast."

After a full meal of scrambled eggs, bacon, toast, orange juice and coffee, they sat on the couch and whiled away the morning, talking and drinking more coffee. With both parents at work, they had the house to themselves.

After lunch, they walked for about an hour. Back at the house, they sat on the couch and kissed some more. Annie told him it took a long time to catch up on five months of missed kisses. So when Brian's dad came in and asked what they were doing, Brian's quick reply was, "Annie says we're catching up on five months of missed kisses."

His dad had a quizzical look on his face. "Can you do that?"

Brian grinned, and said, "We'll let you know."

With a pitcher of iced tea, Jon invited them to the patio. As soon as they'd settled around the table, the telephone rang. Brian went to answer it.

Jon turned to Annie and asked, "Tell me about your family."

She started by telling him that her dad had been killed in a tractor accident when she was thirteen. Her brother Tom had been managing the farm ever since.

"He was a senior in high school when the accident happened. He had planned to go to college, but decided he needed to stay home and help Mom. A year later, Mom started working at the bank so there would be enough money to send me to college.

Tom married Marilyn, his high school sweetheart and they rented a farm about four miles away. They have a little boy eighteen months old. We're a very close family. My brother is very protective of me and is really wonderful help for our mom. She prefers that I come home from school and help her rather than try to find a job, as she gets so far behind with all the extra work in the summer. So I go home and wash and iron, cook and clean, mow the yard, weed the garden, make jams, jellies and pickles and do whatever else is needed. I also try to go every week and help my grandmother while I'm home. I sometimes help Tom in the hayfield and I love to babysit little Paul. He is precious." Jon sat quietly and listened as Annie told him the story.

Brian came back to the patio. An old high school friend had called to invite him and Annie to a cookout and dance at Bob Cooper's home on Saturday night. It would be a get-together for all of the college students on summer vacation. Touching Annie's shoulder gently, he added, "Amy will be there. If that's a problem, we don't need to go."

Annie didn't hesitate. "It's fine with me if we go."

"Are you sure? I don't want you to be uncomfortable."

"Yes, I'm sure. You'll enjoy seeing your friends and I look forward to meeting them." She didn't admit to Brian that she was curious about Amy.

Jon added nothing. His raised eyebrows may have indicated he was simply surprised at Annie's reaction.

Bob Cooper's backyard was set up with tables for the picnic. Some of the guys were charcoaling hamburgers and hot dogs, and a buffet table offered baked beans, coleslaw, potato salad and brownies. Nearby, the cement basketball court would serve as the dance floor. The band began with a lively tune from the Beatles, "I Want to Hold Your Hand." The group loved it and some sang along. As they danced to "Love Me Tender," by Elvis Presley, Brian told her about some of his closest friends and tried to help her with their names. Annie knew she would never be able to remember all the names of the people she met. Brian was a great dancer. "Unforgettable," by Nat King Cole, was a "ladies' choice" and of course her choice was Brian. Annie thought *this tune was very apropos.* Halfway through the number, a cute girl with short dark hair and huge brown eyes tapped Annie on the shoulder to cut in. Annie just smiled, walked off the dance floor and went to get a Coke.

She didn't have time to worry too much about her competition as a guy she'd just met said, "I would ask you to dance, but this is 'ladies' choice' and that wouldn't be right."

For the life of her she couldn't remember his name when she looked up at him and asked, "May I have this dance?"

Just as they started to dance, he told her, "The girl dancing with Brian is Amy; she still has 'a thing' for him."

Annie raised her eyebrows. "Really?"

When the music stopped, Annie turned to see where Brian was. She couldn't believe what she was seeing. Brian was standing on the dance floor with Amy all but hanging from his neck by both arms. Music stopped, *why were they just standing there talking?* Annie's heart was pounding. *What is he doing?* She wasn't the only one wondering. Everyone was looking at them and then looking at her to see what her reaction would be. She started taking deep breaths to calm herself. It seemed like an eternity before Brian walked over, Amy at his side. By the time he reached her, her heart was beating in her throat. He introduced her to Amy. Annie could tell Brian was uncomfortable with the situation and when the music began again he took her back to the dance floor.

"I really didn't expect that to happen," he said, pulling her close.

As soon as they got in the Mustang, Brian apologized. He hadn't wanted to make a scene and that was the reason that he had remained on the dance floor with Amy. Suddenly, all the pent-up emotion that she had felt overflowed and she snapped. "Well, perhaps you didn't want to make a scene, but you did anyway. It appeared to me that everyone there was watching you and Amy, then staring at me to see what my reaction would be. Why couldn't you have just walked away? I didn't appreciate your behavior one bit!"

Brian defended himself. "Annie, I did ask you if you wanted to go to the dance and you said that you did."

Annie's eyes narrowed. "The reason I said I wanted to go to the dance was because I was thinking of you. I knew you'd want to see your friends. But make no mistake, you miss the point if you think this has anything to do with going to the dance. It was your behavior at the dance that is the problem for me." She was silent for a moment before adding, "I somehow thought that you were serious, cared for me so much that you brought me home to meet your family."

"I do care about you, Annie. I'm sorry that I put you in a terrible situation. Surely, you know that I love you. I wouldn't purposely do anything to hurt you."

"Somehow, I didn't feel very loved with you standing on the dance floor with Amy's arms around you, and you not doing anything to stop it." Her emotions were showing. Tears welled in her eyes.

When they pulled in the driveway, Brian stopped the car and apologized again. They sat there and talked for quite a while. Brian told her, "Amy was flirting with me on the dance floor. She told me that she missed not seeing me any more."

"What did you tell her when she said that?"

"I told her again that I wouldn't be seeing her anymore. She didn't like my answer."

Annie was emotionally spent. She told Brian goodnight. They didn't have their lingering goodnight kisses that they had had since they arrived. Annie walked upstairs by herself, went to her room and closed the door. She put on her nightgown and sat up in bed hugging her knees to her chest. Moonlight was streaming in the window as she stared at the wall. She was bombarded by thoughts of wonder and with doubts about Brian. *Was he being honest? Does he really love me? Was he enjoying Amy's flirtations?* She sat there and mulled these thoughts over in her mind. She had no idea how much time passed before she realized she needed to get some sleep. She slipped out of bed and went down the hall to the bathroom. On the way back, Brian was standing in the hallway. He pulled her into his arms. "Annie, I can't sleep because I've upset you."

She whispered softly, "I haven't been able to sleep either. I've been sitting up in bed thinking about us."

"I'm so sorry that I upset and embarrassed you. Please see it in your heart to forgive me," he whispered in her ear. "I love you, Annie." He kissed her and held her close. Her tension drained away as he held her in his arms. She said goodnight and started to walk back to her room, then turned around and saw him standing in the moonlight. The smile on his face beckoned her to him. She walked back for another kiss. *Sometimes you need to stop and do something that purely delights you.*

On Sunday they went to the First Methodist Church as a family and, afterward, joined Grandma and Grandpa Kendall at the Chicken House Restaurant for lunch so they could meet Annie. Grandpa Kendall had Annie sit down beside him. He was a tall, wiry man with a head of thick white hair and bushy eyebrows. He asked her dozens of questions about school and where she grew up. Then he said, "I think it is a real shame that you two have to wait a whole year to get married, since Brian can't get married while attending the academy."

Annie was a bit overwhelmed at this and sheepishly replied, "Brian hasn't asked me to marry him."

Grandpa Kendall frowned and said, "Well, that boy isn't as smart as I thought he was!"

They finished lunch and said their goodbyes. When they were walking back to the car, Annie said, "Why didn't someone prepare me for Grandpa Kendall?"

Sue laughed. "Because no one could. We never know what to expect from him."

The next day, Annie and Brian drove to Ames, Iowa, less than an hour away, to meet his sister Susan. Brian hadn't yet met Kendall, his newest nephew, since his birth in April. Susan had gone to Iowa State University where she met Daryl her freshman year. They married the following summer. She was pregnant within a month. Daryl had a summer job with an accounting firm, while Susan was coping with a baby that hadn't yet slept through the night.

She met them at the door of the apartment, a diaper over her shoulder and her finger to her lips. She had just put him down to sleep. Susan was a pretty girl with short curly brown hair and big blue eyes. She was clearly exhausted. She hadn't had time to fix lunch, but offered to make grilled cheese sandwiches and tomato soup.

After finishing lunch, Susan led them on tiptoe into the bedroom to see little Kendall. He was lying on his stomach with his head turned toward the wall, so it was hard to see his little face. Back in the kitchen, Susan complained she hadn't been out of the apartment in over a week. Daryl was absolutely no help, not with her or with the baby. The baby was awake almost every night crying and slept during the day. She was on the verge of tears. Brian hugged her, taking this moment to present the gift he had brought along. Susan reigned in her emotions, opened it, and was so pleased with the outfit Brian had chosen.

They talked for awhile before Brian said they needed to go. Susan thanked them for coming and said she was going to take a nap before the baby woke up again. Annie felt deep concern about her as they hugged their goodbyes.

Back at the house, Sue was anxious for their report on Susan and the baby. Brian shrugged his shoulders and shook his head. Annie caught Sue's eye. "I'm concerned about her. She's exhausted beyond just being sleep deprived. And she's also lonely and frustrated. I think she needs her mom." Sue wondered aloud if she could go up on the weekend and help her.

The next day they returned to Kansas. Annie shared with Brian that these were the happiest days of her life. She loved being with him. He had convinced her that Amy was no longer in his life. Now she could look forward to Christmas when Brian would come to spend it with her and her family.

Annie invited Julie over to the farm the next night to have strawberry shortcake and meet Brian. The three gathered around the kitchen table. Julie sat directly opposite Annie. When their eyes met, Julie crossed her eyes. She had always done this when she was at a loss for words. Annie knew what she meant, but wanted to kick her under the table before the crossed eyes made Annie laugh. Brian noticed that some type of exchange had taken place and glanced at both of them. "Did I miss something?"

Annie glared at Julie. "Yes, and it's a good thing that you did. Julie is up to her usual comic behavior."

The girls got up to serve coffee and Julie was clearing the plates. In front of the sink, Julie whispered, "Wow, where did you find this guy?"

Annie glared at her again and told her to hush. She and Julie had been friends forever and understood one another. Nonetheless, Julie could get out of control.

When Brian left the next morning, seeing him go was heart-rending. She was already lonely, but knew that she needed to get busy and try to catch up on ten days of work. She decided she would go down to the creek after supper and sit in her special place and write a letter to Brian. Having that to look forward to would make the chores seem easier.

The next afternoon Tom came by and asked Annie if she

would help haul hay to the barn. "I have hay all over the field and it's supposed to rain tonight." She hopped into the pickup. On the way to the hayfield, Tom asked her about Brian.

With a twinkle in her eyes, she shared the obvious, "I've never felt this way about anyone, Tom."

At the hayfield, Tom took charge. "Annie, you drive the tractor and pull the wagon while I load it." Every time they had a full load, she pulled the wagon with Tom atop the hay to the barn, then Tom unloaded the hay into the loft.

It was almost dark when they picked up the last bale. He was unloading it in the barn when their mom appeared with cold drinks for them all. The rain began just as they sat on a bale of hay to rest. Tom hugged her gratefully. "Thanks, little sister, I couldn't have done all this work without you."

Annie was hungry, tired and dirty, but was pleased to have helped Tom. She hoped she'd always be there for him. She and her mom ran in the rain back to the house. Annie was more than ready for a nice hot shower and a good bed. She would have something new to tell Brian when she wrote to him.

Chapter Three

Summer passed, and Annie returned to college. She looked forward to having her dear friend Martha as a roommate. Martha was an intellectual who studied constantly. It was no surprise that she was an excellent student. She was studying veterinary medicine, and was one of the few women in the field. She was as compassionate as she was delightful and humorous.

The Collegian, the school newspaper, announced tryouts for the swim team. Annie told Martha she was going to try out. A week later, when the list was posted, Annie was pleased to see her name. Practice was grueling, but it was great exercise and she loved to swim. Unfortunately, she had a real issue with the swimsuits they had to wear for swimming class. The flimsy unstructured aquamarine suits came in three sizes, but none fit Annie, who was so tall. She couldn't wear the "small" one at all. "Medium" was not long enough; when she dived she felt like she was being cut in two pieces as she fell out of the top. The "large" suit hung like a sack. When Annie walked into the pool area wearing the horrid medium-size suit, Mrs. Brewster, the swimming instructor, assured her it looked just fine to her. *What is it with gym teachers?*

Frustrated, Annie turned around. "This is what I'm talking about, Mrs. Brewster." As she raised her arms over her head, a large portion of her bottom was hanging out.

Shocked, Mrs. Brewster couldn't help but exclaim. "Well, we can't have that, can we? What do you propose to do about this?"

"That's what I'd like to know. How about letting my mother alter a large suit so it would fit me properly? I cannot participate in swim meets dressed like this."

Mrs. Brewster was totally baffled. She'd been on the faculty for twenty-two years, yet, had never been confronted with this problem. She said she would have to ask Coach Rhodes, Head of Athletics.

The next swimming class, Mrs. Brewster gave her approval for alteration. She gave her an enormous safety pin to put on her suit so she could identify it from the others, when she put it into the gym's laundry bin. Annie was so relieved. She felt like she fell into the category of "indecent exposure" in what she was wearing.

That weekend at home, she put the "sack" on inside out so that her mom could pin the side seams to fit. The harder part was shortening the straps, but her mother worked some magic. Annie thought these shapeless swimsuits had been in the inventory as long as Mrs. Brewster had been there. *Isn't it wonderful when a plan works?*

Annie usually enjoyed her classes in the Foods Department, but this semester her instructor was old and irritable. One of the things the class was supposed to learn was how to identify herbs and spices. The samples were so old they had lost all their aroma and scent. Everyone was complaining about the class, but Professor Burns was unmoved. She had been doing the same thing for many years and change was not an option. Spices were easier to identify, but the herbs had lost their scent long ago. It was impossible to tell marjoram from oregano. Gwen, a very spirited co-ed, wanted to take up a collection, go to the grocery store and buy new containers of herbs and spices. She would dump out the old and replace with the new. How else could they learn, let alone pass the class? Everyone gave her money.

By the next class they were all amazed at how well they did identifying herbs and spices. Gwen saved the partially full new containers. Her friends were welcome in her room to study anytime. Gwen was a daring soul who loved living life on the edge. No one dared to know how she got into the classroom to make the switch. Most of the girls in the class probably secretly admired her, but no one was quite as brave as Gwen. She was given to practical jokes, as well as things for the common good. Famously, she was known for lifting up the toilet seats and stretching plastic wrap over the toilets before putting the lids down. When she found life dull, she would smear bits of peanut butter on the toilet seats. She would laugh about these pranks until she cried.

Crazy antics at the dormitory continued. They were never sure which stunts were Gwen's or someone else's. Annie would soon find out.

Fifty girls shared a central bathroom on their floor of the dorm. A changing stall was next to the shower. While Annie was in the shower someone sneaked in and removed her pajamas, slippers and towel. When she finished her shower and reached for her towel, nothing was there. Her only recourse was to walk back to her room dripping wet with nothing on, carrying her washcloth, soap and shampoo. This was getting very annoying and expensive after three times. On each occasion she had to replace her pajamas, towels, and slippers.

She was taking a shower one night when she saw movement through the shower curtain. Jumping out of the shower, she ran after the girl who had grabbed her things. She was soaking wet and the floor was slick. Annie bounded up the steps to the floor above and ran around the corner. She was running down the hall when she saw the girl duck into a room. That's when Annie realized she had just streaked past the assistant house mother. Miss Laplander stood stock still in utter amazement as she watched Annie running stark naked down the hall, dripping water everywhere. Annie knocked at the door where the girl had disappeared. She demanded her things back. The assistant house mother soon followed, arriving at the door with a horrified look in her eyes and utter confusion on her face.

"May I ask what is going on here?" clearly utterly disgusted. Turning to Annie she was indignant. "Will you please put on some clothes!"

"I will as soon as I get them back!" Annie was defiant. "She took my pajamas while I was taking a shower. This has happened to me three times this month and I have just had enough!"

Annie's pajamas, slippers and towel were handed to her by a very embarrassed girl. Annie dried herself off and put on her pajamas, still in the hall beside Miss Laplander.

Disciplinary action was taken against the girl who reimbursed Annie for all the things that she had taken.

Thanksgiving vacation finally arrived. Annie was pleased to be going home, even though Brian could not be there. Walking into the house, she was embraced by the familiar smells of her mom's cooking. The pumpkin pies cooled in the pantry where fresh baked bread and several different kinds of cookies awaited her arrival. Thanksgiving at home was special, but Annie's attention was already on Christmas when Brian planned to spend a week with Annie's family and then they would spend a week with his family in Iowa. Annie thought Christmas vacation would never arrive.

The first week in December, Annie was sleeping soundly when Gwen burst in her room and turned on the light, announcing, "Phillip and I are pinned." She twirled around the room in ecstasy and flopped on the empty bed. Annie's roommate had gone home for the weekend.

Annie sat up and sleepily gathered her thoughts. In a groggy haze, she softly said, "I'm so happy for you, Gwen; let me see the pin." Gwen took off her coat and there wasn't a pin on her sweater. She shrieked and fell to her knees, thinking perhaps it had dropped on the floor.

"Oh, how could I have lost it, I've just had it for such a short while! She was desperate, so Annie crawled out of bed to help with the search. Annie started laughing hysterically, falling back on her pillow.

Gwen was not amused. She snapped, "This is not funny, Annie. I've lost Phillip's fraternity pin. He will be furious with me. Help me find it!"

Annie tried to control her laughter enough to say, "It's okay, Gwen, your pin is on the back of your sweater." Embarrassed, Gwen stood up and quickly turned her sweater around and looked adoringly at the pin. A wry smile came across her face. "What have you been doing, Gwen?"

As her face reddened, Gwen's quick response was, "Annie, you don't want to know."

They talked well into the night, Gwen babbling about what Phillip meant to her and Annie listening to every word. They compared how love made them feel and where life would hopefully lead them. Before Gwen left, she swore Annie to secrecy about her adventure.

The three weeks between Thanksgiving and Christmas seemed endless. She couldn't wait to get home. Annie tingled with excitement just thinking about spending the holiday with Brian. The drive from Colorado Springs was at least twelve hours, so he would be arriving very late. Annie decided to stay up and read. She had dozed off to sleep in the chair when she heard a car come in the lane. She hurried to the back door, and there he was with arms outstretched. "We just have a few days to catch up on six months of kisses, so we'd better get busy."

They went into the kitchen and she got him a plate of cookies and some milk and took them into the living room, where they sat on the floor by the Christmas tree. Brian took her in his arms and kissed her. She had waited for such a long time to be next to him, drinking in the fragrance of his aftershave, she just melted in his arms. She massaged his neck and shoulders and he stretched out on the floor totally exhausted. Her first reaction was to join him, but she controlled her emotions and just sat next to him. She couldn't take her eyes off of him. After Brian devoured the whole plate of cookies, Annie went to get some more.

As she knelt down with an adoring look, "I have a surprise for you." She had gone to the pantry and put three different kinds of cookies on the plate for her starving visitor.

He tried each one, and then whispered, "I have a surprise for you." Reaching into his pocket, he took out a small ring box and opened it and said, "Annie I love you and I want to spend the rest of my life with you. Will you marry me?"

"Oh, yes, Brian, I will. I love you so much." She was ecstatic! This is exactly what she hoped would happen. She had had a hint that this might be coming by the way Brian had talked during their many phone calls. He had told her for months how much she meant to him and how much he missed being with her.

They kissed. He put the ring on her finger. Annie gazed at the beautiful emerald cut diamond and simple platinum setting. She said she had never seen anything so exquisite in all her life. Brian stretched out on the floor again and this time Annie joined him. She thought her heart would burst with joy. They talked and kissed for a long time.

Suddenly Annie couldn't wait to show the ring to her mom. "What time is it?" She ran upstairs, knocked on the door, not waiting for her mother to answer.

Her mom hugged her and said "Oh Annie, I'm so happy for you. If your father were here, he'd be even happier, as if that were possible, sweetie."

When Annie turned out her bedroom light, she was too keyed up to sleep. Wedding plans were racing in her mind. She had a lot to accomplish before June. She hadn't even considered what to do about her internship. For now, she'd be like Scarlet in *Gone with the Wind* and "think about that tomorrow."

Annie was wrapping presents for her mom when Brian came down in the morning. It was a treat to share the holiday preparations with him in her home. She fixed him breakfast, then they went to the living room and sat by the Christmas tree to drink their coffee.

He kept her company while she made the dough for cinnamon rolls. This was a tradition that Grandma Hanson had started and it had become a Christmas Eve ritual. Annie looked forward to the spicy warm cinnamon delicacy on Christmas morning. She knew it would be one tradition that she would continue in her own family.

On Christmas morning, she was up early to help her mom get the turkey stuffed and ready to put in the oven. Grandma and Grandpa Hanson were coming for dinner at 2:00, and so were Tom, Marilyn and little Paul. When it was about nine o'clock, she went upstairs to wake up Brian with a cup of coffee. She slipped into his room and set it on the night stand. He seemed in deep slumber and barely moved when she called his name. Finally opening his eyes, he reached for her pulling her down for a kiss. Those flashy dimples did their thing. She just melted at the core. As she reflected about her luck in meeting him only a year before, she gave him another kiss.

"Rise and shine, you sleepyhead. You need to eat some breakfast before it's time for Christmas dinner. The cinnamon rolls are still warm, but you've got to go to the kitchen."

Christmas dinner was a beautiful and delicious feast they all enjoyed. Brian met her grandparents, Marilyn, and her little nephew Paul. He was a darling boy who looked just like Tom's baby pictures. As if there weren't enough joy at the table, Tom and Marilyn brought the news of another baby on the way.

Brian and Annie loved that. Brian squeezed her hand. No one had noticed the ring on Annie's finger, so Brian said since this seemed to be the time for announcements, he had one to make.

He had asked Annie to marry him. Everyone except Annie's mom seemed surprised. Questions poured from those around the table.

Marilyn came around the table so she could get a closer look at the ring. "When is the wedding?"

Tom asked, with concern in his voice, "Where will you do your internship, Annie?

"It all depends where Brian goes to pilot training." This was as far as Annie had thought in the rush of events.

"What will you do, Annie, if there isn't a teaching hospital where Brian goes to pilot training?"

"I don't know, Tom. We'll have to cross that bridge when we come to it."

They lingered at the table, celebrating the happy announcements with apple pie and coffee.

Once everyone left in the fading light of afternoon, Brian and Annie went for a walk through the pasture and down to the creek. It was cold, but they were dressed warmly, Annie in her winter coat, and Brian in a ski jacket. They sat on her favorite rock and listened to the creek trickle under a thin layer of ice. This was a sheltered area near the creek. The landscape was barren; all the leaves on the trees were long gone, a few volunteer cedars dotted the pasture.

It was a private opportunity to talk about the wedding. Brian wanted the wedding to be at Air Force Academy Cadet Chapel. Annie loved the idea. She had been so impressed a year ago. Brian's job would be to check for open dates. He finally got to tell Annie how thrilled his parents were about the engagement and also his grandparents, especially Grandpa Kendall. He had called his brother, Marc, an Army doctor who was stationed in Landsthul, Germany, to tell him that he had proposed to Annie. Marc, his wife and their two little girls, loved their assignment in Germany. He also called his older brother, Drew, a second year law student at Georgetown University in Washington, D.C., to tell him. Both brothers were happy to hear the good news and sent their congratulations. Susan was also happier than she could say. She had sounded like a totally different person who was enjoying motherhood, now that the baby was sleeping all night.

Annie asked Julie to be her maid of honor after she shared the news of the engagement. Annie was already making lists of things she needed to do. This wasn't going to be easy, planning a wedding that was to be held so far away. How had Sarah managed to do it so perfectly? Annie planned to write for advice about the florist and wedding cake.

Three days after Christmas, the engaged couple left for Iowa. Annie was looking forward to meeting Drew and Daryl, Susan's husband, and seeing baby Kendall, already eight months old. Every time she had extended time with Brian, she counted her blessings. The long car ride was perfect for talk. They hit all the topics randomly, from the wedding and starting a new life together, to what kind of things they liked and disliked. She told Brian that he had made her so happy and when he smiled at her, the dimples did her in. He was the most handsome man she had ever met. *Oh! Be still my heart.*

At Brian's parent's, they found Drew sitting on the floor in front of the fireplace wrapping Christmas presents. He was shorter than Brian and definitely had longer hair, but the family resemblance was unmistakable. They talked easily as Annie joined in wrapping gifts. Drew gratefully accepted the help and promptly went to find more gifts that needed to be wrapped.

That night she, Brian and his dad stayed up and talked for hours. Jon hugged Annie to him. "I'm overjoyed that you are going to be part of the family, Annie."

"Thank you, Jon. I can't wait to join your family. Brian has made me happier than I have ever been before." They talked about Sue and their early marriage and how difficult it was to find time for each other when he was still in medical school and she was trying to support them on a nurse's salary. Annie felt closer to the family as she learned these stories. She had great admiration for Brian's dad and felt a bond with him. He was easy to talk to. She felt she had missed so much by losing her dad at such an early age.

The next day Susan came in the door carrying Kendall; Daryl followed loaded down with presents. After he placed them under the tree he hurried over and gave her a hug. "I've heard all kinds of good things about you."
Grandpa and Grandma Kendall arrived a little while later. Grandma Kendall came in carrying pies and bread, as Grandpa held the door for her. Annie and Susan helped her unload everything. She was a little woman with a beautiful head of grey hair and a sweet smile; now Annie knew the source of the gorgeous dimples. Annie hugged everyone. Grandpa Kendall was delighted to get his hug and grabbed her for a kiss on the cheek. "You'll fit in great with this family, girl."
They sat down to a dinner of rack of lamb, Romanoff potatoes, Grandma's broccoli casserole, sunflower seed bread, and fruit ambrosia. There were three different kinds of pies; apple, pecan and lemon meringue.
After the gift exchange in the living room, Susan played Christmas music on the piano. Annie held baby Kendall, a very playful little one, who preferred playing with the wrapping paper from the gifts rather than the gifts themselves.

The following week they were back in Kansas with Annie's family. *It was just a year ago when I met Brian and, oh my, how smitten I was with him. What a wonderful year it's been.* Just being with Brian she felt content. She didn't want him to leave.

As soon as she returned to school, Annie asked Martha and Gwen to be her bridesmaids. Annie and her mom planned a trip to Topeka to find a wedding gown.

Annie's mom picked her up from her dormitory early Saturday morning. Being together on a shopping spree was a rare occasion; they both were looking forward to the day together. They found a lumpy, but stylish old woman in the bridal department at Pelletier's who had been fitting brides for many years. She was a tremendous help. In she came with an armload of wedding dresses and Annie tried on each one until she found exactly what she wanted. It was the one dress that caused her mom to tear. It had Chantilly lace sleeves and a lace bodice that extended to a V below her waistline and fastened in the back with tiny lace covered buttons. The skirt was tulle and matching Chantilly lace, extending to a wide sweeping train. It was Annie who got teary eyed when they placed the veil of French silk illusion that fell in misty tiers to her waistline. She felt like a princess.

Exhausted, they went to Furr's Cafeteria for lunch, to garner strength for the afternoon search for a dress for the rehearsal dinner and a going away suit. At Crosby's, the racks were filled with newly-arrived spring dresses. Annie found a shimmering pale blue dress, perfect for the rehearsal dinner. Later in a small boutique, she found a stunning linen suit with an elongated peplum.

Packages filled the back seat as they drove back to Kansas State. They were tired, but elated with their finds and with their time together. Brian called that evening and Annie excitedly told him that they had bought her wedding dress.

"What does it look like?"

"You'll just have to wait and see!"

She was counting the days until she would be married. Every week she made a list of things to ask Brian when he called each Sunday afternoon.

Sue had been efficient and sent a list of names and addresses of people to invite to the wedding. The invitations arrived at her mother's, awaiting Annie's attention. She would have plenty of time to address the invitations over spring break.

A dressmaker was sewing the bridesmaids' dresses from a pastel floral fabric that Annie had found in Manhattan. Everyone loved the Vogue pattern that Annie had chosen. Sarah had been such a big help supplying the names of the same florist and bakery; everything was falling into place. Annie told Martha that she felt like pinching herself. No one could be this happy. The wedding was planned for the fifth of June.

The weekend before mid-term exams, Brian called on a Sunday night. It was later than his usual call and he wasn't his usual jovial self. Annie was about to ask why when he said, "Annie, I really hate to tell you this, but we need to call off the wedding."

Annie sat in stunned silence; finally she found her voice and said, "What's the matter, why are you saying this? What has happened?"

There was a long pause. "I still have feelings for Amy."

"How do you know this?" Her heart was racing out of control.

He told her that Amy had come out to see him over her spring break. He hadn't known she was coming.

Tears streamed down Annie's face as she tried to compose herself. She couldn't say a word.

"Annie, telling you this is one of the hardest things I have ever had to do, and I am really sorry. I really wish I didn't have to do this over the phone." His voice trailed off.

She swallowed and took a deep breath before she said, "Brian, you cancel the chapel. I'll take care of everything else." At this point she was crying and couldn't talk anymore. She told him goodbye.

When she went back to her room, she sat on the bed and sobbed uncontrollably. Martha came in from taking a shower, and Annie told her everything Brian had said. Martha tried to console her, but Annie was shaken to the core. She went to call her mom and tell her what had happened, but she could hardly talk without crying. Her mom just listened, and then tried to comfort her.

Annie couldn't sleep at all that night. The next day she had two exams. She got up feeling sick, and only drank a cup of tea and some apple juice before going to take her exams. After the first exam, she came back to the dorm and knew she needed to study for her next test. She simply couldn't concentrate. The news spread quickly in the dorm. Every time someone hugged her and said they were sorry, she cried some more. She asked the kitchen staff if she could just have some soup and crackers for supper, and she had a difficult time even getting that down.

Somehow she made it through the week, taking one test and trying to study for the next. She finished her exams on Friday. That afternoon there was a swim meet. She had hardly eaten all week, but tried to eat lunch before the swim meet, but couldn't choke it down.

The last event was a relay; Annie hoped she had enough energy to do her part. She was weak, emotionally spent and physically weary. She tried to concentrate on what she was supposed to do, but felt drained. As the final swimmer, and using all the strength she had, she pulled it off. They won the relay. Her teammates were jumping up and down, yelling as they pulled her out of the pool. She started jumping up and down, too. It's the last thing she remembered.

The next thing she knew she woke up in a hospital and they were asking her a lot of questions. She knew she was in a hospital, but wasn't sure why. She felt extremely weak when she sat up. Her hair was still damp. *Why am I in a hospital in a wet bathing suit?* She was dehydrated and they had hooked her up to an IV. They took blood from her arm and checked her from head to toe.

When she awoke again, it was morning. Dr. Stone came into her room and started asking questions about what she remembered. He said her mother and brother had come last night. They'd been unable to wake her. "Your mother and brother were very worried about you."

"What medication did you give me, Dr. Stone?"

"I gave you a mild sedative."

"Well, sometimes I have a difficult time with medications. Is there a telephone that I can use to call my mom? She'll be frantic."

"I'll call her as soon as I finish talking to you. Now, tell me how you managed to get yourself in such a state?"

Annie told the doctor about Brian and, in the process, started crying and just couldn't finish a sentence. He tried to console her and then departed to finish his morning rounds. A breakfast tray arrived and she tried to eat some of the food, knowing that if she didn't eat she couldn't go home.

Tom and her mom arrived about mid-morning. How relieved she was to see them, and they, equally so, to see her alert and sitting up in bed. She told Tom what Brian had said when he called. She could tell that her brother was getting angry just by the way his jaw was clenching.

"Brian did the right thing," she tried to reassure him, "but that doesn't make it any easier. It's better to find this out now than after we were married." She barely had enough energy to talk.

"If he had really loved you, he could have never done this to you."

Annie's mom tried to get him to hush. "Tom, you're not helping her at all."

Dr. Stone wanted to give her a new medication while she was still in the hospital to see if she could tolerate it before she was discharged. Annie just wanted to go home and get in her own bed. She promised she would rest over spring break. Remembering this was when she had planned to do the wedding invitations, she felt deeply saddened.

After taking the medication, she slept all afternoon. Annie was sure she would be fine if they would just let her out of the hospital, but they kept her overnight. The next morning her mom came to pick her up. Thank goodness her mom brought clothes for her, as all she had with her was her bathing suit.

As soon as they arrived at the farm, she went to her room and saw her wedding dress hanging in the closet. The sight of it left her numb. She went to the guest room closet, found the box for it, and carefully put it away. *I don't need to be reminded every time I come into my room, that I'm not getting married in June.* She sat on her bed and thought of all the money she had spent on the wedding. The sadness seemed to envelop her and she couldn't control her tears. She knew she wasn't getting married, but she couldn't keep Brian out of her thoughts. He had touched her heart the way no one else had ever come close to doing. *How can this be happening to me? How can something so wonderful go so wrong?*

Chapter Four

Annie had always loved spring with so much new life emerging. The tiny leaves began to unfurl on the trees and sprouts pushed up out of the ground. This year the season of new beginnings applied to her own life as much as the nature that surrounded her.

Her spring break was calving time for the cows. When she went to the barn to see what Tom was doing, Annie learned that Cora Belle, one of their heifers, was having a difficult time birthing her first calf. Tom had her closed off in the barn and had put straw down, but she just wasn't making any progress. She would lie down and strain, then stand up and do the same thing. Finally after several hours, two little feet presented themselves, then a tongue and part of the nose.

Annie was concerned. "Do you think she is going to be okay?"

Tom smiled, reminding her that this was normal. Annie just couldn't take her eyes off the whole miraculous process. She had watched so many times, yet every time she marveled at how wonderful it really was. Finally, Cora Belle delivered a huge calf. She licked it and mooed. After a short while the calf tried to stand up on her very wobbly legs. She kept falling down. Cora Belle licked and mooed some more, and the calf wobbled some more, seeming fragile and helpless. In truth, it was only a few minutes before she stood and leaned against Cora Belle. But, to Annie, it seemed like forever before the baby was nursing. Annie was amazed that she could stand up at all after just being born. She named the calf Belle.

Annie's rest over spring break meant she was feeling much better when classes resumed. Her appetite still hadn't returned, but her mom had tried to prepare all her favorite foods over the vacation. She was concerned about Annie's weight loss. At the first swim practice she realized she'd lost twelve pounds, a tenth of her body weight. The coach noticed too, and was shocked. Annie was brief with her explanation, but felt she had to say something.

One night she was in her room typing on her term paper when she was called to the phone in the hallway. It was Brian's dad, Jon.

"How are you, Annie?"

She took a moment to gather her composure. "I'm better now than I was a couple of weeks ago. I collapsed at a swim meet and ended up in the hospital." She took a deep breath before continuing. "I couldn't have loved Brian any more, and this has been very difficult for me. I thought of him the first thing every morning when I woke up; the last thing at night before I went to sleep, and many times during the day the thought of him would make me smile. I'm trying to keep him out of my thoughts now, but I'll have to be honest with you, I'm not doing a very good job of it." She paused for a moment as she was becoming emotional. "I have always thought, it isn't what happens to you, it's how you deal with it. But, I'm not dealing with this very well. I was totally unprepared. I wish I could just switch off my feelings, but I don't know how." She hadn't meant to blurt this all out so breathlessly.

"I'm so sorry, Annie. We love you so much and we're very sad about the whole thing, too."

Annie felt tears forming in her eyes and didn't want to start crying. "I'm a person who puts all her eggs in one basket, and when I fall I have a real mess. I guess that about describes how I am doing. You are so very kind to call and check on me. I really appreciate your thoughtfulness."

She told him goodbye and went back to her room, closing the door to her room softly.

She had taken the engagement ring off the night Brian called, but not yet mailed it back. She ruminated about putting a note in with it. She would just mail the ring. She would do that tomorrow, without any words from her.

In the days that followed, she studied, went to class, and tried not to think about Brian. When she least expected it, he crept into her thoughts. She loved him so much; it was hard not to think about him. She wasn't sure she could ever feel this way about anyone again. *What do you do when this happens? Now I know exactly what it feels like to have a broken heart.*

Although several guys asked, she was not ready to date again. Bob Spencer kept calling, telling her she needed to "get on with her life." She knew he was probably right, but somehow she just couldn't. Bob had been a friend since her freshman year. They had had several classes together and she liked him as a friend. He and Marie had dated for five years, and this year they mutually decided they would see other people. Bob called Annie almost every week and finally she told him to please stop calling, that she was still in the healing process. Several weeks later he asserted he wouldn't take "no" for an answer. Reluctantly, she let him take her to a movie. She was glad afterward; he was fun. She enjoyed being with him. She had liked him from the first time they met, but she just considered him as someone who was not available, given that he had dated Marie exclusively.

Bob had been Annie's biology lab partner her sophomore year and together they had dissected a fetal pig. One day Bob came to class totally unprepared. This was the lesson on how to tell if the pig was a male or a female. The lab instructor came around to each table and asked each person which sex their pig was. Bob's answer was that it was a female. Annie was very surprised to hear him say this. Her answer was that it was a male. When the instructor asked her where the testicles were, Bob looked at her with raised eyebrows and waited for her answer. Annie's reply was, "They haven't descended yet." The instructor said that was correct and walked to the next table. Needless to say, Bob was embarrassed. He told her later that he was thankful she had kept this to herself and not informed the entire class that he hadn't read the lesson. They had more than a few giggles over this. She teased him unmercifully about not knowing a male from a female.

The more time she spent with Bob, the more she liked him. They had mutual respect for each other and also for the situation they were in at the moment. Bob talked about Marie in such loving ways that Annie was sure that they would resume their relationship. He knew Annie was devastated about the broken engagement and encouraged her to talk about how she felt. They sat and talked for hours and were never at a loss for words.

Annie was in Gwen's room one night studying for the final exam in their Foods class. They were reviewing herbs and spices, trying to identify them by smell. As they sniffed, they giggled.

Gwen could even make studying seem like fun. "Why are we doing this? Do they think the grocery stores are going to take all the labels off the jars and tins?"

Annie loved Gwen's sense of the ridiculous.

Gwen was a very bright girl, but sometimes her actions made you think otherwise. She found a way to sneak in the dormitory after hours and it had worked for her several times. On the nights that she planned to do this, she just neglected to sign out at the desk. She put a stone in the door that led to the parking lot behind the dorm. This kept the latch from catching, but the door looked like it was closed. She would leave her car parked on the street and come in the back door unnoticed. One night when she was out, someone had discovered the stone in the door and had removed it. When she tried to get in, the door was locked. Gwen slept in her car and came in the dorm the next morning. Her roommate was frantic, but hadn't told anyone she was missing. Everyone wondered when she was going to get caught.

The day of the Foods final exam, the weather was unseasonably warm, even for Kansas. There was no air conditioning in the building and the windows were all open, even the wooden Venetian blinds were pulled clear to the top of the window. It was oppressively hot. Miss Burns, the professor, wore one of the three suits she rotated during the year. The old wooden floors creaked as she walked down the aisles and handed out their tests; she fanned herself with them as she walked around the classroom. They all had tests face down on their desks and were waiting for the instructions. When she walked up to the blackboard the heat was getting the best of her, so she took off her suit coat and hung it on the back of her desk chair before she started to write their instructions on the blackboard. What she didn't realize was that she wasn't wearing a blouse, only a dickey. The dickey had a lovely lacy collar and a little strip of fabric in the front, but that was all. The entire class was ready to explode with laughter. Everyone sat there trying to control themselves. Miss Burns stood for what seemed like forever in her slip and dickey and wrote instructions on the blackboard. Watching the flab on her arm jiggle as she wrote was hilarious. The entire class looked straight ahead and tried to stifle their laughter. Finally, the stoic Miss Burns turned around and faced the room of giggling girls. She picked up her suit jacket and went to the back of the room and put it on. Even Gwen wasn't brave enough to turn around.

Three days later, when the grades were posted, they celebrated in Gwen's room and laughed uncontrollably. They had both made A's. Gwen had helped the entire class by replacing the herbs and spices with new ones. Annie knew she would never forget this young woman. She was lively and fun and you never knew what she was going to do next.

Annie knew she needed to forget about Brian. She was grateful that graduation and the new season provided perfect reasons to make new plans. So, with the car packed, friends bid goodbye and a fond farewell with Bob, she drove toward home, passing by huge fields of golden wheat waving in the wind. A tranquil feeling enveloped her as she watched the ever present wind blowing the amber waves of grain. The sun was shining and there were puffy white clouds in the beautiful blue sky. The winter wheat that was planted in the fall was now just weeks from harvest time. She had always loved the beauty of the wheat fields just before they were harvested. It was a glorious day; she needed to be thankful for all her blessings and not dwell on Brian. She looked forward to being home with her mom and awaiting the arrival of a new little niece or nephew. Julie would be a most welcome sight. She had such a great sense of humor and always looked on the bright side of things.

When they were pre-teens, Julie would come to the farm after school was out in the spring and spend a week with Annie. After Annie's morning chores, the girls played for the rest of the day. They loved playing with the barn kittens and Junior, Annie's tomcat, who allowed them to dress him in doll clothes, bib and bonnet. They'd even put him in a doll highchair and fed him Cheerios and milk with a spoon. They also pushed him in a doll buggy, and he loved that. An unusually docile tomcat, he would let them play with him for hours.

One year they decided to play "beauty parlor" and cut each other's hair. At first, they just trimmed the ends, and then Julie decided she wanted bangs, but she didn't want them hanging in her eyes. Annie combed her friend's long black hair over her face and cut it off. It looked pretty good until it dried, and then Annie was horrified. She looked at Julie, and her bangs were sticking straight out. They definitely weren't hanging in her eyes! Determined, Annie wet Julie's hair and put Scotch tape on the bangs to hold them down. When they dried they stuck out straight again. Julie was such a good sport. She said, "I'll just tell my mom that I washed my hair and it shrunk."

The only good thing about the whole situation was that her hair had the whole summer to grow. They laughed about this for years.

The twosome played outdoors, too. They'd fish for crawdads at the creek for hours, tying chicken livers on a string for bait. They always threw what they caught back in the creek, but this was such fun. Sometimes they would try to dam up the creek with rocks. They waded upstream and downstream for hours searching for rocks, carrying back the good ones; it did slow the water just a bit. But when a good "gulley washer" came along, the rocks would all spread out again, ready for their next engineering project.

As Annie approached the lane to the farm, she knew she would enjoy this summer with Julie, who had helped her through so many rough spots in life. She was encouraged just thinking about it.

Chapter Five

While home for the summer, Annie tried to spend one day a week helping her grandmother. Sometimes she would do her grocery shopping, but usually she washed windows or helped clean the house. At other times she weeded the garden or picked vegetables. When it was harvest time, she always helped her grandmother cook for the harvesters.

One day she drove in the lane and saw Grandma standing by a flower bed with an ice pick in her hand. She wondered what was happening. By the time she reached Grandma, there was a mole impaled with the pick. This creature had torn up her flower bed; the flowers that she had planted were limp and lifeless. So was the mole. Apparently, she had waited silently by her flower bed until the dirt moved and then stabbed him with her ice pick. Grandma was usually a gentle woman; Annie had never even heard her raise her voice, so this was quite a surprise. Grandma had worked hard to have a pretty garden and had finally lost her patience with this little critter.

Annie helped repair the flower bed and got some water from the well to water what was left of the flowers. Grandma, who had been silent through the whole event, finally said in a soft voice, "Well, he won't mess up my flowers any more, the little wretch." Annie smiled inwardly, and thought, *This is a side of Grandma I didn't even know existed.*

Annie stopped at the wood pile to pick up some wood for the cook stove. As soon as she walked into the kitchen, she could smell the yeasty aroma of the bread and rolls rising. The stove was already hot, but needed more wood before the ovens would be ready to bake the bread. Grandma had long ago mastered the art of cooking on a wood-burning stove. Just by holding her hand in the oven, she knew if it was the right temperature to put the bread in. She made all of her own bread and wonderful pies. It was a joy to work with her, as she could make any chore seem like fun.

When the harvesters arrived, Annie stayed with her grandparents because there was always so much to be accomplished. As soon as the noon meal was finished, they started working on something to take out to the field about four o'clock. She usually fixed hot tea and iced tea, or lemonade and sometimes sandwiches and cookies. This was a special time with her grandma. It seemed as if the entire day was spent in the kitchen, but there were still all the regular chores to do. Annie was amazed at how much her grandmother could accomplish.

The blue sky was filled with puffy clouds as they walked to where the combine was in the field. They both carried baskets that were filled with delicious treats. Seeing the golden field of wheat wave in the breeze was a favorite time for Annie. She looked forward to this time every year, as it truly thrilled her heart. Walking through the stubble in the field, they reached the men and served them tea and lemonade.

When the harvest was finished, Annie returned home, exhausted. She marveled at the energy that her grandmother had and she hoped she had inherited those genes.

Tom called at 6:00 a.m. to say Marilyn was in labor and they would bring Paul over on their way to the hospital. Annie was excited to be able to take care of Paul and also at the thought of a new little life coming into the world. She knew it would be a busy day, as Paul was two and a half years old and full of energy. When they arrived, Paul was still in his pajamas, and Tom just handed him to Annie and hurried back to the car.

They ate breakfast and Elizabeth went on to work. Annie and Paul went outside. Paul had his toy tractor with him and played in the dirt in the garden while Annie picked peas and strawberries. Paul wanted to see the new baby calves that were "playing chase" in the pasture. After watching them for a while, Annie fixed peanut butter and jelly sandwiches and some milk for both of them and they went down to the creek for a picnic. Sitting on her favorite flat rock, they ate while Annie told him this is where she and his dad had played when they were little. When they finished eating she took off his shoes and socks and let him wade in the creek and squish mud between his toes. The water was very cold, so that didn't last very long. She picked him up and carried him back to the house, taking him straight up to the bathroom to give him a bath and wash his hair. She wrapped him in a towel and dried his hair, then gave him a hug and he hugged her back. *What a precious little boy. He smells so fresh and wonderful.* She put on his underwear and they went to the bedroom.

She told him, "This is where your daddy slept when he was a little boy." She had several of Paul's favorite books and they sat in bed and she read to him before he took his nap. Paul loved tractor books and made sound effects while Annie read to him; which always amused her.

Tom called late in the afternoon. "Annie, we have another little boy! His name is John Michael, and we're going to call him Mike. Marilyn and the baby are fine."

Annie called her mom to let her know the news, then called her grandparents. What a blessing this new little boy was for everyone. She couldn't wait to hold him.

Marilyn's mom came to help with the new baby, and Annie kept Paul during the day. She didn't accomplish much, but she loved being with him. He was very well behaved, but such a busy little boy. Baby Mike was so sweet and she loved holding him. Annie thought, *Someday…*

Although she had already been accepted for her internship at the Kansas University Medical Center, she had to go to Kansas City for an interview with Dr. Gaston, the head of the hospital, before she started. The interview went well, now she needed to find a place to live while she was there. She looked at several apartments and decided on a garage apartment that was close to the hospital. She was pleased with her decision. She returned home excited to be starting on a new adventure and leave the past behind.

Brian's dad called about once a month to check on her, but she hadn't even asked about Brian the last few times he had called. She knew that he was going to pilot training, but had no idea where. The calls seemed to help, as Jon was so easy to talk to and never seemed to pry or ask about what had happened. He just seemed genuinely concerned about how Annie was coping. He did tell her that Amy was pregnant, but had had a miscarriage. She wasn't sure who the father was. It could have been Brian or perhaps someone else. Annie was shocked to hear that maybe Brian was the father. Jon said they had heard that Amy was running with a rough crowd of people.

On the fifth of June, Annie went down to the creek. This special place had always brought her comfort. She slipped off her shoes and stepped in the sand at the edge of the creek and let the icy water spill over her feet. She smiled and thought, *Sometimes you need to stop and do something that purely delights you.* She then sat on the rock and tears clouded her vision. *This was supposed to be my wedding day.* Hearing the water trickle over the rocks had always had a soothing effect on her, she hoped it would now. She closed her eyes and envisioned the chapel at the

Air Force Academy. She was walking down the aisle with Tom at her side; Brian was waiting for her near the altar…. After a good cry, she walked slowly back through the pasture with her head down. She knew she had to put this out of her mind. *Will I ever heal from this ordeal?*

Chapter Six

Annie was looking forward to her internship at the Kansas University Medical Center. The garage apartment was close to the hospital and she could walk to work. The apartment was small, but it was clean and well furnished and even had a washing machine and a dryer in the kitchen. Living alone would be different, but she was sure she would adjust. There were always lots of girls around when she was in college.

On her first day, Annie was met by Paula Collins, a registered nurse, who was to be her escort around the hospital. Paula was an attractive girl with a mass of curly dark hair; she seemed perky and full of life. After orientation the two women planned to meet at noon for lunch in the cafeteria, where there was more to offer than food.

As Paula explained, "Let me warn you, Annie, these interns and residents in this hospital have pure testosterone running through their veins. The only thing that keeps us safe is that they work very long hours, and they are so exhausted when they are finished that they go to their rooms and study or collapse."

The cafeteria was buzzing with activity; it looked like a sea of green with everyone wearing "scrubs."

"I'm being motioned to the table in the corner," said Paula. "I think you have been spotted already. These guys want to meet

BE STILL MY HEART

you." As they approached the table, all three guys stood up. Paula made the introductions. "Annie, this is Jerry Nicholson, Jeff Greer, and Greg Miller." They chatted briefly, then she and Paula went to find a table. Paula was such fun and Annie enjoyed her company.

Annie quickly got into the routine of working from 7:00 a.m. to 3:00 p.m. She didn't mind getting up early, and she really liked having time in the afternoon to study or go for a walk. She was learning so much and it was a good feeling to be using some of the things she had learned in college. She had been there several weeks. She usually took her lunch and ate at her desk, but one particular Friday she planned to meet Paula in the cafeteria. As she went through the line and was walking toward a table, she saw one of the interns she had met on the first day, Jeff Greer. He greeted her warmly. "Hi, Annie, how are you doing?"

She only smiled and said she was fine. She found a table and was waiting for Paula when Jeff came over to introduce her to the guy he had been sitting with, whom Annie had barely noticed.

"Annie, this is Rick Henslee."

Rick sat down beside her and said, "I haven't seen you around here. Are you a nurse?"

"No, I'm doing an internship in foods and nutrition."

They talked for a few minutes, and then Rick asked her if she had seen the movie, *Dr. Zhivago*. She told him she hadn't, and to her surprise, he asked her if she would go with him on Saturday night. She said she had heard it was a great movie and she would love to go.

Rick was tall, probably six feet three inches, had blond hair with a little wave in the front and beautiful blue eyes. Annie was impressed. Paula came to the table and Annie started to introduce her to Rick, but she already knew him.

Rick said, "I'll see you on Saturday at 6:30."

As soon as he left, Paula stared at her with big eyes and said, "I've been here for two years and he hasn't even looked at a girl. How did you do that?"

Annie just shrugged her shoulders.

Saturday night Rick came in his VW Beetle and they went to see Dr. Zhivago. Just after the intermission, he put his head on her shoulder and went to sleep. When the lights came up, he stretched, then realized what he had done. "How long have I been asleep?"

"About half of the movie."

"I'm really sorry, Annie, I just never get enough sleep."

She laughed. "It makes me feel like a really exciting date!"

He took her home and apologized again. "How would you like to go out to eat Chinese food on my next day off? Maybe I can stay awake." She was happy to say yes.

Two weeks later, Rick arrived at her door exhausted, but cheerful. The Chinese restaurant was a local hangout for the hospital people, as it was fast service with great food and inexpensive. Rick recommended the "Hunan Pork," which was spicy and very good. They finished with tea and a fortune cookie. When Annie read her fortune she smiled, and Rick asked what it said. "It says, prepare for exciting times." They both laughed.

As they were leaving the restaurant, Annie suggested they go to her apartment for some dessert. "I can do better than fortune cookies." She laughed and said, "Maybe I should rephrase that before you get the wrong idea."

Rick smiled and shook his head and said, "Annie, let me be 'big brother' for you and tell you that you can't go around making comments like that. You'll get yourself in trouble in a hurry."

"Thank you, Rick, I know I'm a bit naïve, but I did correct myself."

At the apartment, while they ate brownies and drank coffee, Annie asked Rick about his family. He'd grown up on a farm in Kansas with his mom and his grandparents, and when he was about ten, he and his mom had moved into town. He had never known his father. His mom had never married and had been a devoted mother to him. His grandparents had been a very important part of his growing up, and so had his Uncle Charlie and Aunt Grace. Grace was his mom's sister. Rick had worked on the farm, had his own paper route when he was eleven and had stocked shelves in the grocery store after school. In the summer he had mowed lawns and done odd jobs for anyone that needed help. He had saved all his money for college, in order to fulfill his dream to become a doctor.

"Would you like to come here for dinner on your next day off?"

He seemed pleased with the invitation, and said that would be great and told her when his next day off would be. After he left, she thought, *What a really nice young man.*

There was a nip of autumn in the air, leaves were falling and the trees were changing colors. What a glorious time of year! Annie loved the springtime, with everything emerging and coming to life again, but she thought fall was probably her favorite season. She was carrying groceries to her apartment and crunching the leaves as she walked. She had just purchased all that she would need for the dinner tomorrow night: meat loaf, baked potatoes, baked butternut squash with maple syrup, three bean salad and apple crisp and coffee. She needed to get started on the things she could prepare ahead of time.

The following evening, when Rick arrived, he gave her a hug and said he was looking forward to a home cooked meal. "Something smells wonderful and I'm starved. I got interrupted right in the middle of my lunch."

When they sat down to eat, he asked her if she was seeing

anyone else and she said that she wasn't. She told him that she had been engaged to Brian, and he had called off the wedding. He didn't ask any more questions and she was relieved.

"Paula told me that you weren't going out with anyone and that you and Jeff were confirmed bachelors."

Rick smiled and said, "Jeff and I have been roommates for a long time and decided that we didn't have time for girls until we finished medical school. That day in the cafeteria when you spoke to him, I asked who you were; he said he would introduce us. Well, I had no intention of asking you out when I went over to your table, but I just couldn't help myself, so I guess I've broken my own rule. I really like being with you, Annie. You just weren't part of my plan."

She was confused. She wasn't sure if this was a compliment or not. He was at least being honest with her.

After dinner, Annie cleared the table and put the dishes in the sink to soak while she fixed coffee and put the apple crisp in bowls.

Rick came in the kitchen with a little twinkle in his eye and said, "I'm coming for 'dessert kisses.'"

She smiled and said, "What are 'dessert kisses?'"

She was standing at the sink when he came and stood behind her and put his arms around her waist and started kissing her neck. He turned her around and took her in his arms and kissed her.

He smiled and then said, "Now you know."

They hugged and he kissed her again. Annie felt the feelings inside her awakening. She was sure she had been emotionally dormant since the breakup with Brian, but this was a wonderful feeling. She didn't want it to end...

They ate apple crisp with ice cream and drank coffee, then he pulled her next to him and they kissed again. When he kissed her goodnight, Annie wished he didn't have to go. Sitting in bed that night, she felt a warm glow soar within her. She was almost afraid to hope that she had stirred something in him, too.

The next evening she was studying when Brian's dad called. She told him that she had met someone and he was such a nice young man, but was a medical student and didn't have much time to see her. She then decided to tell him how much she appreciated his friendship.

"Jon, (he had asked her to call him that when they first met) I want to tell you what a kind and wonderful man you have been to me. I'm sure you realize that under such circumstances most people wouldn't even try to contact an ex-fiancé of their son. For you to care about me and what I'm doing really means a great deal to me. My brother and I were always close, but after the breakup with Brian, Tom doesn't even want to hear his name. I hardly ever talk to him anymore, and this makes me very sad. Now you are the only male that I can confide in, and it seems a bit strange that this is the way it has worked out. You have been a tremendous help to me and I just want to say thank you for all your kindness."

Jon never mentioned Brian, and Annie didn't ask about him. She felt this was the only way she would ever heal.

Chapter Seven

Rick and Annie went on a picnic on his next break. It was a beautiful fall day, chilly in the morning, but warm during the day. The trees were still ablaze in red, orange, yellow and russet. It was glorious to be outside. She made a picnic lunch of cold fried chicken, potato salad and coleslaw with lemon bars for dessert. They drove to a park and walked in the woods for a while, then sat down on their blanket to eat. When they finished eating, he told her he would wait for lemon bars and settle for "dessert kisses." They didn't get to see each other very often, but he made her feel very special when they did. With his head in her lap, he told her he didn't have much experience with girls, as he had worked several jobs while in college at the University of Kansas. He had worked two jobs during the summer so he could help pay for his tuition. He just didn't have the time or the money to go out with anyone. He didn't think it was right for her to keep having him over for dinner because he couldn't afford to take her out, even if he had the time.

"Annie, I'm up to my eyeballs in debt for all of my years in medical school."

She tried to explain that she loved being with him and she would be happy if he just came over and sat with her on the couch and held her hand and talked to her. She smiled at him and said, "Every now and then you can give me 'dessert kisses.'" He was so serious, she couldn't even get him to smile.

"I feel like I'm mooching" he said. "You do everything for me and I don't do anything for you. That's just not right."

"I don't need to be 'wined and dined' and taken to fancy places, I just want to be with you. Besides, I enjoy cooking for you." She tried again to get him to smile, and said, "You are a joy to cook for; if it doesn't move on your plate you eat it." That brought a little smile from him.

"Annie, before I met you, all I did on my day off was study, do my laundry and sleep."

She smiled and said, "I have a solution. You can pick up Chinese take-out every other time and bring your laundry with you and we can still be together."

"You are impossible, Annie." He agreed that they could try that for a while.

One night when Rick was coming over to see her, he called and asked if she had enough food if Jeff came along. She had made a pot of chili and was making cornbread and said that would be fine. Annie didn't know Jeff well, but she thought perhaps he was very soft spoken until you got to know him. These poor guys acted like they had never eaten a decent meal. They raved about everything she put on the table. Perhaps they had had too many years of cafeteria food.

The favorite table conversation was about surgeries they had done and about patients they had treated and diagnosed. They talked about Mrs. B's gallbladder they had removed, and in more detail than Annie wanted to hear, Mr. R's hemorrhoidectomy. Every little while they would stop and apologize, and within a minute they were at it again.

The telephone rang just as they were finishing dinner and it was for Rick. While he was talking, Jeff asked if they had worked out their problems.

"I hope we have come to a compromise. Does Rick tell you everything?"

"Rick is a very proud young man and that is a good character trait, but it can also create problems. He really cares about you, Annie; just try to be patient with him. He has had a hard life, but he'll never tell you that."

Rick came back to the table and they ate baked apples with cream. Rick and Jeff had lived together for so long and knew each other so well that sometimes they finished each other's sentences. They fed off of each other, and when they got started kidding they were hilarious. They had mutual respect for each other and never were unkind.

When Annie was called to Dr. Bauer's office, she didn't have any idea why he wanted to see her. She knew he was a general surgeon, but that was all. She walked in and shook hands with him and he asked her to sit down.

"You have been recommended by Dr. Gaston as someone who might be interested in babysitting." She smiled and said she loved children and asked how old they were. "We have two, a boy that is three and a girl that is nine months."

She agreed to go to Dr. Bauer's home and meet Mrs. Bauer and the children. She was surprised that Dr. Gaston had remembered their interview. He must have taken copious notes after their thirty minute conversation.

Rick seemed to be comfortable with their new arrangement, or at least he didn't comment about it. The weeks went on as he brought his laundry to her apartment and they ate meals together. He always seemed to be tired, but she tried to enjoy the moment, avoiding any type of confrontation with him. When he let her know several times that she was not in his "plan," she didn't know what to say. It made her feel that maybe he would be happier if he had never met her. It was an uncomfortable feeling.

As the holiday season was approaching, one night Rick said,

"Don't buy me anything for Christmas, because I don't have any money to buy you anything. I've had to have some work done on my car and it cost a lot more than I thought it would."

She agreed, because she didn't want to get into an argument with him.

The first time she went to babysit for the Bauer children they both wanted her undivided attention. She was changing Lauren and getting her ready for bed; Johnny was upset because he wanted Annie to play with him, so he locked himself in the bathroom. Annie had never been confronted with a problem like this and wasn't sure how to handle him. She got Lauren settled and went to see if she could coax him into opening the bathroom door.

"I'll play with you now if you will unlock the door and come out of there."

Johnny was silent.

"Would you like for me to read you a book?"

There was no response.

Annie decided she would try a different approach and said, "I'm going to be in the family room." She walked down the hall and left him in the bathroom. She just hoped he wasn't still there when his parents came home. She was also concerned that he might get into something in the bathroom. No one had prepared her for this type of behavior. She sat down and started reading a magazine, but she couldn't keep her mind on what she was reading. She wished she had taken some child psychology classes. *I'm feeling more inadequate by the minute. This three-year-old child has gotten the best of me and I have no idea what to do about it.*

She was trying to think what she would tell his parents when Johnny appeared with a pile of books and asked if she would read to him. She read several stories to him and put him to bed. Now he seemed like a perfect angel.

When Dr. and Mrs. Bauer returned home, Annie told them what had happened and what she did and they didn't seem concerned at all.

Annie would have a week over Christmas to go home and see everyone. She hadn't been home since she had come to Kansas City. She still had shopping to finish and cards to send out, but the break was going to be most welcome.

She called Julie as soon as she got home. The next day Julie came to Annie's house and they baked cookies. Both of them loved raw cookie dough and ate so much they felt sick. The recipe was supposed to make four dozen and they only had two and a half dozen when they finished. Neither one wanted to eat warm cookies just out of the oven.

When she returned after Christmas, she didn't hear anything from Rick for several weeks, and this concerned her. Maybe he'd had a change of heart and thought it would be better if his "plan" worked. Annie thought, *Why are men always so difficult?* She thought about him all the time. *Maybe she would see him at the hospital...*

Jon called to see how she was doing and she told him the whole story of Rick. "Jon, sometimes I don't think he cares about me at all or he would at least call."

He tried to comfort her and reminded her that medical school was a grueling time. Everyone was sleep-deprived. He was sure Rick would call her at some point. Jon always made her feel better. He then told her that Amy was pregnant again.

Annie shuddered when she heard this. "Are she and Brian going to get married?"

"No, she isn't sure the baby is Brian's."

Annie was shocked. "Was Brian home for Christmas?"

"Yes, and he and Amy did go out together."

Annie could tell Jon was distressed and she could understand why. "Do you think they will get married if it is Brian's baby?"

"Brian hasn't had much to say about it. He's very concerned that Amy is in with the wrong group of friends."

Annie wished she had something positive to say, but the words didn't come easily about such a horrible mess. Jon said he would keep her posted.

Through Paula, Annie was asked to join a potluck supper and bridge group. She met several nice girls and really enjoyed their company. She started joining them for lunch in the cafeteria instead of taking her lunch every day, but she never saw Rick there. *Maybe I should just try to forget him?*

She was doing well with her studies and was beginning to get suggestions of places she might apply for a job. Working on her resume was an interesting task; she hoped she was doing it correctly. Every few days she got information about the different hospitals that had openings. Rick was in her thoughts more than she wanted to admit to herself. She really liked him and missed seeing him.

One evening in February, Annie was in the kitchen preparing for the potluck bridge she was hosting that evening when the telephone rang. It was Rick and he asked if he could bring Chinese take-out up in about an hour.

"I'm sorry Rick, but I already have plans for tonight. It's good to hear from you."

He gave a rather abrupt reply, "Well, I guess I'll just have to eat with Jeff tonight. Take care."

Annie thought he at least knew she was still alive. This gave her a spark of renewed hope that he still cared; she wasn't sure what was going on with Rick. She tried to caution herself about even thinking of him, because she was afraid she would get hurt once again.

She enjoyed the group that she met with every other Friday night for potluck and bridge. She had even splurged and bought a card table and chairs. There were eight girls and they rotated to each other's apartment. The food was always a topic of conversation, as some of them had never cooked before and were experimenting with recipes. They always had an enjoyable evening.

Rick called the next week and asked if he could bring Chinese take-out on Saturday night, and Annie said that would be fine and she added, that he was welcome to bring his laundry. She hadn't seen him for two months.

Rick arrived with his laundry bag, took off his coat and came over and gave her a hug. She was reserved outwardly, but she was moved emotionally just to be in his presence. He looked exhausted. She wanted to talk to him about what had happened for the last two months, but he looked positively drained. He started the laundry and came back over to her and took her in his arms and kissed her and said, "Annie, I've really missed you."

When she asked how he was, he told her he had gotten strep throat after Christmas and had been really sick. He had gone back to work too soon and had a relapse. He was so far behind that he had worked double shifts trying to catch up. She was sorry he had been sick, but she asked why he hadn't called to tell her about what was going on. "I was concerned about you. At least, if you had let me know, I could have made some chicken soup for you." There wasn't an explanation from Rick.

They ate supper, then he loaded the dryer while Annie cleaned up the kitchen. Then they relaxed on the couch and enjoyed some of her homemade cookies and coffee. He asked what she'd been doing last Friday night, and he seemed relieved when she told him it was an evening with the girls. He scooted next to her and pulled her into his arms and kissed her as his hand went under her sweater. She pulled away from him and said, "Please don't do that, Rick."

"Why not?"

"Because, that just leads to other things that I don't want to do until I get married."

Rick had a stunned expression on his face. "Well, I knew you were a nice girl, but I didn't know you were a prude." He got up and stuffed his laundry into a bag and left.

She sat on the couch, tears welling up in her eyes. *How can I be so happy one minute and so upset the next?* Tears were streaming down her face when there was a knock on the door. When she opened it, Rick was standing there.

"I forgot the shirts that I hung on hangers." He looked at her. "What's wrong with you? Why are you crying?"

She shook her head. "It doesn't make any difference." She went into the kitchen and started putting things in the sink and got a Kleenex and blew her nose and wiped her eyes. She always looked so awful when she cried.

He came over to her. "Will you talk to me about this if I stay?"

She nodded her head and he led her to the couch. She was very emotional at the moment and she didn't want to cry anymore. He took a deep breath and was patiently waiting for her answer. Before she said a word, he yawned.

She tried to control her emotions, and hopefully explain to him how she felt. "Rick, I don't even know where to begin. I'm going to be very honest with you. I really do care about you, but I'm a little confused when two months go by and I don't hear a word from you. Then you come over here and you start putting your hands under my sweater, something you have never done before, as you have always been a gentleman, and you get upset with me for stopping you and call me a prude. If you can't deal with that then you need to walk out that door and not come back. I want to wait until I get married for intimacy. Marriage is something that is very meaningful and sacred to me, and I have no intention of changing." Annie felt tears starting to build in her eyes and wished she could control her emotions better. She took a deep breath and tried to calm herself.

Rick hadn't taken his eyes off her since she started talking. "Why haven't you talked to me before about this?"

"Because there was no need to; you have been a perfect gentleman up until tonight," she blurted out.

He sat there for a few seconds, then said, "Annie, I'm so sorry to upset you. I told you I didn't have any experience with girls."

"Well, let's keep it that way."

He laughed at her and hugged her to him.

"Paula told me that all of you had pure testosterone running through your veins, and now I believe her!"

He kissed her tears away and then said he had to go.

She and Rick continued to see each other on his days off, and in April he arrived at the door with a bunch of daffodils. She was very touched, and while she looked for something to put them in he said, "These are my favorite flowers. I've been fascinated with them since I was a little boy."

He had been so kind and considerate with her since the night she had gotten upset. She was sure he would be a wonderful human being if he ever got enough sleep.

Pleased with her job interviews, she told him where they were. One was at St. Luke's in Kansas City, St. Francis Hospital in Tulsa, and one was at Parkland Hospital in Dallas.

"Annie, I would love it if you would stay here and work at St. Luke's so we could be together." He stood up and pulled her in his arms and kissed her.

She had a busy six weeks ahead. She told Rick what her schedule would be and said about the only time they could get together for dinner at her place was on the 22nd of May. One weekend she was going home, another she was babysitting for the Bauer's, and she had two friends that were coming into town. She felt she needed to explain to him that she had guys coming to visit her. One was a guy, Ed, she knew from the swim team. He was coming to town for a wedding and had called to see if they could get together. She'd invited him over for lunch. She said she had never gone out with him, that he was just a friend on the swim team. The other was Bill, a boy from her hometown, whom she had known since kindergarten. He was coming for a meeting and she had invited him to dinner. She made a card with her schedule on it for Rick so he would know where she was, and when she gave it to him he looked upset.

"Why are you having guys come to your apartment? You really worry me sometimes, as naïve as you are."

She didn't like how he was treating her, but knew he was tired and just didn't want to get into a confrontation with him. She assured him that these were nice young men and that there was nothing to worry about.

He was not pleased with her when he left, and said, "Well, as much of a prude as you are, you will probably be fine. I don't have time for you anyway."

The weeks seemed to fly by. She went to all her interviews, took her tests, did babysitting for the Bauer's, and spent a weekend at home. She hadn't talked to Rick once. *He didn't even call to see how my interviews went. He says he wants me to stay in Kansas City, but doesn't even bother to call to see how that went.*

Some of the tests were grueling, but she hoped she had done well. She was excited about finally finishing school and going to work. She was hoping for a letter from St. Luke's saying that she had the job, so she could stay in Kansas City. However, she had really liked the hospital in Dallas. She had been met at the airport by Valerie, a registered nurse at the hospital, who was her escort for the day. Valerie also took her to her apartment complex and Annie had looked at a new apartment and was impressed.

She checked the mail anticipating a letter every day. Excitement was soaring when she saw the envelope from St. Luke's; she opened it and was delighted to see she had a job offer. *This has worked out perfectly.* Rick was coming to dinner tonight. She decided she would splurge and buy steaks and they would have a celebration. She also bought fresh asparagus and some strawberries and rhubarb to make a pie. There were even flowers for the table. Happiness soared through her and she could hardly keep her mind on what she was doing. The apartment was cleaned and she had just had a shower. She had everything ready and would broil the steaks as soon as Rick arrived. *I know now what it feels like to float on a cloud.*

She had missed seeing Rick and was overflowing with anticipation. He was supposed to come at 6:30 and it was after 7:00 and he still wasn't there. This wasn't at all like him. She called him at 7:45 and there was no answer. She had never called him before, because he was rarely in his room except to sleep, but tonight she was getting upset. She put the steaks back in the refrigerator and ate one of the baked potatoes and some salad. She called him again at 8:30, and still there was no answer. She started thinking about their last meeting and she thought, *You really are naïve, dear; he has called you naïve, he has called you a prude and he told you he didn't have time for you. You are a bit slow at figuring this one out.* She sat down and cried, then went to bed and cried some more. *Why is it that as soon as I think life is wonderful, the rug gets pulled out from under me?*

The next morning she got a letter from Parkland Hospital in Dallas with a job offer. The salary was much higher than the one in Kansas City. *Perhaps this is the solution to my problem.* She pondered her predicament and was still smarting from what had happened the night before. Her decision was made, she would go to Dallas. She had no reason to stay here. *This has got to be better than staying in Kansas City and waiting for Rick to know that I'm alive.*

She called her mom and told her what had happened. She was on the verge of tears, but controlled herself enough to tell her that she thought it would probably be for the best if she went to Dallas. Her mom was sympathetic and tried to calm her down. Annie knew by the tone of her voice that she thought Dallas was a long way away.

Monday morning she called and accepted the job at Parkland Hospital, then called the apartment office in Dallas where she had seen the apartment she liked. It was in a great complex with a swimming pool, tennis courts and a barbeque area. She then called Valerie to tell her she was coming and started packing her things. Throughout the day she became tearful and cried, wondering why Rick didn't come. Was he angry, did he forget? She was deeply hurt and disappointed.

She had lots of books, a few cooking items, her clothes, a vacuum cleaner and an ironing board which would all fit in her car. She cleaned the apartment and started loading the car. She called her mom to let her know when she was leaving for Dallas, and told her she would call her when she got there.

"Mom, I'm not having very good luck with men in my life. As soon as I like them, they dump me. I'm looking at this as a new beginning, and right now I think I need one."

Her mother tried to comfort her and wished her well.

The next morning when she finished loading the car, she decided to stop at the hospital. She would tell Rick goodbye, if she could find him, and she prayed she could do it without being emotional. Her heart was beating in her throat when she entered the hospital. She met Greg Miller in the hall and asked if he knew where Rick was. He said he was in a meeting and it would probably last an hour. She thanked him and returned to the car.

Chapter Eight

It took Annie all day to get to Dallas. She had tearful moments along the way, but tried to be positive and not think of everything that had gone wrong in her life. She just couldn't keep from thinking about Rick and wondered why he had treated her like he had. She was hurting, but knew she shouldn't dwell on him anymore. *What am I doing wrong?*

She stopped by the apartment office to get the key after she managed to make her deposits and pay the rent. Finally, she walked upstairs and all through the downstairs of the apartment; it was new and still had the smell of fresh paint. The décor was appealing; she made mental notes as she went through each room about what accessories it needed. This was a first for her; she had a feeling of pride to have a place of her own.

Her cupboards were bare, so she went to a pay phone to call Valerie and ask where she could find a grocery store. Money was a problem at the moment, as she had spent almost all her money on deposits and rent. She did have her deposit money from her last apartment and she would have to live on that for the next two weeks until she got paid.

Her first day of work went well. She met many nice people and everyone was very friendly. There were so many things to learn; she came home with a stack of papers and handbooks to read.

Being just fifteen minutes from the hospital was a great asset. She loved getting off at three in the afternoon. When she got home, she would walk for about thirty minutes, then swim laps in the pool before relaxing in the sun. Every Friday night the residents held a barbeque. Everyone brought something to eat, a salad or a vegetable, bread or dessert and their own meat to grill. The evenings were casual and they usually went for a swim after the barbeque. Annie met lots of new people, most of them young and unmarried. There were several people from the hospital who lived there and quite a few airline pilots. Being with others helped her think of something besides Rick. This was a lively group. Valerie had lived there for two years and seemed to know everyone. She and Valerie usually ate and danced with the guys or swam, then went back to their separate apartments, but many of their friends stayed until the wee hours of the morning, partying around the pool.

Saturday morning, Valerie and Annie went to the pool and swam for a while. They were relaxing in the sun, when Sam and Rob brought chairs over and started talking to them. These were guys that they had met several weeks earlier at the barbeque. When they said they were hungry, and wanted to know what was for lunch, they all decided to go to Annie's apartment for lunch. Everyone wanted bacon, lettuce and tomato sandwiches, so she fried a pan full of bacon. After she put all the sandwich fixings on her patio table, everyone helped themselves.

The phone rang and she went in the kitchen to answer it. It was Rick. He didn't even say hello, he just said, "What are you doing in Dallas?"

"I'm working here. I took the job offer from Parkland Hospital."

"Well, I went by to see you and your landlady told me you had been gone for three weeks! Why didn't you tell me you were leaving?"

"Well, Rick, I did come by the hospital to tell you goodbye, but Greg Miller told me you were in a meeting and wouldn't be finished for an hour. When you didn't come to dinner on the 22nd, I decided you didn't care about me." She took a deep breath and tried to steady her voice. "I had splurged and bought steaks and was really looking forward to an evening with you. I had just gotten a job offer from St. Luke's and couldn't wait to tell you. I was planning a celebration."

There was silence for a moment. "I forgot all about dinner. I'm really sorry, Annie."

Annie took another deep breath. "Rick, this has all worked out for the best. This isn't a good time for me to talk to you, I have friends here. I need to get back to them. I'm sorry."

She went back out to the patio, but now she wasn't thinking about making a sandwich. They ate lunch and the guys asked if they would like to go out to eat at a newly opened Mexican restaurant that evening. They all agreed that was a great idea.

Sunday afternoon Rick called again. Annie found herself apologizing for not being able to talk to him. "There were friends here eating lunch when you called yesterday."

"Were those guys you were having lunch with?"

"Yes, there were two guys and a girl."

"What did you mean yesterday, when you said that it has all worked out for the best?"

"I meant just what I said. You are in Kansas City doing what you want to, and I am in Dallas. I'm sorry it didn't work out between us, but it didn't."

"Can you be more specific?"

"Sure Rick, I will certainly try." She thought for a moment and then said, "I really don't know where to begin. You have called me naïve, which is true, and you called me a prude, and I guess I am in your eyes. You have told me numerous times that you didn't have time for me, that I didn't fit into your 'plan.' I don't like being treated like that. I haven't heard from you in over two months. You didn't even think to call and ask how any of my interviews went or if I got a job offer. It was like I didn't exist. Do you think you can call now and act like everything is fine between us? Well, Rick, it isn't. You have hurt my feelings and I'm trying to get on with my life. Please allow me to do it."

Rick stopped her, "Annie, please?"

"Let me finish this, Rick. You asked me to be more specific, and I'm trying to tell you what is on my mind. Right now, I just don't need anyone as inconsiderate as you in my life. I know you are busy, and I tried my best to be considerate of you and deal with you when you were exhausted. I was not at all demanding of you, and I just wanted to be treated with respect." She took a deep breath and tried to gather her thoughts. "Just count your blessings. You now have time to do whatever it is that you want to do, and I'm not there to mess up your 'plan.' The naïve, prudish girl is not there to deal with anymore. Just be happy that I'm gone, it will make your life a lot simpler." She paused for a moment, then added. "Is that specific enough for you?" She was more emotional than she wanted to be.

Rick seemed stunned; there was a long pause. "Annie, I've made a big mess of our relationship. You have always been so kind and good to me and you didn't deserve to be treated the way I've treated you. I don't have any excuses for my behavior. Please listen to me. I'm in love with you, Annie." Then in a pleading voice, he continued, "Please give me another chance to work this out with you. I promise to be considerate and respectful of you. I've never felt like this about anyone else and I've never told anyone that I loved them before. I want to come and see you and talk to you about this. I really think we can work this out, and I think you still have feelings for me or you wouldn't have been so upset."

Annie was shocked to hear him say he loved her. "How are you going to get the time off to come down here and see me? You've never had time for me before?"

"I don't know, but I'll do whatever it takes. I'll try for the Fourth of July weekend; if that doesn't work, I'll try Labor Day weekend."

She thought for a minute and then said that was fine. Her mind was whirling after listening to him say he loved her. She knew they had many problems to work out if the relationship was ever going to get back on track. Perhaps this was the best way to see if they could talk it through.

"Annie, I miss you so much. Please forgive me for hurting your feelings and not calling to check on you. There aren't any excuses for treating you like I did." He then asked her, "Have you gone out with anyone since you've been there?"

"Yes, I have. This place is full of single guys and girls. Every Friday night there's a barbeque for anyone who wants to go and there's usually swimming and dancing afterwards. It's a great place to meet people."

"I wish I hadn't asked the question." He said he needed to go and ended the conversation with, "I love you, Annie."

Annie sat down; her mind was a blur.

When, Rick called back a few days later, he said it would have to be Labor Day weekend when he came. Annie said she would see if he could stay at one of the airline pilot's apartments, as some of them would be gone over the holiday weekend. "I think Walt Cushing will be gone, I'll ask him and let you know."

"That would be great, Annie. I miss you so much. I can't wait to see you and hold you in my arms. I sometimes wonder how I ever let you get away."

"I miss you, too. I've been doing a lot of thinking about us and I need to talk to you. We definitely have some things to work out. Is there anything that you want to do while you are here?"

"I want to be with you every minute that I can. I love you, Annie."

Valerie introduced Annie to antiquing, and they spent a whole weekend going to antique shops. Annie found a beautiful walnut bedroom set that she really liked. The bed had a high headboard with carving at the top, and the dresser had marble on the top. The chest of drawers had a piece on the top with the same carving as the bed, and there were two night stands with drawers. Annie had some birthday and Christmas money she hadn't used and decided she would put this as a down payment on the whole set. The dealer said she could send money every month until it was paid off. She was thrilled; she was going to have a real bedroom set very soon! She wanted to look for more antiques, but she couldn't afford it.

Terry, a nurse that Annie met at the hospital, invited her to a quilting party. Terry and her mom, Beverly, had been quilting for years. They taught classes, and Annie thought it would be great fun to learn. This was a whole new world for her. She had gone to school for so many years and had never had time to do things like this. She was overwhelmed by all the patterns and the history; she borrowed a book from Terry to learn more about quilts. She thought, *Perhaps I can make a quilt for my antique bed!*

In August, Jon called to say that Amy had given birth to a little boy two weeks premature. She named him Jonathan Brett. Jon said he looked exactly like Brian and they felt sure the baby was his, but they would do a blood test. Brian was coming home over Labor Day.

"We can only pray that things work out for the best," was all that he would say. Annie wasn't sure what he meant by that.

Rick was very good about calling Annie on weekends and she looked forward to his calls. She told him she had a place for him to stay when he came. Walt would be gone and he was willing to let Rick stay there. She really did miss him and knew she cared for him probably more than she wanted to admit. She hoped that they could work out their differences.

Annie had been planning menus for the weekend Rick was scheduled to come. She knew that flying to Dallas was a huge expense for him, and she didn't want him to have to spend money on food. She had several things she wanted to say to him and didn't even know where to begin. She really believed that leaving Kansas City was probably the best thing she had ever done for their relationship. If she had taken a job there, she would still be dealing with the same old Rick. Perhaps this had opened his eyes. Sometimes she wondered if she wasn't to blame for the way she was treated. *Perhaps I should be more assertive. Oh, enough of that!* She needed to get on with menu planning and grocery lists, and start making the things she could put in the freezer before he arrived.

When Friday night finally arrived, Annie went to the airport. She was sure her heart skipped a beat when Rick first appeared around the corner. She tried to calm herself as he walked up to her; he looked so good. He gave her a hug, but Annie wouldn't let him kiss her. She knew that if he did she would melt inside and all the things she wanted to talk to him about would be gone from her mind. She took him to Walt's apartment, where he left his luggage and then they walked over to Annie's apartment.

As soon as they got in the door, he said "Why wouldn't you let me kiss you at the airport? You don't think that I came all the way down here just to talk, do you?"

"Rick if you kiss me now, I won't even be able to think and I need to talk to you. I need a clear mind to deal with you."

His eyes lit up when he said, "If I affect you that way, why do we even need to talk? Let's just kiss, and we may not need to discuss a thing." He grabbed and hugged her and kissed her neck; she enjoyed every minute of it. She didn't want him to stop.

"I don't think you have heard a thing I've said!" Annie had lost all of her thoughts and composure. *Why does he affect me this way?*

"Can you get this discussion over quickly?" He knew he was bothering her and quite enjoyed the process. "Can I put my arm around you while you talk to me?" He pulled her next to him. "You are beautiful, Annie. You have a wonderful tan and the sun has bleached your hair—you are just gorgeous. Please tell me what you need to talk to me about."

She couldn't help but smile at him. He looked really great to her, too. She took a deep breath and tried to clear her mind, and wondered, *Why haven't I done this all on the telephone? It might have been easier.*

"Rick, there are some things about you that I don't like."

He stopped her and said, "Yes, I know, I've already told you that I was sorry for them. I've learned my lesson. I won't call you naïve, even if you are, and I won't call you a prude, and I won't tell you I don't have time for you, and I won't tell you that you don't fit into my 'plan.' What you don't know is that I have another plan, and this one you do fit into, Annie. I love you very much, and I want to marry you." He took her in his arms and kissed her.

"You will go to great lengths to get out of a discussion, won't you?" *This isn't the time for a discussion. So much for my plans.* She lay in his arms and was content with him holding her and kissing her. It was after midnight when he left for Walt's apartment. She told him to sleep as late as he needed, then come over for breakfast.

She sat in bed and tried to reflect on what Rick had said to her. She smiled to herself at how dear he was and that his "plan" did include her now. What a precious man he was. He made her happy and he was full of surprises. She knew she loved him. She was sure that much of Rick's behavior had been caused from lack of sleep.

When the doorbell woke her up, she looked at the clock and it was 6:15. She got up and hurried downstairs to see who was there. The doorbell was still ringing. She looked through the peephole, and there was Rick, smiling. She opened the door and he looked like he had slept twelve hours.

"I woke up and started thinking about you and had to come."

She was in a daze when he took her in his arms and kissed her. His hands went around her waist, and he was holding her bare skin under her pajama top. She didn't flinch.

He was surprised "Annie, you didn't even react to me touching you."

"I know, I'm half asleep and it really felt wonderful."

"If that's the case, I'll be here tomorrow morning at the same time."

She hugged him again. "I need to get dressed; it isn't proper for a young lady to entertain a young man in her pajamas."

She put on a pair of shorts and a blouse and came down and fixed breakfast. Having breakfast with him made her feel content. *I could get used to this.* She smiled at him across the table. Rick was complimentary about everything she cooked. The bacon was crisp, just like he liked it, the eggs weren't runny.

They decided to go to the pool after breakfast. Annie came down the stairs in her bathing suit and Rick took a deep breath. "Wow, do you spend a lot of time at the pool? From the looks of your tan, I think I've already answered my own question. You really look great, Annie."

"Well, if you like, I'll go put on my string bikini."

"You're kidding, I hope," he said with wide eyes.

She answered with a smile, adding shyly, "However, you might see some at the pool. There are two girls that sunbathe in their string bikinis. About a month ago, they were lying on their towels with the strings on their tops untied, so that their backs would tan without string lines. Some of the guys walked by and poured ice water on their backs and then stood back and watched the show. It was hilarious! I think they probably sunbathe on their patio now."

They spent the morning at the pool, swam for a while, then sat in the sun and talked. After they got out of the pool, Annie rubbed suntan lotion on his back; he was pasty white. He told her he rarely saw the light of day. When they walked back to the apartment, Rick said he was starved.

She had roasted a chicken, and she made chicken sandwiches and had a fruit salad in the refrigerator. She cut him a piece of apple pie. It was a new recipe that she tried with sour cream in it; she hoped it would be good. She made some coffee so they could stay awake. Rick thought the pie was great and she was pleased.

They sat on the couch with their coffee. "You're being very quiet about the marriage proposal, Annie. Are you trying to keep me in suspense?"

"No, I'm not; you really took me by surprise." She turned and smiled at this handsome young man. "Rick, I'm sure I've loved you for a long time. But the way you treated me, I felt like you liked me one week and the next week I wasn't sure if you even knew I existed. You've tugged at my heartstrings for a very long time, and sometimes I've felt like you've severed them. I've just never been sure where I stood with you. There were times when I wanted to talk to you, but because you were always tired, I put it off. This is my fault, and I will take full responsibility for it. I just cared about you too much to upset you, and so I never talked about what was bothering me. When you told me I didn't fit into your 'plan,' I didn't know what you wanted me to do. That wasn't a very nice thing to say to me. You have so many outstanding qualities that I love about you. You've worked since you were a youngster to earn money and reach this goal of becoming a doctor, and you have never once acted like you had a tough time. You've just accepted life as it comes, and dealt with it. I have great admiration for you and all that you have accomplished." She stopped, looked into his eyes, and smiled. "I'm very proud of you. Rick, I do love you. You are precious." She snuggled next to him and he kissed her. He was watching her carefully; she smiled at him and said, "I would be very happy to be your wife."

He hugged her to him and kissed her. "I was hoping and praying you would say that." He held her and wouldn't let her go.

The telephone rang and it was Jeff, calling from Kansas. "What are you two doing?"

Annie answered, "We are playing 'kiss and make up' and having a good time doing it."

Jeff laughed. "I'm so happy to hear that, because I've been living with a love-sick little puppy and only you can straighten him out. I need to talk to him for a minute."

She handed the phone to Rick. After a brief conversation he hung up. Apparently, Jeff was just reporting on a patient and all was well. "If it weren't for Jeff, I wouldn't be here now; he is covering for me this weekend. I'm so glad that he is. I was sure that if I didn't come and see you I would lose you to someone else. Annie, you have made me a happy man."

She leaned against him and was glad he had come. "You've made me very happy, too."

"The first time I called you, I was really worried. I told Jeff that I wasn't sure you ever wanted to see me again. You were really ticked with me, weren't you?"

"I was very hurt by the way you had treated me. After two months, and not a word from you, what did you expect me to think?"

"I love your kind heart, Annie. That is just one of the things that I love about you; there are so many more." He kissed her and said he was sleepy.

"That's what happens when you get up at the crack of dawn." She handed him a pillow and he slept on the couch for a little while.

After his nap, Annie asked Rick if he would like to go to the antique shop to see the bedroom set she was buying, and he said he would. Annie was pleased when Rick said he liked it. She showed him the dovetails on the drawers and how well it was made. She still had several months to pay on it, then she could have it delivered. While they were there, Rick saw a beautiful roll-top desk that he admired. It had pretty carving on the drawers and it was in good condition.

Annie whispered to the owner while Rick wasn't looking, "Please put a sold sign on that desk and I'll call you about it on

Monday." Rick was extremely frugal and she knew he wouldn't buy it for himself. She thought it would be wonderful to surprise him. They drove around for a little while and Annie showed him where she worked, then they went back home.

Rick started the charcoal for steaks while Annie put the potatoes in the oven to bake and started cutting up a salad. They sat on the patio and Rick told her how happy he was. He was a different person when he was rested. She loved his gentleness.

"Annie, I hope this won't upset you, but I really don't want a wedding with people invited, I just want to marry you. Weddings cost too much money, and I don't have any money to spare. I don't even have money for an engagement ring for you."

She hugged him. "Please don't worry about a ring for me; I'll be perfectly happy with a gold wedding band. I don't mind not having a big wedding; I just want to marry you. Marriage shouldn't be about having a big wedding." He seemed relieved to hear her say this.

"Annie, you are wonderful." He told her again that he had loans for his medical schooling and he just couldn't see spending money he didn't have. They decided they would get married over the Thanksgiving holiday. Annie would fly to Kansas City on Tuesday and get the blood test, and they would get married on Friday. Rick would send Jeff to the hospital to spend the night so they could have the apartment all to themselves.

He laughed and said, "There is just one problem, I sleep in the room with twin beds and Jeff has the room with the double bed."

"Well, trade with him! I don't think we will both fit in a twin bed."

They ate dinner and then called their mothers to tell them the news.

On Sunday they went to church. Rick was so calm and relaxed. Annie realized that this weekend was probably the first time she had ever seen him when he was rested. She was amazed. He was even more wonderful than she had thought he was! After church they ate chicken salad sandwiches and more apple pie for lunch, then sat and talked about how many children they wanted. Rick said he wanted her to be a stay at home mom. She was pleased to hear that. They talked about buying a house. Annie said she was saving money and she knew she could do even better since she wouldn't have very many needs. She told him about her quilting classes and she said she was looking forward to quilting all winter and maybe she would have a quilt for their bed by the time she moved back to Kansas City in June. The thought of getting married, then having to come back to Dallas was distressing. She had signed a contract for a year and knew she would have to abide by it. *Don't worry about the things you can't change.*

While Annie was preparing supper, Rick came in and stood behind her like he had done on the first night he kissed her. He started kissing her neck, then turned her around and took her in his arms and kissed her.

"Rick, whatever made you think of 'dessert kisses?'"

He laughed, and said, "I just made it up."

"Your 'dessert kisses' will always be special."

Annie loved her time with Rick. They laughed and talked and cuddled and kissed and she wished it would never end. She told him again how proud she was of him. They talked about spending Christmas with both of their families. Rick said his mom wasn't in very good health; she had smoked since she was a teenager and had emphysema. He had tried for years to get her to stop smoking.

Monday morning they went back to the swimming pool and swam for a while, then sat in the sun and talked for a long time about getting married and spending the rest of their lives together.

Rick asked her to please tell him any time she didn't like what he was doing. "Annie, I want to make you happy. It really distressed me when you said you couldn't talk to me because I was always tired. I want you to always be able to talk to me and tell me what you are feeling."

"You are irritable when you are exhausted, and you aren't very patient, that is why I didn't want to talk to you. I didn't want to upset you because you had enough on your mind. When you are rested, you are an absolute dear, so kind and considerate and loving. I know you have had to put in long hours with no sleep; I admire you for what you have done."

They went back to Annie's apartment and ate lunch. Rick told her again how sorry he was to have neglected her and that it would not happen again. "I just didn't know being in love could make me feel like this." He had touched her heart, and she loved just being next to him.

It was time to go to the airport. Annie was sad to see Rick leave, but thrilled with how things had turned out. The entire weekend had been delightful. He started to leave, then came back, kissed her again and whispered in her ear. "I can't wait to be your husband, Annie. I love you."

"Please tell Jeff how much I appreciate him filling in for you so you could come and see me. I couldn't be happier. I love you, Rick." She watched until he was out of sight.

Chapter Nine

Now Annie had real incentive to get started on her quilt. She had such fun with the quilting group and was learning a great deal. This was a whole new adventure for her, and she loved it. She decided to do a "double wedding ring" quilt, and Terry and her mom helped her pick out fabrics. The fabric stores were filled with so many pretty prints and calicos that it was hard to decide which to select for the quilt. Terry and her mom even offered to help her quilt it when the pieces were sewn together. The quilting group had become her main social life. She eagerly looked forward to sewing the pieces of the quilt together every night after work. As she stitched, she thought of Rick and smiled. All the time she worked, she thought that this would be for their bed in their very first home.

The quilting group gave her a surprise bridal shower just before she left to go to Kansas City for her wedding. Annie had no idea this was planned. It was the regular quilting night, and Terry and her mom had invited friends from work and friends from her apartment complex. She received so many lovely gifts. They gave her some of the dishes she had picked out and lots of cooking items. Several of the girls had gone together and bought a beautiful nightgown and robe. She was overwhelmed with everyone's generosity.

Rick met her at the Kansas City airport and told her she had never looked more radiant. She still had the hint of a suntan. Paula had invited her to stay at her apartment until the wedding. Rick said they had been cleaning and scrubbing for days preparing for her arrival. The place looked spotless. The wonderful aroma of a pot roast in the oven greeted them. He told her Jeff had traded rooms with him and was pleased to accommodate them for their honeymoon.

While they were waiting for Jeff, Annie told Rick about the shower her friends had given her and about the beautiful nightgown and robe she had received. Rick got a big grin on his face. "What are you grinning about?"

"I was just thinking how nice it will look hanging on the bedpost."

She couldn't help but laugh. "I can tell you are going to be fun!" She went over and sat on his lap and kissed him.

They were invited to Jerry Nicholson's apartment for Thanksgiving. He was doing the turkey and dressing, potatoes and gravy and everyone was bringing something to contribute to the dinner. Rick had offered to bring a pie and Jeff was bringing a vegetable. Rick said he knew Annie would be a great help. Surprisingly, the guys had been to the grocery store and purchased what she needed to make the pie and the green bean casserole.

On Thanksgiving Day, Annie knew a lot of the folks who were there and met some new ones. The food was delicious. She was very happy and thankful to be with Rick on this special day. He sat down beside her after they had finished their pie and coffee and whispered in her ear. "We're getting married tomorrow."

She whispered back to him, "I was just thinking the very same thing! You make me so happy."

Rick worked part of the day on Friday and picked Annie up at 4:00 so that they could be at the courthouse by 4:30. The old

VW sputtered and chugged, and Annie was wondering if they should have taken a taxi. This little car was on its last legs. However, they arrived in plenty of time and found the office, and in about fifteen minutes they were married.

Hand in hand they left the courthouse; Rick looked over at her. "Thank you for being such an angel about all of this. That is just one of the reasons I love you."

They had directions to the Italian restaurant where they were going to eat. It was family owned and everyone raved about how good the food was. When they walked in, they were asked if this was a special occasion and Rick answered proudly, "It is very special, we just got married." The whole staff pulled out all the stops and they were treated like family. They had a complimentary bottle of wine and when the delicious meal of seafood ravioli was finished, they brought them dessert on the house. It was a delightful evening and one they would never forget.

On the way back to the apartment the car started sputtering and jerking, until Rick finally pulled off the road. He took off his suit coat, rolled up his sleeves; getting out his tools, he asked Annie to hold a flashlight for him while he worked on the engine. He said "Old Lizzie" had never failed him. Finally he thought she was fixed and they got back in the car. Annie was shivering she was so cold. Rick tried to start the engine, they both held their breath. It sputtered and backfired, but it was running.

Just as they got near the apartment, Annie started laughing. "I thought I was going to have to tell my grandchildren that I spent my wedding night in a VW Beetle." They were still laughing by the time they got to the apartment.

The next morning the sun was streaming in the window. Annie was cuddling next to Rick and loving every minute of it, when the telephone rang.

Rick grudgingly answered, "What am I doing? I'm snuggling in bed with Annie." He was silent for a moment, then he said,

"Great," a short pause, "Great," another short pause, and "Great, we'll see you in a few minutes."

"What were all the 'greats' about?"

"Jeff asked how the wedding went, did we enjoy the dinner, and he asked about you."

"Do you tell Jeff everything?"

Rick smiled. "Almost everything. He has known me for so long, if I don't tell him he pretty much knows what I'm thinking."

He kissed her and said, "You need to get dressed; Jeff is coming home to sleep."

Jeff told them if he could sleep for a few hours he would fix steaks for dinner, so Rick and Annie headed to the Plaza to do their Christmas shopping. The Plaza in Kansas City was always a great place to shop, but at Christmas time it was very special with its beautiful decorations and stunning array of Christmas lights. Rick hadn't even started his shopping, and Annie had just a few more gifts to buy. She realized she had never been shopping with Rick, but then he had hardly been out of the hospital since she had known him. He knew exactly what he wanted for his mother. He said the last time he was home her robe was threadbare and she needed a new one. Each went their separate ways. Annie was sure Rick was buying her a present; his eyes sparkled when he said he had some things to do alone. They would meet for lunch at a small soup and sandwich shop.

As Christmas music played, they watched little children sit on Santa's lap and tell him what they wanted. From the time she had nephews, Annie had always bought books for Paul and Mike. She knew just what she wanted and the book store was the last stop before they went to the car. It had been a fun day with her husband.

When they got home, Jeff was in the kitchen cutting up a salad. "How are the newlyweds?"

Rick stood behind Annie and put his arms around her and hugged her to him. They stood and smiled at Jeff.

"You don't even need to answer, I can tell already." Jeff went out to check the charcoal fire, and while he was outside Rick turned Annie around and kissed her. They were still kissing when he returned. "Don't let me interrupt anything."

Rick smiled at him and said, "Don't worry, we won't." They sat down to a delicious steak dinner. These guys knew how to cook, and Annie was impressed.

Sunday morning she packed her suitcase and Rick took her to the airport.

"I'll be back in three weeks, but I think I should come in my car. That will guarantee us a more reliable vehicle when we go to see everyone." Rick agreed, but was concerned that it was such a long drive for her. They said goodbye, and he kept hugging and kissing her until finally she had to get on the plane. This had been a wonderful weekend. She felt so blessed to have Rick for her husband.

Chapter Ten

Annie spent the month of December sending out wedding announcements and writing thank-you notes for the gifts they had received. She also sent Christmas cards and worked on the quilted angels that she was making for gifts. She had wanted to make these angels for a long time, but never had the time to do it. They were for the top of the tree, and they had quilted wings and a skirt of lace. She was making five of them; one for her grandmother, one for her mom and Marilyn, and one for Rick's mom and his Aunt Grace. She knew she wouldn't have time to work on her quilt for the bed until these were finished. She looked often at her wedding ring and felt such love for this man that she had married.

Getting Christmas cards was always such fun. Annie loved hearing from all her friends from school. She got a card from Steve and Sarah. They had a little girl and Sarah sounded happy. She also had a funny one from Gwen.

In the middle of December, Jon called and Annie could tell he was upset. He told her that Carol, a friend of Amy's, had gone to Amy's apartment on Saturday morning, as Amy had invited her to come over for coffee. Carol rang the doorbell and knocked several times and no one came to the door. She waited and tried again, and all the time she waited, she heard the baby crying. She finally went to the apartment office and told them what had happened. They tried calling the apartment, but no one answered. They decided something was wrong and opened the door for Carol.

When she went in, Amy was on the couch, unconscious, and Brett was screaming. The apartment was cold, and the baby was on the floor with a wet and dirty diaper. They called an ambulance for Amy. Carol called to tell Amy's mother to go to the hospital and meet the ambulance, and she called Jon to tell him what happened.

By the time Jon and Sue got to the apartment, Carol had changed the baby's clothes and warmed a bottle. Carol told them that the baby was soaked and hadn't been changed for a very long time. She showed them the diaper, and they were appalled. They took Brett home with them, and then Jon went to the hospital to see what was wrong with Amy. The emergency room nurse told him that she had overdosed on heroin. They were working frantically with her, trying to keep her alive. Jon talked to Amy's mom in the waiting room and told her they had Brett at their house.

Sue gave Brett a warm bath and then used a heating pad next to him, because he was still shaking. She was so upset when Jon got home she could hardly talk. When they called to tell Brian what had happened, he said he would be home early for Christmas. He was very upset that this had happened, and asked his dad, "How could anyone do this to a baby?"

Annie asked, "Have they determined for sure that this is Brian's baby?" Jon said a blood test had been done, Brian had "AB" type blood, and so did Brett. This was not a common blood type.

"Annie, this baby is a carbon copy of Brian. We are sure he is our grandson." Jon's voice sounded very determined.

Annie told him to please let her know what was happening and ended by telling him she would keep them in her prayers. She wondered what would happen to Brett.

While having lunch in the cafeteria one day, Annie met a girl from Wichita who said she needed a ride home for Christmas. This was just what she had hoped for. Five days before Christmas, she picked Peggy up at her apartment and they headed north. Annie was so thankful to be on her way to Kansas City. From the time she had left Peggy in Wichita, her mind had been on Rick and when she would be back in his arms. She wondered how she was going to manage not being with him from January until May. She hoped she could have a long weekend over Easter. She was also sure they wouldn't have been married if she had stayed in Kansas City. She was sure her moving to Dallas was a wake-up call for Rick. Love was hard to understand, but it was wonderful when everything turned out right. She loved him so much.

She was a weary traveler when she arrived, and Rick was such a welcome sight. She just wanted him to hold her and never let her go. With Jeff away visiting his parents, they had several days to be alone before going to Annie's home for Christmas Eve, and then on to Rick's for Christmas day. He gave her a back rub after her shower, which was sheer bliss.

These days were better than any honeymoon could possibly be. Even though it was dark and seemed like the middle of the night, when the alarm clock went off, she was content just cuddling next to her wonderful husband. She fixed them breakfast and smiled at him across the kitchen table. A rush of happiness came over her; she couldn't take her eyes off him. When he looked at her she felt very loved and adored. *I hope he always makes me feel this way.*

They packed all the presents the night before, and Annie was excited to be going home. She had missed all of her family, especially her little nephews. Rick said next year they would have a place of their own with their own Christmas tree, and he was really looking forward to that. He seemed to focus on home and family and Annie loved that about him. The thought of owning a home and sharing life together was so appealing. This living apart was not what marriage was supposed to be.

When they arrived at the farm, the house smelled of wonderful aromas. Annie's mom welcomed Rick with open arms and treated him like he was one of her own. Tom and Marilyn, Paul and Mike arrived with armloads of presents. Annie introduced Rick and there were hugs from everyone. The boys had grown like weeds and were so adorable. The family sat down to pork roast, scalloped potatoes, a squash casserole and copper penny salad, and for dessert there were three different pies; an apple, a chocolate cream and lemon chess. Then they all gathered around the Christmas tree and the little boys started passing out presents for everyone.

The next morning Annie and Rick ate breakfast with the traditional cinnamon rolls, then said goodbye and left for Rick's home. They would go to his house and meet his mom, and then to Aunt Grace and Uncle Charlie's for Christmas dinner.

Katherine Henslee was a tall, thin woman and looked in very poor health. Annie thought she had been a very pretty woman when she was young, but now her wrinkled face looked drawn and she had deep lines around her mouth. She was happy to see them and kept hugging them again and again. The house reeked of cigarette smoke and Annie could see the yellow stains on her fingers.

They sat down on the couch while Rick was bringing in the luggage, and Annie told her what a wonderful young man she had for a son. "I am so proud to be his wife. He makes me very happy." They talked for a little while, then it was time to go for dinner. Katherine had made scalloped corn and a strawberry Jell-O salad and Rick loaded them in the car.

They drove down a country road to the farm where Aunt Grace and Uncle Charley lived. The farm had been in the family for several generations. When Katherine's parents died, Grace and her husband Charlie had moved into the house, and Charlie had been farming it ever since. Rick was very fond of his aunt and uncle. When he was growing up he had worked on the farm in the summer months, helping Uncle Charlie. It was a lovely old Victorian house with a wrap-around porch and a picket fence enclosing the garden inside. Hospitality just oozed out of Aunt Grace as she wanted everyone to feel "at home." She had a pleasant, happy face and she dearly loved to entertain.

Uncle Charlie said, "Well, it's about time you brought this young woman you married to see us." There were hugs and kisses all around. Uncle Charlie was a huge man with a weathered look and a jovial face. When he finished carving the turkey, the food was carried to the table. It was a sumptuous feast. They all said they had eaten too much and would wait for dessert.

After the dishes were finished, everyone gravitated to the fireplace where they opened presents that were under the Christmas tree. Rick's mom and Aunt Grace both seemed pleased with their quilted Christmas angels that Annie had made. Rick's aunt and uncle gave them a beautiful wedding present: a walnut coffee table that Uncle Charlie had made for them. He was so pleased that they liked it. Rick kept feeling the lovely satiny finish on the coffee table and Annie could see that Uncle Charlie was pleased.

Annie thought, *I'm so glad we didn't come in the VW, we wouldn't be able to take this back with us.*

They fixed turkey sandwiches for supper and had applesauce spice cake, which was one of Aunt Grace's specialties. They said their thank you and goodbyes and went back to Katherine's house.

On the way, Katherine started coughing and couldn't seem to stop. She said it was just the cold air and she wasn't used to it. She said she never went out at night. Concerned, Rick brought his "little black bag" in from the car. He listened to her lungs and asked if she had seen a doctor lately. She hadn't.

She smiled up at him, looking very proud of her son. "Well,

I'm seeing one now." Annie wished she could capture that look on her face, as it was a precious moment between a mother and her son. By nightfall, Katherine was wheezing with every breath. Sitting down beside his mother, Rick told her, "Mother, you can't continue to smoke; you're killing yourself."

She became teary eyed. "I know, but I have tried so many times to quit and I always start back."

She was getting emotional, and Rick put his arm around her. The coughing started again, and Rick asked if she had any cough medicine in the house. She nodded that she did and went to get it. She had enough relief from the medicine to be able to sit and talk a while before going to bed.

After they went to bed, Rick talked to Annie about his concern for his mother's health. He felt helpless when it came to his mother and her smoking problem. He had seen too many people suffer from cancer and heart disease because of smoking, but somehow he had failed to communicate this to his mother. He had told her what lungs looked like when people smoked, even if they didn't have cancer. Nothing he said seemed to make any difference.

The next morning Rick insisted that his mother see her doctor so she could have a chest x-ray. He was concerned about pneumonia. Katherine promised to call the doctor and make an appointment as soon as the office opened. In the car, Rick said again that he really felt helpless; his mom had tried to quit smoking so many times and always started back.

When they got back to the apartment, Rick called his mom and she had done as he said, but they were waiting for the report on the x-rays. The doctor had already started her on an antibiotic. Three days later they found out she had bronchitis.

Annie made an appointment with Dr. Gaston while she was in Kansas City to talk to him about a job in June. He said there was an opening and she filled out the paperwork for it. He told her she had married a very nice young man and he would be happy to have both of them working at the hospital.

Annie was content to have Rick all to herself. She fixed dinner for him and when he came home from work he came in the kitchen and said he was coming for "dessert kisses." She told him she wished she could enjoy this every night. She dreaded the thought of returning to Dallas and living alone until June.

Rick decided they should start looking for a house. He wanted something close to the hospital. They had no idea what they could afford. Annie said she was putting a lot of her salary into her savings. He said he would start looking and when she came back for Easter, maybe they could decide on something they could afford.

Chapter Eleven

During the long drive back to Dallas, Annie decided she would try to finish the quilt during the winter. Looking forward to making a quilt for their new bed was a pleasing thought. When she picked up her mail at the post office, she ended up with a carload of wedding presents and Christmas cards. It was almost like having another Christmas. She loved getting Christmas cards from all of her old friends and catching up on the news. There was a card and a long letter from Martha. With this load of presents, there would be lots of thank you notes to write.

Jon called to say that Amy had gone to a rehabilitation center and that Brian was going through the process of custody for Brett. While Brian was home, he was feeding, bathing and caring for Brett. He said Sue was helping, but Brian was doing most of it. She wished them the best and promised to keep them in her prayers.

Annie was thrilled to have the antique bedroom furniture delivered. It was beautiful and it was an elegant touch in the bedroom. She tried to imagine the quilt on the bed.

She talked with Rick every weekend and always looked forward to his calls. Katherine was making a slow recovery from the bronchitis and was on another round of antibiotics. She knew Rick was extremely worried about his mom.

Annie called Rick several weeks after she returned to Dallas and told him, "You are going to be a daddy!" She was delighted and she hoped he was, too. She said, "I'm feeling fine, just a little tired."

"Are you sure, Annie?" She could tell by the tone of his voice that he was overwhelmed with joy.

"I'm sure, honey. I just want you to know how happy you have made me. I wanted to call and tell you as soon as I suspected, but I wanted to be sure. I've wanted to be a mother since I was a little girl, even before I knew where babies came from. Babies have always fascinated me. This is a dream come true for me."

Rick was excited and said he would make her an appointment with Dr. Gill when she came back over Easter weekend. He had worked with Dr. Gill during his time in Ob-Gyn and said he was the best. Rick said he would like for her to deliver by natural childbirth, because he had seen too many sedated babies and he also wanted her to breast feed. This was best for mother and baby. Rick asked so few things of her and she loved him so much she would do just about anything to please him. This was a life long dream of Annie's. She would be thrilled to be a mother.

Annie called Jon and Sue to let them know that she was pregnant. Sue answered the phone and was elated when Annie shared the news with her. She handed the phone to Jon and he kidded her, telling her she didn't waste any time getting pregnant. Jon told her he was sure she would be a wonderful mother. He told her that Brian had Brett with him in Arizona and was a bit overwhelmed with the responsibility that went with being a single father. He had hired an older woman to help care for the baby and had purchased dozens of books about baby and child care. Jon said that Brian called often to ask his mother questions. She, of course, loved this and Brian seemed to enjoy being a father. Jon also said that he and Sue really missed having the baby with them. They both adored him.

After Annie hung up the phone, she sat and thought about Jon and Sue. She had great admiration for both of them. She knew they must have heartache over Brian's behavior, but they had never criticized him or said a negative word about him. They had unconditional love for their son and for their grandson. She was also very touched by the way they treated her. Nothing had changed when Brian called off the wedding; they treated her with the same love and affection as they had before. Jon called often and his care and concern for her well being had been genuine. She valued his friendship and felt she could talk to him about anything. She knew this was a most unusual relationship.

Annie had used most of her vacation time when she got married at Christmas, so she just took off the Friday before Easter and flew to Kansas City to be with Rick. Rick had daffodils on the table when she arrived, and she was very touched that he had done this for her. She had longed to be with him since returning after Christmas.

Rick had looked at several houses and decided that a townhouse was probably the best choice for them. On Saturday, they looked at the options and decided on an end house that had a garage. Annie loved the house; it was really bigger than they needed, with four bedrooms, but they both were pleased with their decision. Two of the bedrooms were small, and Rick said they would be good for a nursery. The kitchen was large, and there was a place for a table and chairs. This was where they would begin their family life together. They felt truly blessed.

Annie had her first appointment with Dr. Gill. She told him he came highly recommended. He was such a gentle soul, and Annie liked him immediately. He said she was fine and the baby was due in September.

Annie was sad to leave for Dallas, but knew in just a short time they would be together again. Her heart quickened just thinking about being with Rick in their new home.

When the final stitches were put in the quilt, she put her initials and the date in the corner. Carefully folding it, she carried it upstairs and put it on her bed. The quilt was stunning. This had kept her busy all winter, and she thought *at least we have a bed to sleep in when we move into our house!* The rest of the house would have to be sparsely furnished.

The roll-top desk was delivered and Annie knew Rick would be surprised and pleased when she gave it to him. This was a perfect gift for him at the completion of many years of hard work and studying, and the fact that he was finally finished with his schooling. The townhouse had a small study with one whole wall for books, which was great because Rick had kept every book he had ever owned. The desk would be a perfect addition for the room.

Boxes were stacked everywhere and Annie was ready for the movers when they arrived. The car was already packed. She didn't want to waste any time before she returned to Kansas City. She hoped they would never have to be apart again.

The first week in June, they moved into their spacious house with the few furnishings they had. When Rick saw the desk, he first hugged Annie, then stared at it in disbelief. He rarely ever said that he wanted anything, and he really didn't say he wanted this, but had admired it, and Annie just couldn't resist. This would be a great place for him to study for his boards, the exams he needed to pass in order to be certified.

He told her, "You really surprised me with this, but I'm so glad you did."

The house was so empty it echoed when doors closed. Rick didn't want to go into any more debt than he had already incurred with his loans for medical school; more furniture would have to wait. They did have to buy a refrigerator, but that was all for now. They could eat off of the card table, and they had the bedroom set, and that was it. Annie was happy just to be together. They would just have to save and buy furniture as they could afford it. A baby crib would be their next purchase.

That night they were standing on the patio and watching a beautiful sunset. Rick stood behind her and put his arms around her and hugged her to him. They watched the pink sky streaked with blue, fade and change color. It was a glorious Kansas sunset.

Chapter Twelve

Rick came to Annie's office at the hospital one morning and the moment that she saw him she knew that something was terribly wrong.

"We've lost my mom. Aunt Grace just called and said that the people from the telephone company where Mom worked called and said she hadn't come to work. They couldn't reach her by phone, so they called Aunt Grace and she went to the house to see what was wrong. She found Mom dead in her bed, probably from a heart attack, but they don't know for sure."

They hugged for a long time, neither one saying anything. Finally, he said, "I'll see you at home; I've asked to be off until Monday."

That same afternoon, they packed and left to go to his mom's home. This was such devastating news. What a horrible shock. Rick talked about his mom so lovingly on the trip home. She was so very proud of him finally becoming a doctor after so many years of schooling. He had been her whole life from the time he was born. They went straight to the farm to see Aunt Grace and Uncle Charlie, and then on to Katherine's house. Rick went into his mom's bedroom and found her Bible open by her bedside. He sat on the bed and read the pages that were open, knowing that these were the last that she had read. Annie came in and found him with tears streaming down his cheeks. She sat down beside him and put her arm around him.

The next few days were spent planning the funeral, and while Aunt Grace and Rick took care of that, Annie started packing some of Katherine's things. She found cookbooks that had belonged to Rick's grandmother and in the margins she had written things like, "Rickie's favorite" and "This is tasty." One that amused Annie was, "Don't try this again." Annie thought it was a treasure.

When Rick and his aunt came back to the house, Aunt Grace told stories about some of the furniture. Most of it had belonged to Rick's grandparents, and there were some beautiful things. Rick went up in the attic and found an old cradle that Grandpa Henslee had made, and also an old wooden highchair with a tray that flipped over the back. Rick asked if Annie wanted to keep these, and she said she would be thrilled with them. The dining room furniture consisted of a round oak table, eight patterned-back chairs, and a large oak sideboard. In one bedroom there were twin brass and iron beds and a pretty washstand with marble on top. The other bedroom had a walnut double bed with a dresser and chest of drawers and a night stand. Rick said they could sure fill up their empty house with all this.

The funeral was on Saturday. Jeff and quite a few people from the hospital came. Katherine had lived in this small town all her life and probably knew every person that lived in the area. It seemed as if the entire town filled the church. Rick saw people he hadn't seen in years. There was lunch served in the church basement followed by the funeral. Annie could not believe that so many, knowing that Rick was a doctor, told him about their ailments as if he had a prescription pad in his pocket. He was so kind and patient with all of them. It was such a comfort to have Tom and Marilyn and Annie's mom there for the service. Annie tried to be very brave and strong for Rick. She hoped controlling her emotions would improve with age, because she wasn't doing a very good job at the moment. She just could not control the tears.

Uncle Charlie said Rick could use his pickup to move the furniture. The next day, several of Rick's friends came to help load the furniture, and when they filled it up they drove to Kansas City and unloaded it in the garage. All of it would have to be scrubbed. Even the furniture smelled of smoke. They took another load on Sunday and filled the car with boxes of small things and returned. They would need to make several more trips on the following weekends.

On the way back to Kansas City, Rick talked about the high cost of the funeral. He knew his mom had money in the bank, but he wasn't sure if she had enough to cover the expenses. They would need to go back sometime during the week and meet with the lawyer. All the money Annie had saved had gone for the down payment on the house and for the refrigerator. Annie could tell this worried Rick. Money seemed to always be a problem.

When Annie went back to see Dr. Gill, he said everything was progressing normally. She was feeling fine and was happy to get a good report.

Rick received word that he had passed his boards. This was wonderful news! He would be joining two other surgeons in their practice near the hospital. Annie told him she was very proud of him. This was his dream and it had finally come true.

In the evenings after work they started washing and waxing the furniture in the garage. They were amazed that the wash water turned black and some of the furniture was almost a different color. One evening while they were working Jeff came by and walked up the driveway grinning from ear to ear.

Annie said, "You look happy, Jeff, what's happening in your life?"

Jeff looked at both of them with a huge grin on his face and said, "How do you know when you've met the 'right one' in your life?"

Annie laughed and said, "Before I answer, I want to hear what Rick has to say." Annie and Rick exchanged smiles. She went over to stand by him and put her arm around his waist. He hugged her to him.

He looked down at Annie lovingly, and said, "Well, first of all you want to be with them all the time, and when you aren't with them, you think about them all the time and you can't concentrate on anything."

Annie nodded, "I agree."

Jeff grinned and said, "Then I've found the 'right one' for me."

"Tell us about her. And where did you meet her?" Annie was excited to hear what he had to say.

Jeff was grinning and his eyes sparkled. "I met her at a hospital meeting at St. Luke's. She is an Ob-Gyn doctor, who kind of did the same thing I did, just studied and didn't date until she had finished medical school. She is so beautiful and I just love being with her. Her name is Emily McCleery."

Annie exclaimed, "I'm so happy for you! When can we meet her?"

Jeff said he would take them all out to dinner, and they decided on a night.

Rick and Annie liked Emily from the moment they saw her. She was a tiny, lovely young woman with black hair and translucent blue eyes. Everyone had a fun evening and it was evident that Emily thought Jeff was very special.

The almost empty townhouse that they had moved into was slowly beginning to fill up with furniture and looked like someone lived there. Annie appreciated all the lovely antiques that came from Rick's family. She envisioned his mother and his grandmother caring for these pieces and was overjoyed to have them in their home. They still had boxes to sort through, but they had made a lot of progress. At least, the house didn't echo anymore.

Chapter Thirteen

Jon called one evening to say he had some very sad news. "Sue died last night. She said she had a terrific headache and went up to bed very early. I watched the rest of a movie on TV, and when I went up to check on her she was dead. They did an autopsy and found that she'd had a brain aneurysm." Jon was devastated. He gave her the details of the funeral arrangements and when the funeral service was scheduled. This was such a horrible shock. Annie said how sorry she was and asked if there was anything she could do.

She checked with Rick when he got home and he said he had a full surgery schedule that day. There wasn't any way he could go. He really didn't want Annie to go by herself as she was seven and a half months pregnant, so she sent flowers and sat down to write to the family. Sue was such a vibrant woman and loved by everyone. It was going to be very difficult for the whole family. Annie was in tears when she finished writing the note.

Almost every weekend Annie and Rick went to Katherine's house and cleaned and painted and tried to get it ready to put on the market. They were making good progress, and given a couple of more weekends, they would be finished. They always stayed with Aunt Grace and Uncle Charlie, which was such a pleasant experience. Their hospitality was warm and wonderful and the food was delicious. Katherine had owned half of the farm and Uncle Charlie wanted to buy it. Rick was willing to sell and said he would go right to the bank and pay on his loans. This seemed like a God-send.

Whenever they could, they got together with Jeff and Emily and had so much fun with them. They ate together on weekends, and Rick and Jeff still talked about their patients. This usually dominated the table conversation, but it was always a source of laughter.

Annie bought a hundred daffodil bulbs to plant along the side of their house. Rick dug up the bed. They added bone meal and planted all the bulbs. She thought *this will be so pretty in the springtime. Rick will love seeing them all bloom at one time.*

While Rick sanded the cradle, Annie covered a mattress for it. She thought it would be perfect to have downstairs for the baby to sleep in during the day. They bought a crib for the nursery and decorated the room with a pretty wallpaper border with bunnies. Neither one had any experience putting up wallpaper, but they managed to get the bunny border on the wall. Annie laughed at Rick because it looked like he had more wallpaper paste on him than on the border.

Rick's next project was sanding the old wooden highchair that they'd found in Katherine's attic. One of the legs had been chewed on and the paint was peeling, but other than that it was in good shape. Now, they had the nursery ready and waiting for their baby.

Annie had been doing her exercises and was down to the last two weeks before her due date. Every day Annie was so thankful for all of her blessings and thought her life was even more wonderful than she had imagined it could be.

When the girls at work gave her a baby shower, she came home with many lovely gifts, including a stroller, which she was thrilled to have. She kept looking at all the cute little outfits and thinking that very soon she would have someone to put them on.

Annie went into labor a week after the baby was due. Rick seemed almost as nervous as she was when they arrived at the hospital. He was very attentive and stayed with her every minute, talking her through every contraction. And when she turned on her side, he would rub her back and hold her hand. Emily and Jeff came up to check on Annie's progress, and Emily told her she was doing great. Finally, after eighteen hours, Annie delivered an eight-and-a-half pound girl. They named her Katherine Louise after Rick's mother. They would call her Katie. Rick held her in a blanket and brought her over for Annie to see. She was still red and crying, but Annie thought she was beautiful. She couldn't wait to hold her.

Rick called everyone he knew to tell them about Katie. Annie's mom said she would be there to stay and help for a while. Dr. Michele Lane, the pediatrician, had thoroughly examined little Katie and said she was perfect. Of course, Rick had already checked her.

When the nurse handed Katie to Annie for the first time she was overwhelmed with joy. She was sure this was one of life's very special moments. She fed her and held her tiny hand, and marveled at what a miracle she had in her arms. This was surely one of God's most abundant blessings. She was very thankful for this precious little girl.

Every morning Rick was there before six o'clock to check on Annie. She had slept on her stomach for the first time in months, and this was a wonderful feeling. The next morning when he arrived, she was feeling something very strange. Her milk had come in and she told Rick she felt like her breasts were filled with concrete. She had milk clear up to her collarbone and she was hurting.

"How long is this supposed to last?" she asked Rick with wide eyes.

He looked at her and smiled. "I don't know, Annie."

"What do you mean you don't know? You're a doctor!"

He tried to comfort her, and said he was sure she would feel better once she nursed the baby. She was relieved to discover he was right.

It was comforting to have her mom there to help her when she got home. She helped her bathe Katie and they talked for hours about when Annie was a baby. Elizabeth could only stay for a week, but it was a very special time between mother, daughter and granddaughter.

A beautiful baby quilt arrived in the mail from Terry and Beverly, her quilting teachers from Dallas. It was a crib quilt, or could be used for a wall hanging. It had a nursery rhyme in each square and was certainly a gift to be treasured.

Annie thought motherhood was one of the most wonderful things that had ever happened to her. She just loved taking care of this new little darling that she and Rick had created. Rick absolutely adored Katie. He loved to just sit and hold her and smile down on her. When Annie put Katie in the old cradle, she wondered who had used it, and if Rick's mother had slept in it when she was a baby. *I'm sure there are stories here, if this cradle could only talk...*

Aunt Grace and Uncle Charlie were coming for Thanksgiving dinner and to see Katie. Aunt Grace said she would bring pies and homemade rolls. This would be such a special time, and they had so much to be thankful for. What an occasion to all sit around the old oak table that had belonged to Rick's grandmother and grandfather and share Thanksgiving dinner.

Thanksgiving was a most enjoyable day for everyone. Aunt Grace and Uncle Charlie were so kind and helpful and easy to have around. They both thought Katie was precious, and it seemed as though someone was holding her all day long. The dinner was quite good, but Annie would never have had everything ready at the same time if she hadn't had help from Aunt Grace. They had to leave in the afternoon so Uncle Charlie could do chores. Annie was exhausted when they left, but she was pleased that they had come.

At seven weeks old, Katie was a darling. She was sleeping until almost five in the morning, but Annie was up fixing breakfast for Rick anyway. Their first anniversary was on Saturday and they planned to go out for dinner. This would be the first time they'd left Katie with a sitter. Angela Grimes was a neighbor who lived just three houses away, and had said she would be available to babysit. Rick and Annie had another delightful evening at their little Italian restaurant. They decided this would become a tradition.

With Thanksgiving behind them, Annie was ready to put up their Christmas tree. She had a few decorations she had made, and they had a box marked "Christmas decorations" that Katherine had stored in a closet. Rick opened it and a flood of memories came back to him. He found some things that he had made at school and some that were his grandmother's. He helped put them on the tree, and told a story about each one. The quilted angel that Annie made for Katherine was also in the box.

"I didn't have time to make an angel for us last year, so this is a very special angel that will go on the top of our tree every year."

When the tree was decorated, they turned off all the lights except for the tree lights, and played Christmas carols and drank hot chocolate. This was another tradition they would keep.

Chapter Fourteen

Annie was looking through one of the cookbooks she had from Katherine's kitchen and found a recipe for "snickerdoodles." In the margin, Rick's grandmother had written, "Rickie's favorite." She wanted to surprise him, so after dinner she brought in a plate of cookies with their coffee. She sat down beside him and snuggled next to him.

When he took the first bite, he hugged her and said, "I haven't had these in years."

She told him where she'd found the recipe and he said, "You are even more wonderful than I ever imagined anyone could be." They sat there for a long time, and Rick talked about his mother and his grandmother.

They spent Christmas Eve at the farm with Aunt Grace and Uncle Charlie, then Christmas day with Annie's family. They had a wonderful time. Annie got to see Julie and they had a good visit. Rick used an entire roll of film of Katie's first Christmas. She was fascinated with the Christmas lights, so he took many pictures of her gazing at the Christmas tree.

After the holidays, Julie came down to spend a weekend with Annie. They sat and talked until after midnight the first night. There just never was enough time to get caught up on everything. Julie had met a nice young man and hoped Ben liked her as much as she liked him. They had been dating for about three months. Julie was still living at home, as her mom was not well and needed help. Sometimes Annie wondered if Julie's mom didn't enjoy poor health. It was a real dilemma with no easy solution in sight. They both wished they could visit more often.

Rick received word from the realtor that an offer had been made on Katherine's house. He decided to accept it and was pleased to have all their work on the house finally pay off. This would be money to pay on his loans.

In the spring the daffodils bloomed and they were a sight to behold. Rick and Annie stood and watched them sway in the breeze and thought they were gorgeous. Rick took pictures of Katie in front of the sea of yellow flowers. Annie took a picture of Rick sitting on the ground holding Katie with daffodils all around. To say the least, she was a well photographed baby. Annie took her out in the stroller almost every day now that the weather was warm. On returning from a walk one day with Katie, she stopped to pick a huge bouquet of daffodils to take in the house. *Sometimes you need to stop and do something that purely delights you.*

Rick dug up the area around the back patio. There were three sides and Annie wanted to plant a salad garden on one side, an herb garden on one side and flowers on the other. She planted several kinds of lettuce and could hardly wait until it warmed enough to plant the tomatoes, peppers and cucumbers. She planted dill, chives and parsley and would plant basil when it was warmer.

Jeff and Emily came by one evening and they were both beaming. They came to tell Rick and Annie that they were engaged, and that the wedding would be soon. Jeff asked Rick to be his best man. Emily was very happy and said she had even thought of eloping. She said Jeff made her feel like she was in the clouds.

Chapter Fifteen

Jeff and Emily had a beautiful wedding and they were such a happy couple. It was a joy just to be around them. They had a quick honeymoon and went back to work in a week. Jeff moved into Emily's apartment until they could look for a house. It was great to have such wonderful friends.

Finding a night that they could all get together for dinner was a difficult task. Each had busy schedules every day and they all were "on call" some nights and weekends. Emily was the one who never knew when a patient was going to have a baby and she would be at the hospital for hours. When they did get together, usually for dinner, it was always a delightful occasion.

Annie had been so involved with Katie that she hadn't checked on Jon Kendall like she had planned. One evening she called to see how he was doing, and he said he did really well until he came home to an empty house. Being home without Sue was never going to feel right for him. Weekends were so lonely, but he felt he was adjusting. Brian and Brett were doing fine, but he said Amy had gone back to the rehabilitation clinic. She seemed to always go back to the friends that she had known before and get into drugs again. Jon was someone that Annie admired greatly and her heart went out to him. She wished she could do more to help him.

Over Labor Day weekend Katie started pulling up and standing alone, and walking around the coffee table. Rick was there with the camera taking pictures of everything she did. She was so pleased with herself; she would smile at her daddy every time he looked at her. When he would walk away she would get down on her hands and knees and crawl after him. Annie loved watching the interaction between them.

Annie often wondered if life could get any better than it was now. Financially, they were doing well, even with Annie not working. Rick had used the money from the sale of the farm to Uncle Charlie and paid off three of the loans he had for medical school. They were happy just to be together and rarely ever went out. Their favorite thing to do was to spend an evening with Jeff and Emily.

On Katie's first birthday, Rick took a whole roll of film of her eating cake and playing with her presents. She looked adorable in the old highchair. They had padded the sides and back, and Rick installed a strap to secure her in the chair. She loved being the center of attention and was so excited she squealed and laughed. She could say "Da Da" now and she called him every time he came near her. When the garage door came up and she could hear the noise, she called "Da Da." Rick loved this and encouraged her to do it even more.

Jeff and Emily came by one weekend to share their great news. Emily was going to have a baby. Emily planned to work until the baby was born, then stay home with the baby as long as she could. She was thrilled and asked Annie many questions about caring for babies. She was glowing with the prospect of being a mom and Jeff was looking forward to being a father. He and Rick had some funny conversations about babies. They started recalling their days in Ob-Gyn, and some of the babies that they had delivered.

"Do you remember the lady that had eight children and all we had to do was stand there and catch the ninth one?" These guys were merciless sometimes.

Chapter Sixteen

In early November, Rick was on call and had to return to the hospital late one night. Annie went to bed, because she never knew how long he would be gone. She was asleep when she was awakened by the doorbell. She hurried down the stairs, thinking that Rick had forgotten his house key. When she opened the door, there stood Jeff and Emily and a police officer. Annie knew the moment she saw them that something was terribly wrong. She asked them to come in; Jeff took her hand and led her to the couch. She sat down and held her breath, waiting for the news. "Annie, I have some terrible news for you; Rick has been killed. He was on his way home from the hospital, and stopped to help at an accident on the highway. An ambulance and a fire truck were already on the scene. While they were working to help the injured, a drunk driver ran into them and killed Rick, a fireman and a paramedic. As so often happens, the drunk driver was not hurt."

Annie was trembling and tears were running down her face. She didn't want to believe what she was hearing. Jeff and Emily said they would stay there with her. The young police officer said how sorry he was and left. Annie sobbed; she could hardly talk she was so upset. When morning came she called her mother, and got so emotional she asked Jeff to call Aunt Grace and Uncle Charlie. When Katie woke up, calm seemed to come over Annie, and she realized this was her reason to be strong.

Her mother and Tom arrived before noon, followed by Aunt Grace and Uncle Charlie. Throughout the day, friends and doctors who knew Rick came by the house. Most of the day was a blur. At times she felt like she was having a bad dream, and she would wake up and it would all be over. The house was full of people bringing food for her. Reverend Habersham from their church came by and they talked about the funeral and when it would be. They decided that the hymns would be Rick's favorites, "The Old Rugged Cross" and "Amazing Grace." Jeff helped her with all the funeral arrangements. Annie was moved that he offered to give the eulogy.

The following night, Annie sat in bed and decided she would write a poem to put in the church bulletin. She wanted to honor this wonderful man in her life who had brought her so much happiness. She couldn't imagine what life would be like without him. He was the kindest and most gentle soul she had ever known. He was a very loving and affectionate husband and father, and Annie always felt that he adored her. She picked up a note pad and a pencil, and started putting her thoughts down on paper. As she wrote she cried and poured her heart out.

A Fond Farewell

I met him and he loved me
And then he stole my heart
And all I have left are memories
For we are now apart.

My heart has been sorely broken
Your solace I must find
For he has gone before me
And I am left behind.

He dreamed of being a doctor
From the time he was a boy.
And when his goal was finally reached
It filled his heart with joy.

He so adored our daughter
It makes me very sad.
For she will not remember him,
This man, who was her dad.

I know my heart will be healing
But I do miss him so much
His hugs, his smiles and his kisses
And his ever so gentle touch.

As I look to the sky for comfort
And I ask the Lord above
Please send me all Your blessings
And open Your arms with love.

The day of the funeral, Angela came to get Katie, saying she would keep her as long as was needed. The church was overflowing when they arrived. The news of the accident had been on all the TV stations and there was an outpouring of grief. There were ten children that were left without fathers after the accident. The fireman had six children, the paramedic had three, and there was Katie.

When Jeff got up to speak, Annie said a prayer, for she knew how difficult it would be for him. He smiled at her when he got to the front of the church; it was all she could do to not break down and cry.

He started off by saying that he didn't have a brother, but if he had been able to pick one, it would have been Rick. They had met their freshman year in college and had been roommates, and they got along so well that they continued to be roommates through medical school. Only when Annie came into Rick's life did he decide that she would be a better roommate. They had both decided that they weren't going to get involved with girls until they finished medical school. They just didn't have time for both. That all ended when Rick met Annie and he was smitten with her. He told funny stories of them studying for tests together and how they memorized bones, muscles and body parts. He told some very touching stories about how they helped each other when they were sleep deprived and how that they fed off of each other's sense of humor. He made it through to the last sentence without his voice breaking, but when he said, "May God watch over you, my friend. We'll miss you," he choked.

Annie was so proud of him. Tears ran down her cheeks.

A lunch was served at the church after the funeral. There were relatives of Rick's that she had never met. So many people that day had such nice things to say about him. She was dreading going to the cemetery for the burial. Somehow this was the final goodbye, and she didn't want it to happen. But she managed to get through all of the burial service. When it started to rain, everyone hurried to their cars. Annie and her family went back to the house. She just felt numb. Emily went to get Katie from Angela. She knew if anyone could bring joy to a sad day like today, it would be Katie.

Annie's mother tried to persuade her to go home with her for a few days and get some rest. Annie said she had too many things to do, and she needed to get a job. She had the funeral to pay for, a house payment to make and the loans for Rick's medical school. She would also have to have a sitter for Katie. She wasn't sure how she was going to manage. She would call Dr. Gaston on Monday. Rick did have life insurance, but she wasn't sure how long it would take to get the money.

She knew she needed to call Jon Kendall and tell him about Rick's death, but wasn't sure she could do it without crying. She finally dialed the telephone and took a deep breath. He was so kind and comforting after she told him what happened. She wondered what she would do without Jon's support. They talked for a long time and she felt better when she hung up. He still missed Sue, and said he was very lonely sometimes. She knew he understood what she was going through. She kept thinking to herself, *It isn't what happens to you in life; it is how you handle it. I must be strong for Katie.*

The weather had been cold and rainy for days and when the skies cleared and the sun came out, Annie asked Angela to stay with Katie while she was napping one afternoon. After gathering her daffodil bulbs, bone meal and shovel she went to the cemetery to plant bulbs on Rick's grave in the shape of a cross. When they were all in the ground and she had smoothed the soil on the grave, tears filled her eyes and she sat on the ground and sobbed. She felt so alone and sad and wondered if she could ever be a normal person again. *Will life ever be the same without him?*

When Annie went to see Dr. Gaston about a job, he sat and talked to her for a long time. He said they would hire her, and she could start whenever she was ready. She said she really needed to start right away, so she could pay her bills. Angela had agreed to keep Katie while she was working.

The first week she was back at work, she saw Dr. Jerry Nicholson. He had been a resident with Rick, and was now a psychologist. He asked how she was doing, and said if she ever needed to talk to please come see him. She told him she was having a difficult time trying to deal with the whole thing, especially when Katie was sleeping. He asked her to come have lunch with him in his office, and they would talk during the lunch hour. Annie thanked him and said she would be there. He had soup and sandwiches sent up from the cafeteria, and they ate and talked. He told her it was important to go through the grieving process, and it was okay to cry and be sad. She thanked him for his help and he told her to call him anytime.

When Annie received the money from Rick's life insurance, she paid for the funeral and the burial plot. This seemed like a huge amount to her. With the remainder she went to the bank to pay off his loans for medical school. It was a relief to have these huge debts taken care of, but Annie knew that she would still have money problems.

Annie continued to have trouble sleeping. She would wake up thinking she heard the doorbell, and the whole horrible night of the accident would come back to her. She knew she could get medication to help her sleep, but she was afraid to take anything because medications tended to knock her out, and she wouldn't be able to hear Katie if she woke up in the night. She was usually exhausted when she went to bed and didn't have any problem going to sleep; it was in the middle of the night that her dreams occurred. Sometimes she would wake up and be so frightened that it was hard to believe that the dreams weren't real. She missed Rick so much and just sleeping without him was a tremendous adjustment. She tried to keep her spirits up and not be sad around Katie, but the evenings were long and lonely and there was an enormous void in her life. She felt so empty…

Chapter Seventeen

Annie and Katie had Thanksgiving with Emily and Jeff. It was a quiet day; no one mentioned a word about it being Rick and Annie's anniversary. Jeff told her to let him know when she wanted to put up the Christmas tree, and he would come over and help her.

Annie took three days off for Christmas and took Katie to her mom's. Katie loved all the tree ornaments and lights and was such a joy to watch. Sometimes Annie felt like she was just going through the motions of life with no feelings. Katie was the only thing that made her smile.

She managed to get through Christmas and get back home and unpack. Jon called and said he, Brian and Brett would like to come down for the day and take her and Katie to lunch on Saturday, if that was okay. She thanked him, and said she looked forward to seeing them. She hadn't seen Brian in years, but certainly knew what had been going on in his life through her conversations with Jon.

They arrived about 11:30, and Jon came in and gave her a hug, and so did Brian, and then she saw Brett. He was a miniature of his dad and had the same dimples and smile. When Annie gave him a hug, he said he had to go to the bathroom. She took his hand and showed him where it was. As soon as he finished, he came out and climbed up on her lap. Katie was sitting beside Annie, and he said, "What's her name?"

"I'm sorry Brett, this is Katie."

They went to a nearby restaurant to eat and Brett wanted to sit by Annie. He was so cute, and very well behaved. They went back to the house, and Annie said she needed to put Katie down for a nap. She sat down with Brett on one side and Katie on the other, and started reading a story; within minutes Katie was falling asleep. She asked Brett if he would like to take a nap, and Brian said that he should. They put Brett in the guest room, and he snuggled down under the covers. Jon said he thought he would rest while the children did, and Brian and Annie went downstairs. Annie made them a cup of tea and got some spritz cookies out of the freezer.

"Annie, I'm so sorry this has happened to you. I can't even imagine what you are going through right now."

She thanked him and said, "I have good days, and some that aren't so good. Katie is the light in my life right now. Without her I'm not sure what I'd be doing." Then she added, "You have a precious little boy, Brian, and he is so well behaved. You've done a great job with him."

Brian told her that he had a really good sitter and the time he was off from work he spent with Brett. He said he hadn't been out on a date since he took Brett home with him. He said that Amy had just ruined her life and that she had aged ten years. Annie asked about Jon; she was concerned that he looked tired. Brian said Jon had gotten up at 5:00 o'clock this morning so he could go to the hospital and check on patients before they left. They continued to talk until Jon came downstairs and Annie fixed him some tea.

When Brett woke up, Brian went to get him and brought him downstairs. He immediately came over and crawled up on Annie's lap. He was still sleepy and laid his head against her.

Brian said, "I think you've found a friend."

Katie woke up and Annie took them both to the kitchen and

gave them juice and cookies. Brett and Katie played on the floor, and Brett was so good with her. He gave her every toy she wanted and they had fun with the pull-toys she loved. Some of them made so much noise you could hardly talk. Brian suggested that they order pizza, and said they needed to leave as soon as they finished eating.

When it was time to eat, Brett asked to sit by Annie again. She was amused at all the attention she was getting from him. They ate pizza and salad, then Brian said they had better get on the road.

Brett looked up at Annie with a sweet smile on his face and said, "Can I come back to your house?"

"Sure you can, Brett." They hugged and said goodbye. Annie had enjoyed the day with them. She probably needed more days like this.

When she took down the Christmas tree, she remembered all the stories that Rick told her about the ornaments. It seemed that every day was filled with memories that she cherished about Rick. *I need to write all of this in a journal for Katie, so that she will have it to remember her dad and his childhood memories.*

A surprise phone call came on New Years Eve. It was from Gwen, her friend from college. She had just found out about Rick's death and was calling to say how sorry she was. Gwen was a spirited young woman, but tonight she had a soft and compassionate side. They talked for over an hour. Gwen was working as a hospital dietitian in Denver. Annie told her if she ever got back to Kansas to please come and see her.

Annie was still having difficulty sleeping at night, but felt she was doing much better emotionally. The dreams of the doorbell ringing and reliving the whole night of the accident was still so vivid and real to her. She woke up one night and was so sure Rick was sleeping beside her; she reached over to see if he really was there. She knew she would always love him. He made her feel so loved and adored and she never wanted to forget that feeling...

Chapter Eighteen

Annie took Katie home to her mom's for Easter. She thought it would be good to be away from work for a while, and also a chance to visit with the family. Springtime was a source of joy for her. For Easter dinner, they had baked ham, scalloped potatoes, broccoli and a delicious Jell-O salad made with canned green-gage plums. Tom and his family joined them for dinner. When the kitchen was cleaned and all the food put away, Tom asked Annie if she would like to go see the new baby calves. She changed her shoes, put on a jacket and joined him at the pasture fence. They watched a cow licking her calf and another cow nursing her calf. The rest were all grazing. Tom asked Annie how she was doing. She smiled and said she was okay.

He then said, "Mom told me that Brian and his dad came to see you after Christmas. Was this just a courtesy call or is he trying to get back in your life?"

"They came down to see how I was after Christmas and Brian has called to check on me several times since then. Jon calls to talk to me, too. They have both been very kind and thoughtful."

"Annie, I'm going to give you some unsolicited advice. Stay away from this guy. He isn't trustworthy." Annie wasn't surprised that Tom was telling her this; he had always tried to look out for her.

"I think Brian has matured over the years. He has a son now who is very well behaved. Don't be so quick to judge him."

"My judgment of Brian stems from how he treated you. He said he loved you, but when his old girlfriend shows up, he cast you aside. How do you know that he wasn't sleeping with her the weekend she went to see him?"

"I don't know what happened, Tom. He just told me he had feelings for Amy. If that was how he felt, I didn't want to marry him. I think he did the right thing. I was devastated, but I knew I had to get over it."

"I know you have a mind of your own, but please listen to me about this. This guy is no good for you." The wind was beginning to blow and it was getting chilly. They walked back to the house in silence.

When Katie woke up from her nap, Annie had the car packed and ready to return home. This had been a pleasant weekend, with the exception of Tom telling her how to run her life. She knew he meant well, but he seemed to think he was the only one that could judge character and knew what was best for her. Brian's phone calls had been comforting to her, and she actually looked forward to them.

In May, Emily gave birth to a baby boy, and she and Jeff were thrilled. They named him Nicholas Alan. Annie went to see Emily and their little bundle of joy in the hospital. She seemed almost overwhelmed with joy. Emily was so cute when she said, "Now I really know what the mothers that I have been delivering go through. It is a bit different than I imagined."

Annie thought she was doing better emotionally. Now that the weather was getting warmer, she could get outside and get some exercise. Money remained the big problem. She bought items on sale and never bought prepared food. She took her lunch to work every day. She and Katie ate mostly vegetarian meals, because they were cheaper. She barely made enough to pay for everything she needed, and when the car needed tires or any repair she had to save for months to get it done. It seemed like there was always something that she needed money for and didn't have.

The planting of her "salad garden" had always been something that she looked forward to doing. She didn't have much room, but just having her own tomatoes and a few fresh things was a source of joy. Having fresh herbs outside her door was happiness for her. She planted parsley every year and had to make a note to herself to water it every day. It was extremely slow germinating. Her chives and oregano returned every year without fail. Her very favorite herb was basil. She had to smile as she remembered Gwen and the Foods class so many years ago. It had been her introduction to herbs.

In May Brian called and asked if it would be okay if he and Brett came by to see them enroute to Iowa. "Brett keeps asking when we are going to Annie's house."

Annie said that would be fine. Just thinking of that darling little boy made her smile.

They arrived on Saturday morning and it was a beautiful day. Annie had fixed a picnic lunch to take to the park. Katie was twenty months old and was happy to have a playmate to go to the park with her. The children played on the swings and then wanted to play in the sand box. Annie put a blanket down and they ate lunch, then Katie and Brett ran around some more and had a great time. When they returned to the house, they sat with the two children on the step and took off their shoes and socks and emptied out all the sand. Annie said she would go run the bath water. They were too dirty to take a nap without one. After their baths, she read them a story and put them down for a nap. She and Brian went downstairs and Annie sat down on the floor to pick up the toys and put them away. When she started to get up Brian held out his hand to help pull her up. He pulled her into his arms and kissed the hollow of her neck.

"I've wanted to do this for such a long time, Annie."

Annie was surprised at his actions, but the aroma of his aftershave brought back a flood of memories. She just stood there speechless with his arms around her. He kissed her neck again, and she felt like she was frozen in that spot. She felt helpless.

Taking a deep breath, she stepped back from him. "Brian, I just wasn't prepared for this, you are moving a bit fast for me. I'm still trying to deal with the loss of my husband."

He took her hand and walked to the couch and sat down with her. "Annie, I don't want to rush you into anything. I'll wait for you as long as you need, but I just couldn't help myself. I don't want to upset you."

She was stunned by what was happening. "Brian, there are times that I think I am fine, and then something triggers my emotions and I just sit down and cry. About six weeks ago, I put Katie to bed and went outside to take the trash out to the curb. When I was walking back to the house, I saw the daffodils swaying in the breeze. They were Rick's favorite flowers and we had planted them along the side of the house. When I saw those beautiful flowers, I came in and just sat and sobbed and sobbed. I just couldn't stop. As long as I do things like this, I know I'm not ready for anyone else. I loved him so much, and I know he is never coming back, but I still miss him, and I need to work through all of this. I'm emotionally very fragile right now."

He hugged her and said, "I won't rush you, I promise." He held her and she finally relaxed in his arms.

Brian said he would like to spend the day with her tomorrow, if that was okay. He would stay in a motel and come back in the morning. He gave her one of those big smiles with his dimples showing. "I feel just like I did when I first met you, I just don't want to leave you."

She had to laugh at him, and she could see that he was pleased to see her laugh. She thought maybe this was what she needed, but was still hesitant.

The next morning she let them in and said she was having "apple French toast" and bacon for breakfast.

She hugged both of them and Brett kept hanging onto her neck. "I want to sit by you."

Brian whispered in her ear, "And so do I."

"That can be arranged," she said with a smile.

Brett thought the "apple French toast" was the best breakfast he had ever had and wanted more. He had such good manners for a boy who wasn't even three years old. He always said "please" and "thank you."

They had planned to go to the park again, but it started to rain. Brett said he wanted to play "tent," so Annie went upstairs to get sheets and draped them over chairs. Katie and Brett sat under the sheets and laughed and giggled. This was all new to Katie and she loved playing "tent."

Standing beside Brian, Annie shook her head. "We spend all this money on toys, and they are just as happy with sheets draped over a chair."

After lunch the children went down for naps, then Brian said, "I'd like to talk to you, Annie, about what happened a long time ago." Annie was curious. *What could he possibly have to say to her after all these years?* They sat down in the living room. Annie had no idea what he had on his mind. "Not marrying you when we planned was one of the biggest mistakes I've ever made, and I've made numerous ones since then. The whole thing with Amy was a huge mistake."

She looked at him astonished. "How can you call that precious little boy sleeping upstairs a mistake?"

"That's not what I meant. That all happened because I was totally out of control. Amy came to see me over her spring break, and I didn't know she was coming. I went to see her, and we slept together. I felt so guilty that I called you and told you I still had feelings for Amy. I didn't love Amy, I loved you. I didn't think you would marry me after what I had done."

She was stunned! Annie was silent for a long time, trying to concentrate on what he had just said. *Tom was right!* Finally she said, "You could have at least been honest with me. I wish you would have shared all this with me at the time, Brian. It would have helped me get over you. I could have at least had a reason to be angry with you, and that would have really helped. It took me a very long time to stop thinking about you." She felt like she was in shock. This was almost too much to comprehend.

"Annie, will you forgive me for all the misery I put you through? I'm so sorry."

She nodded her head. "Brian, why did you keep going back to Amy if you didn't love her? There must have been some attraction there?"

Brian hesitated. "Amy was always a willing partner, and I wasn't smart enough to figure that out. Sex is powerful, and I just couldn't keep away from her."

She was still trying to digest what he had told her. "Why didn't you ever try to contact me? Did you think that I was so hard hearted that I couldn't forgive you for what you had done?"

"Annie, I was so full of guilt that I didn't want to face you, so I didn't."

They sat for a long time in silence. Brian took her hand in his and finally he said, "Annie, I love just being here with you. It is a joy to watch you with the children. Motherhood really agrees with you. I do appreciate you letting me stay an extra day with you. It means a lot to me."

Brian said he would take them out to dinner so Annie wouldn't have to cook. This was a real treat for Annie, as she didn't go out to eat because of the cost. They went back to the house after dinner and Brian came in for tea and cookies. When he said he needed to go, they hugged and said goodbye.

Sitting in bed that night she had a difficult time trying to think through what he had told her. *How would I have reacted if he had been honest with me?* She would have to think about this some more…

Chapter Nineteen

In the middle of the summer, Brian asked Annie if she would go with him to visit his dad in Iowa for a week. She thought about it for a while, then decided she would go. She needed to find out if she wanted to pursue this relationship or not. She was undecided about Brian. Jon was pleased to hear that she was coming. Brian and Brett would fly to Kansas City, and then they would drive in Annie's car to Des Moines.

When they arrived at the airport, Brian and Brett both had beautiful suntans from spending so much time in the pool in Arizona. Brian hugged Annie and said, "I'm so happy that you've agreed to do this."

They went to Annie's house and started taking her luggage to the car. "Your dad will think we are coming for a month when he sees all these suitcases."

"He would love it if you were; he just adores you, Annie."

The trip went well. The children slept and Brian and Annie talked. She told him she was doing really well, emotionally. She hadn't had one of those horrible dreams for a long time, and she felt that was a good sign. "Katie is such a happy little girl, and that keeps my spirits up. It's hard to be sad when she brings me so much joy."

Jon was excited to see them and welcomed them with open

arms. After they finished eating, Annie and Brian went upstairs to bathe the children. Annie said, "I'll wash and you dry."

"I think we are a good team, Annie."

The children were all settled in bed, and she went into the bathroom to pick up the towels when Brian came in and put his arms around her. She was tired and it felt so good to have his arms around her. She looked up at him and smiled and they kissed. He kissed her neck and then kissed her on the lips again. She thought, *This is another "be still my heart" moment* and just melted inside. She felt weak in the knees, for it was more emotion than she had felt in such a long time. She didn't want him to stop.

They went downstairs and Jon was just finishing cleaning up the kitchen. They all sat down and talked for a while and then Jon said he was going to bed.

"Do you remember the very first time I kissed you, Annie?" She said she did. "Do you remember what you said?" and she said yes.

She turned around and lay in his arms. He kissed her and then he smiled and said, "Why did you let me do that?"

Looking up at him, she said, "Because I wanted you to."

Brian pulled her into his arms and said, "That was a very special moment for me, I've always loved what you said and I've remembered it all these years. I've never stopped loving you, Annie." She snuggled in his arms and felt so content, she didn't want to move. *Was it possible for this relationship to ever get back on track?*

They had a wonderful week. During the day, they took the children swimming and to the park, and at night sometimes Jon kept the children so they could go out to dinner. Brian was a very attentive father to Brett and Annie just loved watching them play together. This is just what Annie needed. The week just went by too fast. She felt so rested and relaxed.

When she returned home, she called her mother and told her about their trip, how great it was and how happy she was.

Her mom said, "Tom is very upset that you are seeing Brian again. He has never been able to forgive him for treating you like he did."

This was distressing to Annie and she wasn't sure how to handle it. Tom had always had a hard time with forgiveness, and she wasn't sure she could say anything that would change his mind.

When Brian called her, she mentioned Tom's attitude toward him.

"My brother has always been protective of me, and he just thinks I'm making a terrible mistake to get involved with you again. I've always told him that I didn't want to marry you if you had feelings for someone else. Now that I know that you called off the wedding because you felt guilty, and not because you loved Amy, it makes it even worse. This is really upsetting me, Brian. I wish you had told me the truth."

"What would you have done if I had told you the truth?"

"I don't know, Brian."

There was a long silence, then Brian asked her, "How do you feel about me now, Annie?"

"Brian, until I talked to my mom I felt really good. I felt like it was springtime, and I was beginning to have new life again. Our time in Iowa was like an awakening for me. I loved spending time with you. Why is life always so difficult? I just want to be happy again." She was almost in tears, and she didn't think there was any easy solution to their problem. "I do have a bit of doubt about your behavior. I know that past behavior is a good indicator of future behavior, and I just couldn't live through something like that again. I know this is difficult for you to hear, but I need to tell you how I feel. I had such a hard time healing when you broke the engagement, and now that I know that you weren't honest with me it makes it even harder. My heart tells me one thing, and my head tells me another. You have definitely thrilled my heart, but my head says, not so fast."

Brian was slow to respond. "Annie, I appreciate your honesty. I want you to know that I haven't been out with anyone since Brett came home with me; I've been devoted to him. All I can say is that I hope I've matured in the last five and a half years, and that I love you very much. There isn't anything going on between Amy and me. I was just young and very foolish and made poor choices. If you want to be part of my life, you will just have to forgive me and we will have to start anew. You need to think about this; I just hope you will find it in your heart to forgive me for all the mistakes I've made. I couldn't love you any more than I do right now. Please think about all of this and let me know what you decide."

Annie was trying to deal with all the emotions she felt and decided she needed to think about the whole situation for a while. She talked to Emily about Brian, and that didn't seem to help make a decision about anything. Emily was a good listener, but didn't have any answers or suggestions.

Annie called Brian one evening and said she just needed to talk, that she hadn't made a decision, but she just wanted to talk to him.

"I hope this is a good sign. It has been weeks since we talked and I was getting worried."

"Oh, Brian, I wish you were here, you are such a comfort to me, and I'm not making any headway on my own. You have a tendency to cloud my judgment, but I miss you right now more than ever."

He decided that they would fly in to see her over the Labor Day weekend.

Angela had said he could stay at her house, because they were going to be gone and would like having someone there.

Brian and Brett arrived on Friday evening and as they were driving home from the airport Brett was telling them about his birthday that he had just celebrated. He was talking about his "big wheel" that he had received and said he rode it almost everyday. It was similar to a tricycle, but had an enormous front wheel and was very low to the ground. Brett was going to spend the night in the guest room.

When the children were both asleep, Brian took Annie in his arms and kissed her and said, "Have you made a decision about what you want to do?"

She said she knew that she loved him, and she could forgive him for what he had done, but there was a matter of trust that still bothered her. "Brian, I love everything about you, but I'm not sure I can trust you. That is the only thing that keeps me from saying yes. You make me feel so wonderful when I'm with you. You are a great father and Brett is so well behaved and polite; you have done such a fantastic job with him. You are so patient and kind with him. I love all those things about you. I'm just going to have to trust you and I'm working on that. Please be patient with me." *I know that he loves me; I do want to trust him.*

"Annie, we've wasted a lot of time because of me and my behavior and the only thing I can do is promise not to do it anymore. I'm so in love with you and want to spend the rest of my life with you. I'm just waiting for you to say you will marry me." He smiled at her with those dimples and she wanted to say yes, but hesitated.

"Oh, Brian, I know we could be happy, you just have a way of making me feel content and I love you for that." She paused for a moment and smiled at him. "When do you want to get married?" He was so excited; he kissed her over and over again.

The next morning when Brian came over for breakfast, Brett and Katie were in bed with Annie. She went downstairs and let him in and said, "You need to come up and see who's in bed with me."

Brett had been snuggling beside Annie and said to his dad, "I like being here with Annie."

Smiling down at his son, he said, "We are going to be a family very soon, Brett."

Brett looked at Annie and back at his dad and said, "Really?"

Annie put her arm around him and said, "Yes, your dad and I are going to get married, and we can all live in the same house and you can play with Katie every day."

"When are you getting married?"

Annie told him they hadn't decided yet. Not sure what was going on, Katie just watched and listened.

"How would you like chocolate chip pancakes for breakfast?"

The pancakes were a hit and when all the syrup was wiped off of their little hands, they went to play with the toys. It was really amazing that they played so well together.

Brian held her in his arms and told her how happy he was. "We should call my dad. He'll be thrilled to hear the news."

Jon was overjoyed; he said he had waited far too long to have Annie for his daughter-in-law. Annie called her mom and she said she was happy for her, she just dreaded telling Tom.

Chapter Twenty

Annie and Brian decided they would go to Iowa for Thanksgiving and have their blood tests so they could get married just before Christmas at Brian's home. Brian was going to be reassigned to Florida and would be moving in January. Brett would stay with Annie while Brian went back to Arizona to move his household goods.

Annie slept better than she had in months. This was the young man that had stopped her in her tracks almost six years ago, and now she was finally going to marry him. She talked to a real estate agent and decided to put the townhouse on the market. She had given her notice at work. Everyone saw how happy she was and seemed pleased that she was getting married again. Only her close friends knew that she had been engaged to Brian when she was in college and that he had called off the wedding.

She dreaded making this call, but knew she had to talk to Tom. She knew he would never give her his blessings, but she wanted him to know how happy she was. She thought of what she was going to say, then dialed the number. When he answered the phone, he seemed surprised to hear from her. They talked for a few minutes, then she broke the news. "Tom, I want you to know that Brian and I are getting married just before Christmas in Iowa. I love him very much."

With concern in his voice, Tom said, "I'm going to be honest with you. I know you don't want to hear this, but I need to tell you how I feel. I don't know what you see in this guy, especially since the way he has treated you. I think you are very vulnerable right now. I wish you would wait and not rush into this. I don't trust Brian any further than I could throw him. I'll tell you right now, I won't be at the wedding."

Annie was almost in tears; she thought she had prepared herself before she called Tom, but she wasn't prepared for this. "I'm sorry you feel this way about him. I just wanted to let you know what is going on in my life." She couldn't talk anymore without crying, so she told him goodbye. She felt sick when she hung up. She broke down and cried, knowing that Tom would never be able to accept Brian as part of the family.

Thanksgiving was a lovely time with Brian's family. Grandpa Kendall welcomed Annie with open arms and said he didn't understand what took Brian so long. They planned the wedding for 20 December and they would be married in front of the fireplace with the Christmas tree in the background. The wedding would just have family in attendance. Jon had offered to keep Katie and Brett so Brian and Annie could spend the night at a local hotel.

Annie found a lovely green suit for the wedding. She was packed and ready to go when Brian and Brett arrived at the airport. There was a snowstorm predicted and they were hoping to leave from the airport before it started snowing. When they arrived in Des Moines just after midnight, it was beginning to snow.

The next morning it was a beautiful sight outside, with at least a foot of snow on the ground. Annie called her mom, and Elizabeth said they too were snowed in, and there was no way she could come to the wedding. The lane to the main road had high drifts and she wasn't sure she could even get to town for days. Annie was disappointed, but understood the situation.

The wedding was very special. Katie dropped rose petals and Brett was the ring bearer. The two children "stole the show" as Grandpa Kendall put it. Brian looked so handsome in his uniform, and Annie couldn't help but remember how this all started six years ago at a wedding when she saw him standing at the front of the chapel. Jon had arranged for a dinner at the hotel where they were staying. It was a lovely evening with Brian's family there. Jon said he would be fine with Katie and Brett. Katie was falling asleep on Jon's shoulder when they left. "We'll see you in the morning."

They were back at Jon's house for breakfast and as soon as Brett saw them he asked, "Are we a family now?"

They both hugged him and said, "Yes, we are a family now."

After Christmas they returned to Kansas City. The first morning they were at home, Annie went to get Katie out of her bed and when she got back, Brett was snuggling with his dad.

Brett said, "Now I can snuggle with my whole family." They all got under the covers and he said, "Can we do this every morning?" They told him that this would probably only happen on weekends.

The children went to Katie's room to play and Brian pulled Annie next to him and said, "Do you know how happy you've made me? I love you so much."

She loved to be next to him. "You've made me very happy, too, Brain. I wish you didn't have to leave."

Three days later, Brian flew back to Arizona to prepare for his change of assignment and ship his household goods to Florida. Brian would drive to Florida and hopefully rent a house for them, then fly to Kansas City to help with the move.

While Brian was gone, Annie sorted through boxes and cleaned. The house had not sold, but the realtor told her there were people who were interested in renting, so that is what she decided to do.

Katie and Brett played so well together. Brett would do

anything to please her, and when Katie lost interest in what they were doing, he would go on to something else—anything to keep her happy.

When Brian returned, he was excited about the house he had found. It was a four bedroom single story house with a fenced in back yard and a carport. He said Annie would love the kitchen, as it had ample cabinet space and a place for a table and chairs. Brian was such wonderful help preparing for the move, he could do anything. Annie was exhausted by the time the movers arrived and relieved when they were finished packing and everything was out of the house. Brian helped her clean, and then they went to a motel room and collapsed.

The next morning they went by Jeff and Emily's to say goodbye. Nicholas was sitting in his highchair. He was adorable. Jeff and Emily were Annie's dearest friends and this was a difficult farewell. They hadn't met Brian before, but were very kind and wished them well. Annie had thought about going to the cemetery before she left, but decided against it because she knew she would be emotional, and that wouldn't be fair to Brian. She knew Rick would always be in her heart and she had a precious little reminder of him sitting in the back seat.

They headed south to Florida, with the car packed to the brim. "Maybe I'll figure this moving thing out after several moves. I'm sure I have too much stuff, but how do you clean your house after the movers leave if you don't keep your mop and vacuum cleaner?" Brian just smiled at her.

They arrived in Florida on a balmy day. Brian showed her the house and she loved it. "Do you think everything will fit in it?" she asked. He said he was sure it would. The move went well and everything did fit in the house. Brian helped unpack boxes, hang pictures and organize the shelves.

Annie was very content to be a stay at home mom. Brett started calling her "Mom" within a month of being together and this pleased her. On weekends, there was always the sound of little feet coming to their bedroom so they all could snuggle under the covers.

The warm weather and the beautiful white sand on Fort Walton Beach were so inviting, especially when so much of the country was plagued with snow and freezing weather. They went to the beach and took off their shoes and socks and walked in the sand and made sand castles. They enjoyed walking along the gulf and having the tide wash over their feet.

The days at the beach were relaxing and Brett and Katie played for hours running through the water and playing in the sand. Sometimes they took a picnic, but they usually came home to eat, because the children were tired and needed a nap. These were such happy times. Sometimes Annie wished Tom could see how content and joyful she was. Brian was very attentive to her and to the children.

Brian asked her if she had thought about having another baby and she said she would love to. Katie was two and a half now, and Annie didn't want to wait too much longer. They had an extra bedroom to make into a nursery.

A delightful discovery happened when they got to Florida. Annie loved Brian in his uniform, but seeing him in his flight suit was even better. When he came home from work and walked in the house, he held his arms out for her, smiled with his dimples showing and she always came for a kiss. From that time on, these were affectionately known as "flight suit kisses." Annie looked forward to these every day.

Brett came in the house one day walking rather strangely with tears running down his face, and when Annie ask what was the matter, he said, "I just pooped my pants." He was so upset and embarrassed.

Annie took his hand and said, "Did you wait too long before you came to the house?"

"Yes, I did," he said in a jerky voice.

Annie tried to comfort him and said, "Brett, I did the same thing when I was a little girl, I just waited until it was too late to get to the bathroom."

He smiled up at her and said, "Did you really?"

She nodded her head. She told him that he needed to come to the house as soon as he felt the urge, and not wait to go to the bathroom until it was too late. She put him in the tub and cleaned him up.

He looked up at her with concern in his eyes and said, "I thought you would be mad at me. I'm glad you're not."

She hugged him, then said, "Now if you do this when you are ten, I might be mad at you." He got tickled at her and started laughing.

When Brian came home she related the whole incident to him and he just shook his head. He said, "It's a good thing you were here and not me."

Annie looked at him sternly and said, "Well, I suppose you never pooped your pants when you were little, did you?"

"I'm sure if I did, I've suppressed it. Thanks for being so kind to him, Annie. You are a wonderful mom and I love you."

About a month later she was folding clothes and Katie and Brett were outside playing in the yard. She saw Katie slowly walking around and Brett said to her, "Katie, do you need to poop?" Katie didn't say anything to him. Brett reminded her, "Mom told me as soon as I felt the urge to poop that I needed to go in the house to the bathroom so I wouldn't poop my pants." Annie was having a hard time not making a noise she was laughing so hard. This was just too funny. Katie came in the house and said she needed to go to the bathroom. It was difficult keeping a straight face she was so amused. What precious children they were. She waited to tell Brian until they were in bed that night and they both laughed.

Annie called her mom and told her she never thought she would ever be this happy again. She told her about Brett and

BE STILL MY HEART

they had a good laugh. She asked her mom to please tell Tom that she was very happy and content. It still bothered Annie that he didn't like Brian.

Chapter Twenty-One

Brian called one Friday night and said to eat without him, that something had come up and he would be late. Brett had an invitation to a birthday party for the little boy next door. Annie and Katie ate, and were reading a story when Dottie came running over and said Brett had been hurt, she thought his arm was broken. Annie rushed out the door. She knew as soon as she saw his arm that it was broken. Brett was screaming and she tried to calm him. Annie knew he was in terrible pain. She supported his arm with a cutting board and made a sling for him, then drove him to the base hospital. Dottie offered to keep Katie for her. Brett was crying and Annie wanted to comfort him, but couldn't while she was driving. She had to carry him to the emergency room. The staff took x-rays of the arm and the doctor said Brett needed surgery to set the bone.

As soon as they took him into surgery she tried to call Brian at the squadron. They said he was at the Officers' Club. She was shaking as she drove to the club. She tried to calm herself as she got to the door and walked into the bar. The lights were dim and the music was loud, and she stood just inside the door, trying to look around and see if she could see Brian. Her eyes adjusted to the dim light and she thought she saw him on the dance floor. She took a deep breath. It was Brian. Her heart was pounding in her throat, as she stood there in disbelief. He was dancing with a girl who had her arms around his neck and he was kissing her on her neck and holding her very close. Annie didn't want to make a scene on the dance floor. She could feel hot tears forming in her eyes. She decided to go to the restroom until the music stopped, and then she would talk to him. She went into the restroom and splashed cold water on her face and tried to stop shaking. As she leaned against the wall, she had waves of nausea. Fighting back the tears, she returned to the bar and the music had stopped, she didn't see Brian. She walked back to the lobby and started to go out the door, when she saw Brian and the girl going up the steps of the building across the street. He had a hold of her hand as they went in the door. Annie went out and sat in the car and sobbed. *How could this be happening to me? Tom must have been prescient.* She would calm herself down, only to sob more. After about twenty minutes, she saw Brian and the girl come out of the building. He had a hold of her hand and was talking to her. He appeared to be infatuated with her. Annie got out of the car and walked up the steps to meet them. Brian was startled when he saw her and blurted, "Hey, what's going on?"

Her eyes narrowed as she looked at him, "That's what I'd like to know!" She was seething and her voice was shaking when she said it. "I need to talk to you, if you can tear yourself away from what you are doing. Brett is in the hospital having surgery on his arm." She turned around and walked away with tears streaming down her cheeks. She drove to the hospital with her eyes so full of tears; she could barely see where she was going. At the hospital, she learned that Brett was out of surgery, but still in recovery.

The doctor took one look at Annie and said, "Mrs. Kendall, your son is going to be just fine." She must have looked terrible.

When Brian got to the hospital, Annie gave him a look of disgust and said she was going home to get Katie from the neighbors. Dottie took one look at her and asked if Brett was okay. Annie just said he had had surgery to set the bone and that she was worried. She thanked her for keeping Katie. Katie was already asleep, and she carried her home, put a nightgown on her and put her to bed. Annie took a shower and got into bed and started crying again. She hardly slept at all.

Brian came home early the next morning and came into the bedroom and sat down on the bed beside Annie. She asked how Brett was, and he said he was sedated and had had a quiet night. He said he came home to shower and change clothes and he would go back to the hospital. "What are you going to do, Annie?"

She could hardly talk she was so emotional. "What do you expect me to do? I'm leaving as soon as I can get my things together; there is no reason for me to stay here. Tom warned me about you, but I wouldn't listen." She tried to keep her composure, but she was shaking and tears were running down her face.

"Annie, I don't know what happened to me, I just lost control. Please Annie, I promise you this will never happen again."

Annie looked at him sternly, "That is what you promised when we got married seven months ago. Obviously promises don't mean very much to you."

Brian went back to the hospital and Annie got up and started looking for boxes she could use to pack her things.

When Brian returned from the hospital Annie was in the storage shed at the end of the carport.

"Can I help you find something?"

"I think I see what I need," and she pulled out a box marked maternity clothes.

Brian looked at Annie and said, "How far along are you?"

"I'm not sure that I'm pregnant, but I think I am."

Brian started to reach for her and she pulled away. "I wish you had told me, Annie."

"I was planning to when you got home last night, but you had other things on your mind."

"When are you planning to leave?"

Tears were streaming down her cheeks. "As soon as I can get our things packed. How is Brett?"

"He has a fever and they are going to keep him until that goes away. He is on an antibiotic and was sleeping when I left. I came home so we could talk."

Annie went in the house to get a Kleenex and Brian followed her. He put his arm around her and she moved away from him. "Brian, there isn't anything to say, you said it all last night with your actions. I saw you on the dance floor and I saw you go in the girls' dorm. There is no explanation that you can give me that will make that okay with me. There is only one thing that I want you to do for me, and that is to go to the legal office and file for a divorce. I've made a horrible mistake trusting you and now I am paying the price." Annie walked away from him and went to see what Katie was doing. Brian followed her and when he got to Katie's room he saw that the toys and books and clothes had all been packed. "Can I help you put these in the car?" he asked, and she shook her head.

Katie looked at her mom and said, "Mommy, why are you crying? Is Brett okay?"

Annie hugged her. "Brett is going to be just fine."

Brian said he needed to go back to the hospital and Annie said, "I want to see him before I leave. If I meet you there would you come down and stay with Katie while I tell him goodbye?" Brian said he would and they agreed on a time to meet.

As Annie drove to the hospital, she knew this was going to be one of the most difficult things she had ever done. She couldn't love Brett any more if he had been her own son. He was such a precious little boy, and she loved him dearly. She saw Brian waiting for her in the parking lot. "This makes me sick at my stomach to think I have to go tell him goodbye," she said with disgust. She prayed she could talk to him without crying and being emotional.

Brett smiled when she walked in the room and she asked how he was feeling. They talked for a few minutes about falling out of the swing, and how frightened he was about coming to the emergency room.

She held his hand and said, "Brett, Katie and I are moving back to Kansas City tomorrow. I just wanted you to know that I love you very much and that I will miss you. I loved being your mom and I will always love you."

Brett looked at her with tears running down his cheeks and said, "I don't want you to go, Mom."

Annie hugged him and said, "I don't want to go, honey, but I have to. I love you." She left his room and went to the restroom and stood in a stall and sobbed uncontrollably.

She went back to the car and told Brian he needed to go to Brett and comfort him. "I'm sorry I upset him, but I couldn't leave without telling him goodbye."

Annie went back home and finished packing the car. It was loaded to capacity. When Katie was down for a nap, Annie stopped for a moment to gather her thoughts. She called Emily to tell her what had happened and asked if she and Katie could stay there until she found a job and a place to live. She knew her old job was taken, but hopefully there would be something she could do. Emily kindly said they could stay as long as they needed. She hadn't called her mom. She thought she would wait until later. At the moment, she was emotionally drained. She was numb and wasn't thinking straight, but somehow she managed to fix something to eat, bathe Katie, read her a story and put her to bed.

Brian came home and found Annie in bed crying. He tried to comfort her and she told him it was too late for that. "I was hoping we could talk before you leave in the morning."

"Brian, there isn't anything to talk about."

"I'm sorry, Annie."

"Sorry that you got caught?" she snapped. "What were you thinking, Brian? You had to have made a conscious decision to go to the club with her and then go to her room. Did you even think of me? This is just too much for me. I just told my mom a few days ago that I didn't think I could ever be this happy again. I was thrilled to be pregnant. Now I'm so sickened by your actions that I can't even sleep."

"Can we talk about this?"

"There is nothing you can say that will make me feel any different about you and your behavior. If you think I'm going to stay here and live with you while you sleep with other women you are wrong. I will not tolerate that. I had so much respect for you that I didn't even want to make a scene on the dance floor when you were dancing with her and kissing her neck. You have no respect for me at all. There is no explanation for your conduct, except you are out of control. Your behavior is just like a bull in a pasture, you get one pregnant and you are off looking for another one."

This was too much for Brian; he gave up and went to sleep in Brett's room.

Annie hardly slept that night. She kept waking up and seeing Brian dancing with the girl and her arms around his neck and him kissing her on her neck. This all seemed too horrible to be true.

Chapter Twenty-Two

By the time Annie reached Kansas City she was drained emotionally and physically. Unable to afford more than one night in a motel, she had driven over 1,100 miles in two days. It was late at night when she arrived at Jeff and Emily's house. Katie was sound asleep and didn't stir when Annie put her in the bed Emily had lovingly prepared. When she returned downstairs, Annie found Jeff and Emily at the kitchen table with a most welcomed cup of tea for her. They didn't ask any questions, but were obviously concerned. When Annie started by telling them she was pregnant, the words stuck in her throat. She sobbed convulsively before she could finish.

Emily helped her to the guest room and said, "I can't begin to imagine what you are going through right now, but you need to get some rest."

The next morning Annie called and talked to Dr. Gaston; he said he could see her in the afternoon. She told him briefly what had happened and why she was back. He said there weren't any openings, but that the girl who had replaced her was going to have a baby in October, and Annie could fill in for her while she was on maternity leave. Annie said she appreciated his offer, but in the meantime she was desperate and would take any job that might be available.

"Would you be interested in house sitting for a doctor who is in England? They are gone for the year and they had a couple staying there, but when the outside work got too much for them they left. They need someone to clean the house and take care of the lawn and gardens. The pay is adequate and you would have a place to live. It would be until the end of the year." Annie said she was interested, and he gave her the name and phone number for the doctor's daughter. She called the daughter, and made an appointment to meet her at the house the next morning.

Annie drove down the driveway of a gorgeous estate and couldn't believe how lovely it was. The house was an old English Tudor style with leaded glass windows, and the grounds were lovely. She met Betty Camorra, Dr. Livingstone's daughter, in the driveway, and they walked around the grounds. There was a lovely rose garden and several flower gardens and an assortment of fruit trees. They went into the house and walked through the upstairs and downstairs. There was a long list of instructions about what needed to be done and when. There were maid's quarters in the house where she and Katie could stay, if she accepted the position.

Mrs. Camorra asked, "Are you sure you can do this all by yourself?"

Annie said she would sure try. She was desperate and this was a place to live and work. Mrs. Camorra told her they had a lawn service since the couple left, and that she would cancel it if Annie wanted the job. Annie said she would take it. She went back to Emily's, picked up Katie and drove back to the estate. As she drove down the driveway, she was hoping that she wasn't in over her head.

She put Katie down for a nap and sat down to read the instructions on what she was supposed to do. The house had fourteen rooms, plus the maid's quarters, and the lawn covered about three acres. Much of the estate was wooded. When Katie woke up they went to the grocery store and Annie bought a few things for them to eat. At the moment, money was a real concern.

Everywhere she looked there was something that needed to be done. The flower gardens were full of weeds and the hedge needed trimming. In the utility shed she found a riding lawn mower and all sorts of tools, mulch and fertilizer. Then Katie spotted an old tricycle and wanted to ride it. "We will have to get permission first," Annie told her. The house hadn't been cleaned in several months and as Annie walked through it she wondered, *what was I thinking when I took this job?*

With pencil and paper in hand, she made a list of all the things that needed to be done. She decided she would have to get up at 5:00 a.m. and start outside while it was still cool. Later, when it was hot outside, she could clean inside. She explained to Katie that she might be in the garden when she woke up, and just come get her and they would have breakfast.

That night the enormity of the task she had ahead was too much for her. She knew she had taken this job out of sheer desperation, but it was absolutely overwhelming. She felt sick and depressed. Crying didn't help; it made her feel even worse. There was an urgency that kept nagging at her; she knew that she needed to call her mom. She didn't want her mom to call and hear what had happened from Brian. At the moment nothing was going right in her life. She picked up the phone and dialed the number.

When her mom answered she didn't even know where to begin. She asked how she was and then said, "I wanted to let you know what is going on in my life, Mom. The last time I talked to you I was bumping my head on the clouds, I was so happy. So much has changed since then..." She told her what had happened with Brian; that she was in Kansas City, where she was living, and that she was pregnant. Her mother was kind and supportive. Annie was upset when she finished, but tried to control her tears. "I know Tom will think all those things that he warned me about Brian have come true. I wish I had listened to him." This was very difficult for her to admit to herself, but she knew it was true. Tears were streaming down her face. She told her mom that she had a lot to accomplish, but didn't go into detail. She didn't talk as long as she wanted to; because she knew she didn't have a lot of money to pay for long distance phone calls. After she hung up, she sat and reflected on what the last week had been for her. *If I keep on like this I'll never be able to get out of bed in the morning. I can't just sit here and feel sorry for myself.*

The first week, she put in sixteen hour days and was tired when she got up and exhausted when she went to bed, but she had accomplished a lot. She started by cleaning out the flower beds in the front of the house. She spread mulch in them and was pleased that at least something looked neat and tidy. She kept a list of all the things that needed doing and as soon as she crossed one thing off, there were three that were added.

One day while she and Katie were having lunch, Dr. Livingstone called from England to see how she was getting along. She said she was working long hours every day, but wasn't caught up yet; she remembered to ask about the tricycle. He said it was fine if Katie rode it. He also said how pleased he was to have her, and if Dr. Gaston recommended her he knew she was trustworthy.

As soon as Katie was asleep that night, Annie felt a cloud of melancholy come over her. She wondered if she could ever make another good decision in her life again. The circumstances of her life were devastating. Dr. Livingston's praise had lifted her spirits, but only momentarily.

When the alarm clock would go off each morning, she could barely reach over and turn it off, she was so exhausted. Finally she had to put it across the room, so she would have to get out of bed to turn it off. Because Katie was in the same room with her, she would jump out of bed before it woke her up. She had never been so tired. She knew part of it was the fact that she was pregnant, but every morning was a struggle. The only time she ever slept in was when it rained.

The second week, there were three days of rain and she was happy to stay inside and get the entire house cleaned. This was a huge accomplishment. Katie played with her dolls while Annie cleaned. Katie talked to her dolls just like Annie talked to her. Her imagination was vivid and she played well by herself. This was a bright spot in Annie's day. She had to smile when she would hear things like, "I've told you this before, haven't I?" coming from Katie. *I need to be very careful how I talk to this little darling.*

Emily came by to see her one afternoon just as she was putting tools away. She said, "I just came by to check on you and see if you were okay." Sitting at the kitchen table, she took Annie's blood pressure and listened to the baby's heart beat.

"You are so kind to do this for me, Emily. I really appreciate it, and I'm so thankful to have a friend like you." They talked for a while and Emily asked if all this work wasn't too much for Annie.

"I don't have any other choices right now. At least I have a little money coming in and a place to live."

Emily said she and the baby were doing fine. She added, "I just wish you would go see Dr. Gill."

Annie was weeding a flower bed one evening and Katie was riding the tricycle when a neighbor, Mr. Delgato came to meet them. He was a distinguished looking gentleman, perhaps in his seventies, with a bald head and tufts of hair around the edges. He said he had lost his wife a year ago, and was very lonesome without her. She was a wonderful cook and he missed her cooking.

Annie asked, "What do you miss most that she made for you?"

"Gina's manicotti was the best I've ever eaten. She made it with love, just for me."

Annie was touched with his answer and asked, "Do you have her recipe for manicotti?

"Indeed, I do. Can you make manicotti?"

"If you give me the recipe, I'll sure try."

Mr. Delgato was so pleased he was grinning from ear to ear.

"If you tell me what you need from the store, I'll go get it for you and we will have a party." His eyes were twinkling.

Annie couldn't help but be amused. He seemed so happy that someone cared about him.

She got the recipe and made a grocery list for Mr. Delgato. It was supposed to rain over the weekend, a good time to make manicotti.

It was quite a complicated recipe. The tomato sauce needed to be simmered for hours. The cheese filling, which had three different kinds of cheese, and then the eggs and herbs needed to be mixed into it. The crepe batter had to be made and crepes that held the filling needed to be cooked. Annie loved trying new recipes, but she wanted this to be perfect and not disappoint Mr. Delgato. She filled the crepes and spread the tomato sauce over the top and put it in the oven. The aroma was wonderful, and it wasn't even baked yet. He had bought a crusty loaf of bread and Annie would cut up a salad while the manicotti was baking. He had mentioned that he liked strawberries and cream for dessert.

Mr. Delgato arrived and said he was intoxicated just smelling "Gina's manicotti." This old man was such a character, but seemed so sad at times. He talked for hours about his beloved Gina, and what a wonderful life they had had together.

Annie served the plates and they sat down at the kitchen table. She was a little nervous and held her breath when he took his first bite.

"Oh, my dear, you have mastered my Gina's recipe. This is delicious!"

They had a delightful evening. Annie was so relieved that it was good, and that it had pleased him. She sent him home with the remainder of the manicotti.

Jeff called one day and said Brian had called and asked if they could give him her phone number. Her first thought was perhaps this was about a divorce, so she agreed that Jeff should give Brian her number. A short while later he called. He asked how she was, and if she had been to a doctor.

"Brian, I don't have enough money to go to a doctor. I canceled my health insurance when we got married, and I can't afford it now. I'm taking pre-natal vitamins, and that is the best I can do at the moment. I wish I could go see a doctor; it is a little scary not seeing one. I don't know what I'm going to do if I can't find a full time job. Not very many people hire pregnant women. I'm having trouble finding enough money for food. The hot water heater had to be replaced in my townhouse, and that took everything I had. I don't have a savings account anymore."

"Annie, I'll be happy to send you money."

"I don't want any money from you," she snapped back at him.

"Well, if you don't have enough money for food, perhaps you should reconsider. Why do you always have to be so stubborn?"

"Brian, at the moment I don't want anything from you." She tried to calm herself, but she was seething inside.

"How are you feeling, Annie?"

"I'm tired all the time." She told him where she was living and what she was doing and that she was putting in very long days. Again, he said he would send her money, and she insisted she didn't want any money from him. There was a long pause. Then she asked how Brett was doing. Brian said he cried for her almost every day. She asked if he had gone to the legal office to file for divorce, and he said no. "I really wish you would do it, Brian. I would if I had the money." He said Brett wanted to talk to her.

She asked Brett how his arm was doing and he said it was still in a cast. He said the cast was heavy and it itched and he couldn't scratch his arm. Then he told her in a weak voice he was going to day care on the base.

She asked how he liked it and he said, "I liked it better when you were here taking care of me and I could play with Katie." He started crying and Brian took the phone. Annie was glad he couldn't see the tears running down her face.

"I'm sorry he is upset. Adults have no idea how their actions affect children."

"I'm concerned about you and the baby. If you don't have enough money for food, you know that will affect the baby. Please take care of yourself, Annie."

"That is rather difficult to do at the moment, thanks to you." She was so disgusted; it was difficult to carry on a conversation with him.

Brian asked if it was okay to give her phone number to his dad and she said sure. She hadn't talked to Jon in such a long time and she knew he would be a comfort to her. It took her a long time to settle herself after Brian called.

By August, temperatures were over 100 degrees every day. It was impossible for Annie to work outside during the heat of the day. At 5:00 a.m. she would work in the yard, by 10:00 a.m. it was so oppressive she had to go in and shower. Katie had to be bathed, too, and after lunch, while Katie napped, Annie cleaned the house. After dinner she started the mowing. Once she got Katie settled for the night, Annie would go back out to weed the flower beds until it was dark.

One night with an aching back and legs, she went in the back door, her arms felt like rags hanging beside her. She got a glass of ice water and was just taking a most welcomed drink, when the phone rang. She picked up the phone and collapsed in a chair. It was Jon.

"I was getting worried about you. I've tried to call for the last two hours and there was no answer."

"I just walked in the door, Jon. I've been outside working."

"Are you okay, Annie?"

There was a long pause, she was in tears she was so exhausted. There was an almost inaudible, "No, I'm not." She began to sob.

"What is it, Annie? Please talk to me." All he could hear was crying.

She started to talk, but Jon couldn't understand her. Finally she calmed down enough to say, "Just talk to me for a minute, Jon, while I calm down. Tell me how you are." He heard sniffling, but told her he had talked to Brian and he was just calling to check on her.

"I'm sorry, Jon, I'm so tired and I ache all over. I'm very overwhelmed at the moment. I took this job because I was desperate. There is more to do here than I can possibly keep up with. I keep making really bad decisions in my life." She started sobbing convulsively and couldn't say another word.

"Annie, I know this is difficult for you right now. I'll call you tomorrow night about 8:30, perhaps we can talk then. Is that okay?" All he heard was a jerky sound and then she hung up.

The next evening she made sure she was in the house by 8:30 when the phone rang. She was exhausted, but had showered and was in a little better state than the night before.

"How are you feeling tonight, Annie?" Jon said in such a kind voice.

"Jon, I've been tired since I arrived here. No one has done anything to this place, but mow the grass in three months. I'm not sure I'll ever catch up. It is depressing and with everything else that is going on in my life, there isn't much happiness. I try to be cheerful around Katie, but I'm not even doing a very good job of that."

"Do you have to do all the work outside right now?"

"Dr. Livingston's daughter lives nearby, I don't want her to come over and see that I haven't done what I said I would do. I started out doing really well, and then we have had a heat wave and it is so hot that I can't stay outside."

"Surely, she will understand that you can't work outside when it is over 100 degrees."

"I hope so, but I'm trying my best just to make headway every day."

"This hot spell won't last forever. Can't you wait and get caught up when it cools off in September?"

"I hadn't even thought about that, Jon. Thanks, you are always such a help to me."

"Have you been to your doctor, Annie?"

"No, I don't have any health insurance anymore and I'm barely making enough here to have food for both of us."

"Annie, please let me send you money so you can at least go see your doctor. What are you going to do when it comes time to have the baby?"

"I have no idea. It's frightening. Nothing is right in my life at the moment. I don't want you to send me money, Jon. I'm sure I'll manage somehow, but thank you for the offer."

"Brian is devastated that he has done this to you, Annie."

"Well, he didn't look devastated when he came out of the girl's dorm holding hands with his newfound friend. How do you think I felt sitting out in the car waiting for him to finish his affair, so I could tell him his son was in surgery? If he wanted that kind of lifestyle, why did he even want to get married?"

Jon was calm. "I can't answer those questions, Annie."

"I'm sorry Jon; I shouldn't have lashed out at you. I'm just very hurt and angry right now. I'm also frightened about how I'm going to look after myself and Katie and have another baby."

"I'll be more than happy to send you money any time you need it, please remember that. Do try to take care of yourself and get some rest, Annie"

"I will, Jon. Thanks for calling, I really appreciate it."

The neighbor across the street came over to meet her one day when she was deadheading roses. He said he was amazed that one person was taking care of this place. He told her that the Livingston's had had a full time gardener until a year ago when he became ill, and that they also had a live-in housekeeper. Annie said she was trying to keep up as best she could.

Another neighbor came over and asked if she would like to pick from their vegetable garden and water for them while they were on vacation for two weeks. She said she would be happy to do it. This was a God-send for Annie. She and Katie were living on beans, rice and oatmeal, and the fruit from the fruit trees and berries. Though it was more work, she would love to have fresh vegetables. She went over to pick every day and what they didn't eat, she put in the freezer. Katie enjoyed going to the garden because the neighbors had a playhouse and playing in it delighted her. They returned home every day with a basketful of vegetables. This was a bright spot in her day.

Katie had been such an easy child to entertain since they moved there. Annie had oiled the tricycle and Katie rode it on the patio while Annie mowed the grass. When Annie got down to the end of the yard she would wave to Katie, and Katie would wave back and they would both turn around. Katie pretended she was "mowing" the patio.

Annie's mom called often to talk. Annie knew that she was concerned that she wasn't seeing a doctor. "Honey, please let me send you some money so you can go see your doctor." Annie refused.

"I'll be okay, don't worry about me. I may get desperate and need some before this is all over, but I'm okay for the moment. Brian wants to send me money, too."

"Do you talk to him often?"

"No, he called to get my phone number from Jeff. Jeff called to see if it was okay. I told him it was. It wasn't a very pleasant conversation, but I did get to talk to Brett. He cried and I was sad just talking to him. This is such a wretched situation I'm in. I wonder sometimes if I will ever heal from this."

"Sure you will, honey. It will just take time."

"I've asked myself how I could ever get myself in such a horrible mess. Sadly, I know the answer; there definitely is chemistry between us. I realized that when I first met him and felt helpless. It was like a magnetic force pulling me toward him. When he came back into my life last summer, I felt it again. He can just look at me and smile and I just melt inside. At the moment, I am so angry and hurt that I don't feel that way anymore. It is frightening to think that he could stir that kind of emotion in me."

"Has he started divorce proceedings?"

"No, he says he doesn't want a divorce. He still wants us to work through our problems.

"How are you feeling?

"I'm tired all the time, there's a lot to do here, but I'm getting plenty of exercise."

Mr. Delgato checked on them several times a week and one day he asked Annie if she would consider making meals for him. He told her he would buy the groceries, and he would pay her for her time. He even said he would watch Katie while she cooked. Annie was already overwhelmed with all that she had to do, but he was such a dear old man that she couldn't refuse. He brought Gina's recipes for her to look at, but he said he would be happy with anything she wanted to fix. Gina's recipes were ones that you could spend all day in the kitchen cooking, but Annie was fascinated with some of them. She just wished she had time to try them all.

They had been having raspberries ever since they got there and now the apples were ripening, and so were the pears and plums. Annie made applesauce, apple butter and apple jelly and then she made pear preserves and plum and raspberry jam. She found jars at a thrift store and decided she would give an assortment of jams, jellies and preserves as gifts at Christmas. Right now she had no extra money for presents.

One day Mr. Delgato came over to pick up the casserole that

Annie had fixed for him and he looked at her and asked, "Annie, are you going to have another baby?"

She smiled and said that she was. She hadn't told him why she was here, and he hadn't asked. She took a deep breath and told him what had happened to her, and why she was here working at the estate. She explained that she was desperate for work and a place to live and this was the first thing that was available, and she took it. He was very distressed to hear her story and said he was sorry.

When the girl that replaced her at the hospital had her baby, Annie started back to work on the 2nd of November. They had opened a day-care center next to the hospital and she could leave Katie there while she worked. Most of the yard work was finished except for leaves that were still falling. Hopefully she could rake them on weekends.

She had only been back to work a week when Dr. Gaston came by. He said that the girl she was filling in for was not coming back to work because her baby had a heart problem and had to have surgery. He asked Annie if she could continue working until Annie's baby was due in April. She was sad to learn about the other woman's baby, but she felt like she had angels watching over her. This is just what she needed. With only five months left before the baby was due, she had been wondering where she was going to get the money to have her furniture sent from Florida when it was time to move back into her house. The best news was she could get health insurance and could go see Dr. Gill!

There were some nice days in November and she started washing windows in the house. She wanted the house to be in great shape when the Livingston's arrived home after Christmas. She had finally finished with all the outside chores and that was a relief. This was a huge house to keep clean, but she admired the beauty of it every time she cleaned. Katie loved to stand at the large bay window and watch the birds. Annie had found a metal trash can full of bird seed and put up a bird feeder she found in the shed.

Mr. Delgato was so complimentary of everything that Annie fixed for him and he tried to give her extra money, now that he knew what her situation was. Annie tried several of Gina's recipes and they were all great, just time consuming. She asked if she could copy them and he said Gina would be pleased.

Chapter Twenty-Three

The holidays were very quiet and Katie and Annie would be spending Christmas alone in the big house. Annie knew if she went home, she and Tom would have a discussion about Brian and she couldn't handle that. She had rented a motel room that had a kitchenette for the month of January and by February she would be back in her own townhouse. Now if she could just save enough money to have her furniture shipped here...

Not having Christmas decorations was difficult for Annie. She had always loved preparing for Christmas, but this year she just couldn't afford anything extra. Her Christmas decorations were all in Florida with Brian. She needed to save all she could. Katie was too young to ask questions. Annie cut some greenery from a spruce tree and some from a fir tree and put it on the mantle and added some pine cones. Then one day she remembered the nandina bushes that were near the woods and went out and cut a basket of red berries and added then to the mantel. She was pleased with her efforts. This lifted her spirits. She vowed to concentrate this year on the real meaning of Christmas.

On Christmas Eve Annie read the Christmas story to Katie and put her to bed. She thought of the cinnamon rolls that were always a part of Christmas and decided that she was too exhausted to make them. A whole recipe of cinnamon rolls was too much for her and Katie anyway. She looked out the window and saw there was snow falling and it was beautiful. The telephone rang and when she answered, it was Jon.

"I wasn't sure I would find you in Kansas City. How are you doing?"

"I'm doing okay, Jon. I decided to stay here. I knew if I went home that Tom would let it be known that I had made a horrible decision to marry Brian, and I didn't want to deal with him. He hasn't liked Brian since he broke our engagement many years ago. He warned me not to marry him and I should have listened. I've been a recluse since I came back, and most of my friends don't even know I'm here. Jeff and Emily are the only ones that I see."

"Annie, have you been to see your doctor?"

"Yes Jon, you will be glad to know that I've been to see my doctor. Dr. Gill was very kind and didn't scold me for waiting so long to come see him, but I haven't gained weight like I should. That is because money has been in short supply and we've hardly eaten meat since we've been here. Also, I've worked very long days trying to keep up with all I had to do. Just one more week and we will be moving to a cubical, a tiny room with a kitchenette in a scruffy part of town."

"I thought you were back to work now."

"I am back to work, but I need money to have my furniture shipped up here, and I also have a security deposit to refund at the end of January. It's always something."

"My offer to send you money is still there, Annie."

"Thank you, Jon."

"How are you emotionally, Annie?"

"I'm doing really quite well until I'm by myself. Then my mind starts working and I start thinking about what has happened to us. I think the fact that I've put in sixteen hour days and I've been too tired to think about what has happened has helped a great deal. I do fine until Katie goes to bed, and then sometimes I get teary-eyed. This has been very difficult for me.

I thought it was tough when Brian broke the engagement, but this has been so much worse. I didn't have a place to live, a job, or any health insurance, and I had very little money. I'm pregnant, and I have a three year old to look after. I still blame myself for ever marrying him. My only hesitation was trust, and I told him that before we got married. I listened to my heart and not my head; now my life is in a shambles. I miss Brett so much. The only time I've talked to him he cried over the phone, and so did I. He sounded pitiful and it makes my heart ache not to be able to comfort him and love him. I have an enormous amount of resentment toward Brian. We had such a happy family and now that is all gone. Enough about me, how are you doing?"

"I'm fine. Slowing down a bit, but I still do a full surgery schedule."

"I do want to apologize for not calling you. First of all, I was sure you didn't want to hear me tell you how awful Brian had treated me, and secondly, I just didn't have the money to call. I always enjoy talking to you, and you've helped me tremendously through the years. I was really looking forward to spending time with you. That is another thing that makes me sad about this whole situation. I really appreciate you calling and checking on me. Merry Christmas, Jon."

She sat and watched the snow falling and thought what a lovely scene this would be on a Christmas card. The snow was a wet one and was piling up on the trees and shrubs.

The phone rang again, and it was Brian. "How are you, Annie?"

"I'm okay. I just talked to your dad." She was surprised he was calling and wondered why.

"Yes, I know. The reason I'm calling is to see if it would be okay if we came by to see you on our way back to Florida? Brett keeps asking when we are going to see you again."

"Brian, I would prefer that you didn't. I just don't want to have anything to do with you. I'm still very hurt and seeing you would only make it worse. You have made such a wreck of our lives. I'm trying to get on with my life, and I'm emotionally drained and physically exhausted right now. Seeing you isn't going to change anything for me and it may make it even more difficult for Brett. There isn't any reason for us to see each other."

Brian was silent for a long time and then he said, "I will respect your decision, Annie. I'm so sorry for all the pain and misery that I've caused you."

"Have you gone to the legal office to file for divorce?"

"No Annie, I haven't."

"Why haven't you? You certainly have had enough time."

"I don't want to get a divorce from you is the reason. I was hoping we could work this out. That is one of the reasons I wanted to come see you, so we could talk."

"That is not going to happen, Brian," she said in disgust. She told him goodbye.

Mr. Delgato came over and brought a book for Katie and one of Gina's recipe books for Annie.

He said with a smile, "She would be pleased for you to have this."

Annie thanked him and went to the kitchen to get a basket of jams and jellies and preserves she had made for him.

He looked at her and said, "When did you find time to do all this? You are an amazing young woman and I'll miss you when you leave." He hugged them both and said thank you for the basket.

Annie cleaned the house for the last time. She left an assortment of jams and jellies and preserves on the kitchen counter for Dr. and Mrs. Livingston. After she packed all of their things, she drove to the motel where they would have to survive for the next month. Annie knew the only good thing about this place was that she would be able to get some rest.

As she was carrying her suitcases into the motel two seedy looking characters were watching her. One said, "Need any help, lady?" She said, no thank you, and just carried in what she needed at the moment. She would get the rest after they left. These men gave her the creeps. *This may be a long month.*

She met Jerry Nicholson in the hall one day. Frowning at her, he said, "What are you doing here, I thought you were in Florida?"

"It's a long story, Jerry."

"Can you meet me in the cafeteria tomorrow for lunch at noon?" She said she would.

When she sat down with Jerry the next day she told him what had happened, and why she was back working at the hospital. She said she was devastated, and was still having a difficult time over the whole situation. He was such a kind man and was perfect for his profession. He listened intently to every thing she said.

"Jerry, a week before this happened I told my mother that I wasn't sure I could ever be this happy again. We had been trying to have a baby, and I was going to tell Brian that night that I thought I was pregnant. To find him on the dance floor with that girl, kissing her neck and dancing so close, was more than I could handle. Then I saw him disappear into the girl's dorm my heart was shattered. He has never denied what he did, and I didn't even want to hear an explanation from him. I just don't think they were up in her room trading baseball cards."

"There is a possibility that he has an impulse problem."

"Jerry, you can put all kinds of names on what he has done, but it doesn't make it any easier for me to accept."

"What I'm trying to tell you Annie, is that it may be treatable."

"At this point, that doesn't make it any easier either." Annie had an appointment and had to go back to work, so their discussion ended. She thanked him before she left.

The next day when she returned to the motel with grocery bags, the same men were watching her. She hurriedly grabbed her sacks and went inside with Katie. She was uneasy, just knowing they were outside. No one was around when she left in the morning, but in the afternoon there were always scruffy looking men around. As soon as she got into the room she locked the door. She never opened the drapes.

Annie had a call from Dr. Livingston at work one morning and he invited her and Katie to lunch on Saturday. She was surprised, but he said they would like to meet her and thank her personally for what she had done.

The following Saturday, Annie and Katie arrived at the front door of the estate and were warmly greeted by Dr. and Mrs. Livingston. They were a lovely couple in their middle fifties. When they went into the living room and sat down, Katie remembered the bird feeder, and asked if she could go to the window and watch the birds.

"Mom, there is my chickadee coming for his lunch." They were amused at what she said.

Dr. Livingston said, "We were so pleased with everything that you did while you were here. You did things that we didn't even expect you to do. The gardens are all bedded down for winter and you have trimmed and pruned and done a spectacular job. We have something for you, to show our gratitude." That said he handed Annie an envelope.

Annie blushed. "Thank you, you didn't need to do anything else for me. You paid me while I was here." She opened the envelope and there was a kind note in it and a check. She was amazed at the amount. "Oh my, you are very generous, thank you so much."

Lunch was ready and they went into the dining room. Mrs. Livingston asked when the baby was due, and then said she was even more amazed that Annie had accomplished all that she had. They hadn't realized that she was pregnant. After lunch Mrs. Livingston and Katie went back to watch the birds, and Annie and Dr. Livingston sat down to talk. He inquired about her situation, and she told him briefly why she was here alone, and that she was waiting to get back in her house on the first of February.

"Where are you living now?" When she told him he just shook his head. "If only we had known, we would have let you stay here. That area is no place for a young mother and daughter to be living."

"Sir, you have done quite enough for me already, and for that I thank you. I arrived here without a job, no place to live and no money. You, on the recommendation of Dr. Gaston, took care of me. I'll be forever grateful." Annie said thank you for lunch and for the very generous check. They again expressed their gratitude to her and requested that she notify them when the baby was born. The money was just what she needed at the moment. She smiled on the way home, thinking *sometimes when you think the bottom has fallen out of your life; a kind gesture can be most rewarding.*

Chapter Twenty-Four

One weekend when Annie was in the kitchenette preparing lunch, she looked and Katie was standing in front of the window; she had the drapes pulled back so she could see out and let some sunshine in the room. It was dreary in this little cubicle. She didn't want to scold her, but she was frightened when she saw the men outside watching her. She gently took her hand and closed the drapes. She had to admit that it was depressing to always have the drapes closed, but she didn't want to have these seedy characters looking in on them. Only five more days and they could leave this place behind.

When the renters moved out of Annie's townhouse two days early, she was able to do some cleaning before the shipment of furniture arrived. Familiar surroundings gave her encouragement. She put shelf paper down and the house echoed just like it did when she and Rick first moved in. She smiled at the echoes, and memories of him flooded her mind. Sometimes this was a way to calm herself; to think of the happy times with Rick. She knew it was not reality, but the real world at the moment was not pleasant. This was her escape from the world.

Annie took Katie to day care and when she returned a moving van sat in front of her house. What a welcoming sight! Finally, she would have her pots and pans put away in the kitchen, and all of her belongings in familiar surroundings. She knew exactly where everything went. The men were very helpful and set up the beds before they left. She would have the weekend to clear a path and get settled. Katie was content to see her toys and books, and played with dolls she hadn't seen in months. Jeff came over to hook up the washer and the dryer for her. Some of the boxes were very heavy, and Annie knew that she probably shouldn't be lifting them. It was a comforting feeling to be back in this house that had brought her so much happiness.

Angela came over to visit and brought them a pot of soup and a loaf of homemade bread. "You are so kind and thoughtful, I really appreciate this. It smells great." She put it in the empty refrigerator. Annie explained to her why she was here alone. Angela was kind and very supportive.

The following week Brian called to see if she was okay and if the furniture had arrived in good shape. "The furniture arrived in great shape and so far I haven't found anything broken, but I still have lots of boxes to unpack."

Brian had concern in his voice when he said, "Please don't work too hard getting the house in order. You always tend to wear yourself out. I'm worried about you trying to do all this by yourself." He was silent for a moment, and then added, "Annie, I would really like to be there when the baby is born, and help you for a while." She stiffened at the thought. This really took her by surprise.

"Brian, this is just going to make it more difficult for everyone. I appreciate your offer, but I know I'll be emotional around you; I don't need that when I'm having a baby. Believe me; giving birth is emotional enough on its own." She shuddered at the thought of him coming to help her. "My mother is going to come help me, but thank you anyway."

"Please think about it, Annie, will you?" She told him she would.

Annie sat in bed that night and thought about what Brian had said. When Katie was born, she and Rick were so thrilled to be parents, and they were joyful. She knew she would feel very blessed to be a mother again, but she felt so alone and sad this time. She still had hostile feelings toward Brian. She just didn't want to deal with him. She wasn't sure she could ever deal with him again. Leaning back on her pillow, she thought about the new life inside her. *Brian will always be this child's father. This little one will need to know him. I'm not being fair about this whole thing. Please God, I need your help with this decision.*

The next week when Brian called again, Annie gathered her courage and said, "Brian, I'm sorry I acted the way I did. I was being very selfish when I refused your offer to help when the baby is born. This isn't just about me. You need to bond with our baby. I should be grateful that you care enough to come." Her voice wavered, "We are going to have to remember that this child always comes first, and not let our feelings for each other interfere. I'm truly sorry for saying what I did, I wasn't being fair to you." She was getting emotional, so she swallowed, took a deep breath and continued. "I'm still very hurt and that was my first reaction to your request. I'm sure we can treat each other with dignity and respect, and get along while you are here. I'll try my best."

He seemed genuinely pleased. "Thank you for being so thoughtful, Annie, I'm relieved that you feel the way you do. I would like to stay ten days, if that's okay? I just hope I can be there for the delivery. That would mean a lot to me." When she hung up the phone, she closed her eyes and prayed she had made the right decision.

Annie finished unpacking and finally got the pictures on the wall. As she washed and put away all the baby clothes, she was feeling good about being prepared for the birth of this little one. Katie had been a week late in her arrival and Dr. Gill seemed to think this one would also be late. Brian would arrive a week after this baby was due.

It was a beautiful spring morning. The sun was shining and

the daffodils were just beginning to bloom. Annie had done her exercises and was trying to finish cleaning the house before they went to the airport. She was apprehensive about Brian staying at the house, but he was still her husband. She just didn't want to get into a confrontation with him. She had blamed herself for ever marrying him. What a rollercoaster of emotions she had been through over Brian. He had made her feel so comfortable and content and loved, and she knew that after losing Rick that she needed all those things. Now, when she thought about the future she became very depressed. *Will I always be a struggling mother trying to make ends meet? That is certainly how I feel at the moment.*

When Annie and Katie waited at the gate for Brian and Brett, Katie was chattering excitedly, she could hardly wait for Brett to play with her again. Annie hoped that she could let all her hostility toward Brian go, and just be kind and pleasant. When they came through the gate, Annie took a deep breath and prayed she could keep her composure. When she hugged Brett, he wouldn't let her go. He kept saying, "I've missed you so much." This almost brought Annie to tears. When she stood up Brian put his arms around her and hugged her to him, and then he stood back and smiled down at her stomach. She saw those dimples and she couldn't help but return his smile. They went home and she took Brian and Brett to the guest room.

Early the next morning Annie woke up having contractions, but nothing regular. She carefully made her way to the kitchen to put Brett's favorite breakfast, "apple French toast" in the oven.

When she told Brian she was having contractions, he said, "May I feel your stomach when you are having one?" After breakfast when the children were upstairs, she sat on the couch and he put his hand on her stomach. She told him her stomach got really tight, but it didn't hurt. She took him to the kitchen and showed him where things were and what she had already prepared in the freezer. She checked him out on the washer and dryer, and said she would love to have a picture of him putting Katie's hair in rollers. Her contractions started getting closer together, so she called Angela and told her to be on standby. Then she called her mom. She would come down to see the new baby, then go home and come back when Brian returned to Florida.

When they arrived at the hospital, Brian was amazed at how calm she was. She filled out the paperwork and a nurse took her to labor and delivery in a wheelchair. A doctor on duty examined her and said she was dilated five centimeters. When her contractions became stronger, Brian looked at her with wide eyes and asked if he could do anything.

She smiled at him and told him, "There isn't a thing you can do, but I'm glad you're here." He took her hand and squeezed it. She had to admit that just his presence was helpful. No one should have to go through this process all alone. Her contractions were really getting stronger and lasting longer, and she was dripping wet. Brian got a wet washcloth from the nurse and wiped her forehead. When the nurses kept coming in and checking her and taking her blood pressure, Brian asked would she be okay? The contractions were coming closer and closer together, and Annie seemed exhausted.

Annie asked, "Are you sure the air conditioning is working?" They assured her that it was. The nurse finally brought her some ice chips which helped cool her off.

Annie was so glad to see Dr. Gill, as he had a calming effect on her. She introduced him to Brian and they shook hands. When Brian said he would like to go into the delivery room, Dr. Gill suggested he get ready as Annie's labor was progressing. Dr. Gill asked if she planned a repeat performance, and she said she did. Within the hour Annie delivered an eight pound, two ounce little girl. They had positioned a mirror so Annie could watch the delivery and she thought it was miraculous. The baby was born with spontaneous breathing and didn't cry at all until they started cleaning her up. She looked just like her daddy, with dark hair and a little curl, blue eyes and dimples. They named her Elizabeth Anne and would call her Betsy.

Brian had her wrapped in a blanket and brought her to Annie. "She's so beautiful, Annie." He was so emotional, he almost choked. Annie was pleased he was there with her to share this very special moment. What had gone wrong between them had to be put aside and this time had to be cherished.

Annie couldn't wait to hold her little girl and nurse her. She was so precious. When Annie's mom came to see her and the baby, she was happy she had come. Her mom said Brett and Katie were excited and waiting for them to come home.

When Brian came back to see her the next day, he gave Annie a hug and kissed her on the cheek. He had a beautiful arrangement of flowers for her. When she started talking about the baby, she just broke down and cried. Brian tried to comfort her, but she just convulsed in sobs and couldn't say a word.

Finally she said, "It's not supposed to be like this, Brian. She is never going to know us as her parents. It'll be 'my mom lives in one place and my dad lives in another place.' It makes me very sad." She knew she had to stop thinking like this. It wasn't going to change anything. Brian looked at her with such sadness in his eyes. He was at a loss for words.

When Annie took Betsy home, Brett and Katie could hardly wait to hold her. Brian fixed lunch, and no sooner did they sit down to eat than Betsy let it be known that it was time for her to eat, too.

Katie thought this was funny and said, "She knows it's lunchtime." Annie went into the living room and said she would feed her while she ate her lunch in there. Later, she put Betsy down in the cradle and called Dr. Livingston. She told them that she had a little girl and that her husband was there helping her. They said they would like to come by to see the baby, but they would wait a while and call before they came.

Annie woke up in the night to see Brian with Betsy in his arms. "I have a hungry girl that's crying for her mom."

Annie was surprised to see him there. "I didn't even hear her, thank you for bringing her to me. This is really great service."

Brian asked if he could stay while she fed her. He sat on the end of the bed and said he was very blessed to have her be the mother of their child.

"You are just a natural mother. This all seems to come so easy for you."

"I really love it, Brian. There isn't anything I would rather be doing. I just wish the circumstances were different."

Later in the night, Betsy was wailing and Annie jumped out of bed and hurried down the hall. Brian was changing her. "I think she's hungry." He picked her up and handed her to Annie. Brian walked back to the bedroom with Annie.

He commented how demanding she was when she woke up. "She's ready to eat when she opens her eyes, isn't she?"

Annie smiled at his comment. They talked for a few minutes and Brian went back to bed. When Betsy finished nursing, she was fussy, so Annie sat in the rocking chair in the nursery and rocked her. The next thing she knew, Brian was standing beside her; she had dozed off to sleep. She put Betsy in her crib.

Brian was standing next to her and whispered, "She is a beautiful baby."

Annie smiled at him and he pulled her into his arms. Her neck was stiff from the way she had been sitting and she leaned it on his shoulder. He held her next to him. This was more affection than Annie had received in months, she began to relax and warmth soared through her body. She hadn't felt like this for such a long time. It felt absolutely wonderful to be in his arms. This was a sleepy daze she was in and she didn't want it to end. He followed her back to her bedroom. After she moved her neck back and forth trying to make it feel better; he motioned for her to sit down and he sat on the bed and started massaging it. She felt as limp as a noodle after a few minutes, and was almost in a state of euphoria when he finished. She knew that hormones ran wild after giving birth, but she didn't want this to end.

He hugged her and kissed her on the cheek, then whispered, "You need to get some sleep before she wakes up again." She collapsed on the pillow and he gently pulled the covers over her. Sleep came almost instantly.

Early in the morning, Brian was back with Betsy in his arms. He was smiling with dimples showing. "I managed to get her to you before she yelled." Carefully, he handed the baby to Annie. "How's your neck this morning?"

"Thanks to you, it is fine, I really appreciate you rubbing it and working out the kinks. I slept really well." He sat down on the bed and smiled at her. Their glance met, and he watched her with loving eyes.

Every day that went by, Annie became more impressed with Brian. He treated her with such love and affection. He was kind and gentle with the children. Great meals came out of the kitchen. Her heart ached to think that their marriage wasn't successful. She had so much love in her heart for him, but she knew there also had to be trust.

One evening, she had just taken her shower and was sitting in bed thinking about her life. Tears rolled down her cheeks, just thinking what might have been. She knew she was going to have to be strong. She was barely making ends meet now and that was always a worry. Brian knocked and came in with Betsy in his arms.

He looked at her and with a look of concern on his face said, "What is it, Annie?"

"I'm just sad thinking what life could have been with you. You are such a kind and caring father and Betsy will never have the benefit of enjoying it. I need to put it out of my mind. It won't do anyone any good." Brian was silent.

The days seemed to pass quickly and Brian managed to do everything well. He washed clothes, cleaned the house and cooked, and took the children to play in the park. He shopped for groceries and when Betsy cried in the night, he took her to Annie to be fed. He was such great help. They got along really well, but they had always gotten along well. That wasn't the problem...

Before Brian returned to Florida, he went to the grocery store and bought everything on the list and more. He knew Annie needed financial help, and she had never allowed him to help her. Her cupboards were overflowing when he finished putting everything away. The freezer was also full.

One evening after the children were in bed she told him about what Jerry Nicholson had said, that perhaps his problem was something that was treatable. Brian said that he really didn't want to go to the mental health clinic, because once that was in his Air Force records; it would probably have a negative impact on his career opportunities. This was disappointing for Annie to hear. She knew she still cared for Brian, but thought it best not to reveal this to him, as he had hurt her so deeply. She knew she could never go back to him, if he wouldn't go for help. She had a heavy heart.

At the airport Annie hugged them both, and told Brian how much she appreciated all his help. She felt sad to see him leave. He was a wonderful father. They had managed to enjoy their time together.

Annie's mom came and stayed for a week after Brian left. She hadn't seen much of her mom and this was a good time to visit. Her mom brought daffodils into the house one day and Annie managed to say how lovely they were without crying.

She called Mr. Delgato and told him she had a little girl and he was very pleased for her. He was such a kind man and he had touched her heart.

Chapter Twenty-Five

The telephone rang while Annie was feeding Betsy. The welcoming voice on the other end of the line was Jon.

"How are mother and baby doing? Is this a good time for you to talk?"

"This is a perfect time to talk. I'm feeding Betsy at the moment and Katie has just gone to sleep. We're doing fine. I must admit that I miss Brian. He was such wonderful help and so kind and thoughtful with the children. He really spoiled me; he would even bring Betsy to me in the middle of the night to be fed. No one has ever done that for me before, except the nurse in the hospital, and I can't think of anything nicer."

"How is that sweet baby?"

"I wish you could see her Jon, she is precious. She looks like her daddy, with dark hair with a little curl and her daddy's dimples. She is very demanding, thinks she needs to eat as soon as she opens her eyes, and wails while she is getting her diaper changed. Once her tummy is full, she is content."

"I wish I could see her. You'll have to send me pictures in the meantime."

"I've taken pictures; I just haven't taken them to be developed. I'll send you some as soon as I do. Running errands has been difficult for me. I just go out and pick up the essentials and hurry back home."

"I'm so glad things went well while Brian was there. Did you have a chance to talk or decide anything?"

"Jon, I asked him about going for counseling, but he doesn't want that on this Air Force record. I was very disappointed when he told me that. It lets me know where I am on his priority list. I might as well get used the idea that I will be a single mom. There needs to be trust there and there isn't any now. It's really a hopeless situation. There is no way that I can go back to him." She paused for a moment, then added, "That is just the down side of things. Let me tell you the good part. I saw how wonderful he was with me and with the children while he was here, and we got along really well. I couldn't have asked for anyone to be any better to me. He touched my heart in so many ways." At that moment, Betsy rolled up a huge burp, and Jon was amused.

"It sounds like she's doing really well." Annie smiled down at her little girl, who was ready to eat some more.

"Sometimes I become very sad, thinking what might have been with Brian. There was such happiness in this house while he was here, despite the situation. Katie and Brett are a joy; they play so well together and are considerate and loving with each other. It's a shame that they can't be together. I miss Brett more than I can tell you. It was heartwarming just to be able to sit and talk to him. And Brian was exceptional in everything that he did. I wish things were different between us, but there isn't a thing that I can do about it."

"What are you going to do, Annie?"

"I don't know, Jon. I've been too busy to think about it. I become overwhelmed every time I think about going back to work. I can't keep up being at home all day. What am I going to do when I work all day?"

"You'll do fine, just like you do everything else."

"Thanks for the vote of confidence. I need it right now."

"I'll let you go so you can get some rest and I'll check back with you later. I love you, Annie."

"I love you, too, Jon. Thanks for calling and being such a good listener." She sat holding her precious baby and just looking at her made her smile. *I've got to be positive about this whole situation or I'll never make it.*

It was time to go back to work at the hospital; Annie had both the girls scheduled in the day-care center. She just hoped she could handle it all. She planned to go down on her lunch hour and nurse Betsy, and she used a breast pump for the rest of her feedings.

She knew she needed to leave the house by 6:15 at the latest to get the girls in day care and get to work by 7:00. Katie was able to put on her clothes most of the time and was a big help carrying things to the car. She liked being mommy's helper.

The first morning Betsy woke up at 3:30 to be fed and was fussy and wouldn't go back to sleep. She fussed while Katie and Annie ate breakfast. Katie smiled and said, "Mom, does she know it is your first day back at work?"

"I don't think so, honey." She had to smile at the comment.

The entire first week was the same. Annie's day started at 3:30. By Friday she was ready to crawl into the house and collapse. She and Katie ate scrambled eggs for supper and as soon as she gave each one a bath she showered and literally collapsed in bed. She didn't even remember putting her head on the pillow.

At 4:45 she heard Betsy and went to get her. *Isn't it wonderful what a good night's sleep can do for you! Never mind that it is a weekend!* She felt rested. Betsy ate and went right back to sleep. Annie was tempted to go back to bed, she knew she could sleep if she did, but she went downstairs and started making a dent in the pile of laundry. She managed to go to the grocery store without Betsy crying, never mind that most of the groceries were still in the car. She did bring in the things that needed to be put in the refrigerator and freezer, but that was all. Betsy needed to be fed. As soon as she sat down to nurse her, Annie's mom called and after a difficult week, she needed some encouragement from her. They talked for almost an hour. *There just aren't enough hours in the day.*

The next week seemed to be the same, somehow Betsy knew when Monday morning rolled around and it was 3:30 when she woke up. Annie had to keep ice water at her desk, so she could stay awake. She was always tired. It seemed she didn't have time to do anything at home, but laundry and prepare meals. She was horrified one day when she saw "dust bunnies" under her bed. She smiled and thought, *Welcome to my world.*

On the day of Betsy's two month checkup, Annie was at the point of exhaustion. Betsy was still waking up at 3:30 and Annie wasn't able to go back to bed and get any rest—she was a walking zombie. When she picked Betsy up after work to go to the pediatrician's office, Betsy was so hungry she sucked Annie's cheek. She usually ate when Annie picked her up, and Betsy was not a patient baby. She asked the receptionist if there was a place where she could feed her. She found the examining room and nursed her, and when a knock came on the door, Annie was sound asleep. The doctor came in, and it wasn't her usual doctor. He introduced himself as Dr. Campbell and said Dr. Lane was on vacation.

"Did I wake you?"

"Yes, you did. I'm sure you've seen sleep deprived mothers before." She explained that she was getting up at 3:30 almost every day and she was tired all the time. After examining Betsy thoroughly, he noted she was gaining weight and she was fine. He sent Annie to the lab for Betsy's shots.

Dr. Livingston called to see if they could come by on Sunday afternoon to see the new baby.

Mrs. Livingston asked to hold Betsy, so Annie could open her gift. Annie handed the little bundle to Mrs. Livingstone and she was looking at her with adoring eyes. She asked if she was a good baby and Annie smiled and said she was very demanding, but when she was fed she was content. The gift was wrapped in

Peter Rabbit paper, and inside was an adorable set of Peter Rabbit dishes for Betsy, with a porringer, plate and a two handed cup, all with Peter Rabbit characters. They brought a book to Katie. They were such a nice couple and obviously loved children.

Brian called twice during the next week and each time Annie was asleep. She explained that she had to get to bed as soon as the girls were asleep, because Betsy was waking up at 3:30 in the morning and she usually couldn't go back to sleep. He apologized and said he would talk to her at another time. Annie looked forward to his calls, as he was a great source of encouragement for her.

On Saturday morning she was up early feeding Betsy, and she decided she would call Brian. She rarely called him, but knew he got up early, so she thought she would surprise him. When the phone rang a woman answered. Thinking that perhaps she had dialed the wrong number, Annie said, "Is this the Kendall residence?"

The woman said, "Yes it is, this is Bonnie, may I help you?"

"Is Brian there?"

"Brian is in the shower, may I take a message?"

"No thank you." She hung up the telephone. She sat there in disbelief. *How could he come up here and be so wonderful and caring and go home and have someone spend the night with him? Why is he doing this with Brett in the house? I'll never understand this man...*

When the girls were settled that evening she sat in bed and cried. She was hurt and angry. *I can't go on like this. I was a fool to think he cared about me.* She knew what she needed to do.

On Monday she called the lawyer that had helped her after Rick's death and asked to see him. She would file for divorce even if she had to go into debt to do it.

If it weren't for Katie she wasn't sure how she would have made it through the next few weeks. She unlocked the door to the house, and dumped all the stuff from the car in a chair. Betsy was wailing to be fed. This was such a demanding child and she screamed when she was hungry. Annie sat on the couch to nurse her and she usually read to Katie while she fed the baby, but today Katie said, "My baby is hungry, too." She picked up her doll and pulled up her shirt and proceeded to pretend she was "nursing" her baby. Annie was so amused; she had a hard time not smiling. Katie got up again and got her doll blanket and threw it over her and her "baby" so no one could see her nursing, just like Mommy would do when she would feed Betsy in the car before they came home. Then Katie said, "I guess I don't really need the blanket, Mom, since it is just you and me here." Annie knew she couldn't laugh, but she was so tickled she could hardly keep quiet. What a precious child her Katie was.

The divorce papers should have reached Brian by now; Annie was expecting a phone call from him and was trying to keep her composure. When the phone rang she somehow knew it was him. He didn't even say hello, his first question was, "Why are you doing this now, Annie? Have you met someone? You really surprised me, I just wasn't expecting this."

Annie had to laugh. "Brian, no I haven't met anyone. I'm a mother with one baby in my arms and another by the hand. This isn't exactly what guys are looking for. I barely have time to sleep, let alone go out with someone. Our relationship isn't important enough for you to seek help for your problem, so there is no reason to continue being married. I'm not asking for anything for me, but I do think you should pay child support for Betsy. I asked you to go to the legal office and do this when I left last year and you chose not to do it. I have had to take out a loan to do it. I just hope you'll be reasonable. This isn't something I want to do, but you leave me no choice. Working through our problems is just never going to happen."

"Annie, I thought when I was there that you were okay. What has changed?"

She quipped back at him, "Nothing has changed, that's the problem."

"I could tell by the way that you looked at me that you still cared about me."

"I do still care about you, Brian. You were wonderful while you were here and I will always be grateful for your help. This is a very difficult thing for me to do. I'll tell you just like you told me many years ago; this is one of the hardest things I've ever had to do." Her voice broke when she said this and she was silent for a moment. She almost brought up the fact that she had called and a woman had answered the phone, but decided against it. There was no excuse for what he had done. Emotions were overflowing now, and she didn't want to cry. She took a deep breath and said, "Brian, I hope you will be reasonable. I need to go now." When she hung up the phone, she sat and dissolved in tears. *I know this is the right thing to do, but it isn't easy.*

When she took Betsy for her three month checkup, Annie felt like the haggard mother. She yawned when Dr. Campbell asked her questions and she told him that she was sleeping until 4:00 now, but that still made a very long day.

"I shouldn't even tell you this, but sometimes I just put a pillow on the other side of her and just crawl back in bed and feed her and go back to sleep. I'm smart enough to know that this is not the thing to do, but my judgment at 4:00 a.m. is a bit clouded."

He just smiled and shook his head. He was tall, probably at least six feet four inches and had huge hands, but was so gentle with Betsy and talked to her while he examined her. She smiled at him when he talked to her. You could tell that he loved children.

Brian did not contest the divorce and signed the papers. The lawyer said it would take a while before the divorce was final. The child support would be deposited directly into her checking account and it would be retroactive to Betsy's date of birth. Annie knew she was doing the right thing, but it still made her sick to think that she would soon be a divorcee. She never thought this would happen to her. Now she thought she would be a struggling single mother for the rest of her life. She felt so alone. She decided she would have to let all of this go and count her blessings. She had two beautiful little girls and they were both healthy.

Chapter Twenty-Six

Annie received a call from Dr. Stillwell, an oncologist, who wanted her to visit with a patient of his. He was a nine year old boy who had been undergoing chemotherapy for a brain tumor, a medulloblastoma. He had been so nauseated he wasn't able to eat and even when he felt hungry, nothing sounded good to him.

Annie went to his room and met Bobby Masters and his mother Mary. Bobbie was propped up with pillows all around him and he gave her a smile when she came into the room. He had lost all of his hair and he looked very thin and pale. He had beautiful big brown eyes that sparkled when he smiled. She asked what he liked to eat before he got sick and what his favorite foods were. He said he loved strawberries and peanut butter and bananas. Annie asked if he thought he would like to try a milkshake with strawberries and he said he would. While she was talking to him, his mother asked if it would be okay if she left the room and made a few phone calls.

While she was gone, Annie talked to him about school and Bobby told her he liked to play soccer and really missed playing since he was sick. He said he was tired and had trouble going to sleep. His foot was sticking out from under the covers and Annie said, "Would you like me to give you a foot rub? I'll try not to tickle you."

He gave her a big grin and stuck his other foot out for her to rub. Annie moved a chair next to the bed and sat down and gave him a foot massage and after a little while he relaxed and went to sleep. Annie stayed with him until his mother returned.

Mary whispered to her when she came in the room. "How did you do that?" Annie told her and said she would have a strawberry milkshake sent up for him for his evening meal.

Annie was always greeted warmly when she went to see Bobby Masters. She checked regularly on him to see if he was eating what was sent up from the kitchen.

He told her, "That peanut butter and banana milkshake was really good. How did you learn to do that?"

She smiled and said she learned it from her mom. She asked him about other foods that he liked, and they decided they would try some soups the next day. When Annie had time, she would stay and massage Bobby's feet. As soon as she walked in the room he would stick his feet out from under the covers and smile at her. He was such a dear little boy and Annie hoped he would recover from this horrible illness. Mary Masters always looked so weary when Annie saw her. She said she had three other children at home and that she needed to be both places at once.

In October she made back to back appointments with Dr. Campbell for Katie and Betsy. It was going to be Katie's fourth birthday in just a week, and Betsy was six months old. He checked them both over and said they were fine. That was good news and the other good news was that Annie was finally getting some much needed rest.

The next day was Saturday and she received a call from Dr. Campbell. "Annie, this is Doug Campbell and I'm calling to see if you would have lunch with me on Tuesday?"

Annie was so surprised she hardly knew what to say. "Thank you, it is so kind of you to ask, but I have a lunch date with Betsy every day. I go down to the daycare center and feed her and I have my lunch. I'm sorry."

"Would it be okay if I picked up Chinese take-out and brought it to your house tonight about six?"

"That would be great; I'll see you at six. Now let me give you directions to the house."

Doug arrived at six with boxes of food. Katie was excited that they were having a guest for dinner. They sat down at the table and Betsy was in the highchair. Annie served Katie's plate with a taste of everything. Katie wanted to say the blessing. She was praying with one eye open. "Thank you God for Dr. Campbell bringing us food, and thank you for the chicken, and the rice, and the peas, and the broccoli, and — Mom, what is this?"

Annie said, "It's an egg roll."

"Thank you for the egg roll."

Doug could hardly keep from laughing and Annie knew she couldn't look at him or they would both laugh. Katie asked Doug if he would read her a story and Annie went upstairs to feed Betsy and get her ready for bed. When both girls were settled she sat down by Doug and he told her that he had talked to Dr. Gill this morning and had found out what was going on in Annie's life.

"I had no idea you were raising the girls by yourself."

Annie told him a brief history of what had happened in her life and then she asked him. "Why is it that a handsome man like you isn't married?"

He smiled at her and seemed to be gathering his thoughts. He told her that he and Leah had dated for four years and planned to get married when they got out of medical school. They were very much in love, unfortunately Leah told him that she didn't want to have children; she just wanted to be a doctor. They broke up and he just hadn't found anyone he wanted to go out with. He said he just couldn't imagine going through life without children. Annie told him that her two little ones were the light of her life and that Katie was what kept her going after Rick's death.

Doug said, "I don't know how you keep a straight face with that one."

Annie related the pretend nursing incident to Doug and he thought that was really hilarious. Annie then added, "Now Betsy is going to be a real character. I was nursing her just last week, and she's cutting teeth and she decided to bite me. Needless to say, this took me by surprise and I yelled and jumped, she just laughed out loud. She got so tickled, she just laughed and laughed. I was not amused, and told her that her nursing days were numbered if she did that again. So far she hasn't tried it again."

Doug asked if he could take her out to dinner next Saturday night. She said she would check to see if Angela could babysit and let him know. He said it was time for him to go and that he had enjoyed the evening with her. Annie thanked him for bringing dinner and for reading to Katie.

The next weekend they went out to dinner at a lovely French restaurant and had a delicious meal. This was such a treat for Annie. She asked if he would like to go back to the house for coffee and cookies and he said he would. Angela said the girls were good, but that Betsy wailed when she emptied her bottle and wanted more. Annie paid her and thanked her for staying. She brewed coffee, then joined Doug in the living room with coffee and cookies. Annie thought he was such a kind and thoughtful man. She enjoyed being with him, but was surprised that he would even want to go out with her. He said he needed to go and she walked to the door with him. He took her in his arms and kissed her, and she put her head on his shoulder and he held her close.

"Thank you, Doug, for a lovely evening. Why don't you come for dinner here next weekend?" He said that would be fine and he would look forward to coming.

The next morning, Annie brought Betsy back to her bed to feed her, and Katie came in to snuggle with them.

Katie said, "Tell me the story about my daddy, when I was a baby."

Annie had told this to Katie so many times. She knew that she didn't remember her daddy, but stories like this would keep his memory alive. Annie began the story again. "When you were a baby about Betsy's age, your dad would wait for me to bring you back to bed so we could snuggle and I could feed you. I would put you down between us and you would start nursing. You would hold his finger while you nursed. Sometimes you would stop eating and turn toward him and just smile and coo at him and then you would start eating again. You would do this over and over again. It was like a little game you played with your daddy."

As soon as Annie finished the story, Katie would say, "Tell it to me again."

When Doug came for dinner they had spaghetti and meatballs, one of Katie's favorite meals. It was a fun evening. Katie seemed to think that Doug came over just to read a story to her and she had a book already picked out for him to read.

Annie said, "I would stay down here and feed Betsy, but she has started throwing off the blanket that I cover us with, so I think I'd better go upstairs and feed her." She got the girls put to bed and came back downstairs. Doug took her hands and pulled her down on his lap and kissed her. Annie put her head on his shoulder; she hadn't felt this content in a very long time.

"You have been really good for me, Doug. I have a different outlook since I've been seeing you."

He hugged her and said, "I'm so pleased to hear that, because I love being with you, Annie." He told her that he thought she was very attractive when he first saw her half asleep with a baby in her arms, but he said that he just assumed that she was married and never gave it another thought. "The last time you were in my office, I noticed that you weren't wearing a wedding ring, and I asked Dr. Gill about you. I'm so glad I did."

Chapter Twenty-Seven

Emily came over one Saturday afternoon with Nicholas. Annie really loved spending time with Emily, they were both very busy and never had enough time to visit and catch up. As soon as they sat down to talk, Emily said she was pregnant again and was pleased. They had hired a nanny for Nicholas and that was working out well.

Annie told her about Doug, how she enjoyed being with him. "Katie adores him and thinks he comes over just to read to her."

Emily seemed pleased that Annie was seeing Doug and enjoyed his company. When Emily was leaving she said they would have to get together more often.

Annie went home for Thanksgiving. She loved spending time with her mom, but Tom was still rather distant and that put a damper on the visit. She hoped the opportunity would arise at some point for her to talk to him. He had always been the one man in her life that had never let her down, and now she felt that she couldn't even approach him.

Annie received a note from Mary Masters saying that Bobby was doing really well and gaining weight. She thanked Annie for her help and said Bobby was addicted to milkshakes. It was heartwarming to know that she had been able to help him.

The weekend after Thanksgiving, Doug said he would take Annie and the girls Christmas shopping at the Plaza. Santa

Claus was going to be at one of the stores and Annie hoped to get pictures made of him with the girls. She knew it would be hectic, but Doug was so patient and was wonderful help with Katie and Betsy. Annie had a long list of things to do and was making great progress. They stopped for lunch and Katie said, "I think we should do this every week." It was a fun, but exhausting day.

Doug helped put up the Christmas tree and decorate it. Betsy was crawling everywhere and was in to everything. He observed her for several minutes, then said, "This is going to be fun. She's going to pull things off as soon as we put them on." Betsy wailed when she was put in the playpen. Then he laughed. "Maybe we should put the tree in the playpen." They decided to finish decorating the tree while Betsy took her nap.

Katie was at the church practicing for the children's Christmas program on Saturday morning. When Annie picked her up she said she had fun and that she was learning Christmas songs. Annie asked what song she was singing and Katie told her "Away in a Manger" and "Silent Night" and then she asked, "Mom, who is Round John Virgin?" Annie knew immediately what she was asking and said, "Honey, it is round yon virgin and yon is just a short version of yonder, meaning over there at a distance." Annie would have to remember to tell her mom about this one.

There was a Christmas party sponsored by the hospital and Doug and Annie attended. It was a lovely event at a local hotel. Doug came in for a few minutes when they got back to the house. Annie paid Angela and when she left, Doug took Annie in his arms and said, "Annie, I wish I could take you to Virginia with me."

Annie smiled and said, "I'm sure that would be fun. Thank you, Doug, for a wonderful evening." He kissed her and said goodnight.

Doug was planning to go to his home in Virginia for Christmas, and Annie was going to be with her mom, but just for Christmas Eve and Christmas day. She didn't want to take too much vacation time. She never knew when one of the girls might get sick, and she would have to stay home from work. She had the car packed, so she could leave as soon as she got off work, and then she would come back on Christmas afternoon.

When she returned to Kansas City, she walked in the door and the telephone was ringing. It was Brian. He wanted to know if he, Jon and Brett could come for the weekend. Jon hadn't seen his granddaughter since she was born and Brian hadn't seen her since she was ten days old.

"Brian, why couldn't you have let me know before now what you were planning? I just walked in the door and I'm not ready for company. This house is a mess."

"Don't worry about a thing; we'll help you. We'll take you out to dinner when we get there and I'll get something to cook on the grill while we're there."

She asked when they planned to arrive, and Brian said they would be there when she got home from work the next day. Annie was already dead tired because she had stayed up late both nights she was gone. She fed the girls, bathed them and put them to bed. When she finished cleaning the house it was after midnight and she was ready to drop in her tracks. After showering, she sat on the bed and was putting on face cream and thinking about the weekend ahead. She looked forward to seeing Jon and Brett, but she wasn't sure she was ready for Brian. She wasn't sure she would ever be ready to see Brian again.

Jon, Brian and Brett were waiting in the driveway when she arrived home. She opened the door and let them in the house. Brett was so happy to see her. Just looking at this darling little boy made her heart ache. She loved him so much. Betsy crawled up to her dad and pulled up on his leg. Annie looked at Brian to warn him. "Please hang on to her or she'll dismantle the Christmas tree." Jon said he would take them all out to dinner.

The next morning after breakfast Annie said she needed to go to the grocery store; Brian said he would take her. He wanted to buy steaks to grill for their evening meal. On the way home he asked how she was doing and Annie said she was okay. She wasn't very talkative. When he asked if she was seeing anyone, Annie said she was. She didn't say any more. There was an edgy silence between them.

Katie and Brett played and were so happy to be together again. They let Betsy play too, or at least they tried to. She had a mind of her own. She would do what they wanted, but when she lost interest, she did what she wanted. Katie and Brett would build towers and houses with blocks and Lincoln logs and Betsy would knock them down and laugh. They were always happy when it was time for Betsy to take her nap.

As soon as they finished the evening meal, Annie went up to bathe Katie and Betsy. She fed Betsy, then read to Katie and Brett. They sat in her bed with one on each side of her; Brett told her he liked this best. Annie could hardly look at him without getting emotional, she loved him so much. Katie was almost asleep when she finished and Brett went to his bed. Annie said she would be in to tell him goodnight in just a minute. Brian was rocking Betsy in her room. She thought as she walked by what a sweet picture it was as Betsy was cuddled down on his shoulder.

Annie sat on the side of Brett's bed and listened to his prayers. At the end he said, "Please God, let Annie be my mom again."

She was so moved by this she hugged him and said, "Brett, I loved being your mom. You are the most precious little boy that I have ever known and I will always love you. I wish I could be your mom as you've brought me so much joy, but right now it just isn't possible. I know you don't understand this, but please remember that I love you and there will always be a special place for you in my heart." She hugged him and was so emotional. She felt helpless.

Then he said, "Now will you tickle my back, please?"

Annie came downstairs and Jon could see she was on the

verge of tears. "What is it, Annie?" As she told him about the conversation she had with Brett, tears streamed down her cheeks.

Brian came down the stairs and asked what was wrong, and she repeated the conversation to him. He sat down beside her and put his arm around her; she sat there teary-eyed trying to control her emotions.

"Brian, that little boy is breaking my heart. I couldn't love him anymore if I had given birth to him. He is too young to understand what has happened between us, and I don't know what to tell him when he says he wants me to be his mom." Annie got up and went to the kitchen for a Kleenex and Brian followed her. He held out his arms and hugged her and patted her back. She stood there for a moment and then backed away.

"Annie, he talks about you all the time. You haven't spent a lot of time with him, but you have made a big impression on him."

Annie was trying not to get emotional again. "I wish there was a solution to this problem."

"There was a solution Annie, I just made a mess of it."

The next morning Annie made pumpkin and pecan pancakes for everyone. Brian took Betsy out of the highchair and held her most of the morning. He played with her and every time he put her down she crawled over to him and hung on to his leg. It seemed as if she instinctively knew he was her daddy. Jon thought she was adorable.

Annie made a pork roast with a garlic and herb crust, and candied sweet potatoes and a green bean casserole for lunch. They were going back to Iowa as soon as they finished eating.

As Jon was loading the car, Brian came into the kitchen and took Annie's hands in his. "Annie, thank you so much for having us. We have a precious little girl and you have done a great job with her. I'm sorry for making your life so difficult, you deserve much better. You mean more to me than you'll ever know."

Brett came in to give her a hug and said goodbye, and so did Jon.

When the girls went down for a nap, Annie started the dishes and laundry and then started taking the ornaments off the Christmas tree. She was so tired she was ready for a nap. The whole week of Christmas was just a blur. She thought about what Brian had said, but she was sure nothing was going to change there. *If he had really cared for me, he wouldn't have had a woman spending the night with him.*

Annie was taking the ornaments off the Christmas tree when the doorbell rang. When Doug came in, he was so happy to see her that he almost lifted her off her feet. "Annie, I've missed you so much, I just had to come by and see you before I went home. I don't ever want to be away from you again." She was amazed how exuberant he was. He was usually reserved and calm. She took his coat and he sat down.

"Can I make you a cup of tea? She went to the kitchen to put the kettle on the stove. While the water was coming to a boil, he came in and hugged her to him and kissed her. They talked about Christmas and what they had done. She told Doug she had returned on Thursday evening and that Brian, Brett and Jon had come on Friday for the weekend and had just gone back this afternoon.

"You mean you asked them to stay here for the weekend?" He looked at her waiting for an answer and by the look on his face she knew he was upset.

"Yes, I did. Brian is Betsy's father, and Jon, her grandfather, had never seen her. I didn't want them to stay in a motel and just come here for a visit. Brett and Katie love playing together. I decided a long time ago that I would never make it uncomfortable for the children. I never want them to feel tension between Brian and me. This is the least I can do for them. Divorce is a horrible thing and it is devastating for the children. I wanted to make this visit as normal as possible and that's why they stayed here."

Doug walked into the living room, picked up his coat and said, "I think it is time for me to go." He walked out the door.

Annie sat down and drank her cup of tea. She was surprised at Doug's behavior. This was so out of character for him to just walk out because he was upset. She felt like she hadn't done anything wrong, and yet she was sorry she had offended him.

Emily came over on the next weekend, and Annie told her what had happened with Doug.

"I really do miss seeing him, but I think the relationship is over. He was so glad to see me when he came in the door and ten minutes later he left. He wouldn't even discuss what I had done; he was just upset that I had asked them to stay."

Chapter Twenty-Eight

Several weeks later Emily came by to return some books she had borrowed and Annie said, "Do you have your bag in the car? Would you check Betsy's ears? She is really fussy and keeps pulling at her ear."

Emily checked her ears and listened to her chest and said, "She has an ear infection and her chest is rattling." She called in prescriptions and Annie went to pick them up before Emily left.

Annie was so grateful that Emily had been there to check Betsy. "Now you need to get out of here before you get sick, Emily."

Emily said she would send Jeff over in a couple days to check and see how Betsy was doing.

When Jeff came by two days later, Annie was running a fever and coughing and was feeling terribly sick. Jeff listened to Annie's chest and said she had bronchitis. He called in prescriptions and asked if they could deliver them to the house. He checked Betsy and she was still running a low grade fever. Annie called her office the next morning and said she would be on sick leave for the rest of the week. She called Angela and asked if she could keep Katie at her house so she wouldn't get sick. She also called to cancel Betsy's appointment with Doug on Friday. This was a well-baby check and she was anything but well.

Annie spent a horrible night with chills and fever. Every time she got up she was wet with sweat and when she would change her nightgown she got so chilled she shook and couldn't seem to get warm. She just went to another bed and tried to pile the covers on until she got warm. Betsy's crying awakened her and when she went to get her she was shaking so hard she could hardly hold her. All she heard were croupy coughs and by the way she sounded, Annie was sure Betsy also had bronchitis. She finally got her settled and went to find the vaporizer. She took more cough medicine, but nothing seemed to help. Sitting up in a chair was the only way she could get any rest that night. After two days of this, she finally began to feel like she was going to survive. However, she was so weak; she hardly had the energy to walk up the stairs.

Late Friday afternoon the telephone rang. As soon as she answered, she heard, "You cancelled Betsy's appointment, why did you do that?"

Annie was so hoarse from coughing, she said in a whisper, "Doug, Betsy is sick, and so am I. She had an ear infection and bronchitis and I have bronchitis."

He sounded a bit annoyed. "Who did you take her to?"

"I didn't take her to anyone. Emily was here and checked her and called in prescriptions, and then Jeff came to see me two days later. It has been a long, miserable week and I don't need to be questioned by you. Do you think I'm irresponsible or are you just upset because I didn't call you?"

"Why didn't you call me, Annie?"

"Doug, I think you know the answer to that."

"Is it okay if I come over and check on you and Betsy now?"

"No, it is not okay. I look like death warmed over right now, and I do not want to see anyone."

"Do you have fever now?"

"I don't know. I haven't taken it this afternoon."

He was really getting impatient with her. "Why didn't you call me? You know I would have come over." She started coughing and just couldn't seem to stop. "I'm coming over to see you." He hung up before she could say another word.

Doug arrived in about twenty minutes. He took one look at her and shook his head. "Annie, you are one of the most stubborn women I have ever met in all my life. Why wouldn't you ask for help? Where are the girls?"

"Katie has been at Angela's all week, and Betsy is asleep. The cough medicine makes her sleep a lot, which is probably a good thing because I've been too sick to do much for her."

"Will you let me listen to your chest, you really sound awful?" She nodded her head, and he got out his stethoscope and listened to her breathe. Every time she took a deep breath she started to cough. She heard Betsy upstairs and started to go upstairs to get her. She was so weak she had to move slowly, and Doug came to steady her. Betsy seemed to be improving each day, but still had a cough. Annie changed her, and Doug listened to her chest.

"Her chest is just a little raspy. Is she still on the antibiotic?" Annie nodded that she was. Doug asked Annie if she had eaten and she said she hadn't. "What have you been eating all week, Annie?"

"Not much, I've had juice, tea, soup and cereal and that's about it." She put Betsy in the highchair and gave her some slices of banana and some apple juice.

Doug told her to please sit down and he would fix her something to eat. He fixed scrambled eggs, toast, juice and tea. He took Betsy upstairs and bathed her, and Annie put clean sheets on her bed. She sat in the rocking chair to nurse her, and Doug said he would clean up the kitchen and start on the pile of laundry.

Annie came downstairs after she had given Betsy her medicine and put her to bed. Doug was putting more sheets in the washer.

"Where did all the sheets and blankets come from?"

"I had chills and fever for so long, and when the sheets were wet with sweat, I just moved to a different bed. I've slept in all the beds in the house and in the chair downstairs." He came over to her and put his arm around her and hugged her to him. They stood there for a long time and not a word was spoken.

Finally, he said, "Annie, can we try this once again?"

"Doug, I don't think it will ever work. Everything is fine between us until Brian's name comes up, and then you stiffen and walk out the door. Brian is always going to be a part of my life. We have a child, and I will always treat him with respect as long as the children are around. I don't like what he did to me, but the children will not suffer because of it. I don't think you will ever accept him as part of my life. It is up to you, not up to me."

"You mean a great deal to me, Annie, and I miss seeing you. I'd like to see if we can get back on track." He hugged her and kissed her forehead.

Doug put a clean mattress pad and sheets on Annie's bed. It would feel wonderful to sleep in her bed again. She was certainly grateful for his help. He had accomplished more in a couple of hours than she had all week. He said he would be back in the morning and asked what she needed from the grocery store. She didn't even know what she had in the kitchen; she said by morning she'd have a list. When Doug was ready to leave he hugged her.

"Doug, I'm sorry I upset you. Surely you know that I wouldn't intentionally hurt you."

He hugged her again and said, "I know you wouldn't, Annie."

Brian called after Doug left and when Annie answered he said, "Are you sick?"

"Brian, this has been the hardest week I've had in a long time. Betsy started out with an ear infection, and then she got bronchitis and I sat up holding her for two nights. Every time I put her down, she would start coughing, so I just sat and held her. Then I got bronchitis and I had chills and fever. I'm much better, but I'm still very weak. Katie has been with Angela all week. Brian I know God meant for children to have two parents."

Brian was kind and said, "I know that Annie, and I've made a real mess out of our lives. I'm sorry. I wish I could be there to help you."

Annie talked to Brett for a few minutes and then Brian asked if he could take Betsy to Iowa with him just before Memorial Day. There was a family reunion and he wanted to take their daughter home for everyone to see. She said that would be fine, then added, "I hope you're prepared for your daughter, she's a live wire."

Doug came over the next day and cleaned the house and went to the grocery store and helped her with Betsy. He wouldn't let her pay for the groceries. Annie looked at him and said, "And you call me stubborn." Annie felt like all she did was laundry and that wore her out. When Angela brought Katie home, Annie hugged her and told her how much she had missed her. They had talked on the telephone, but it was wonderful to have her home. Katie was a big help and put away laundry, and helped Doug put away groceries. She loved being a caregiver for her mom and little sister. They all sat down to eat Doug's delicious chicken soup. He had been such wonderful help. He bathed the girls and helped put them to bed.

When they came downstairs he sat down beside her. "Annie, I'm worn out. I don't know how you do this every day." He pulled her close to him and put his arm around her. "I hope you can get some rest tonight. Please take it easy. I need to go now so you can get to bed." Annie thanked him for all his help and hugged him before he left.

Annie returned to work on Monday and by noon she was exhausted. She went down to day care to feed Betsy and almost went to sleep sitting in the rocking chair. She went outside to get some fresh air before she went back to work, hoping that would help wake her up. By the time she got home, she wanted to crawl into bed she was so fatigued. She was warming the chicken soup when Doug arrived.

"I think an angel has just arrived at my door to help me," she told him. "You have no idea how pleased I am to see you."

He gave her a hug and said, "I thought you might need some help." Doug was such a natural with children and the girls loved him. He cleaned up the kitchen, bathed the girls and read to them, and put them to bed.

Chapter Twenty-Nine

The days were getting longer and Annie could see the daffodils poking out of the ground. After a long winter she was always ready for the signs of spring and a new beginning. Doug had been coming over every weekend or they had been going out to dinner or a movie. They enjoyed each other's company and Annie always looked forward to their time together. One evening they had been out to dinner and had come back to the house. Annie had gone up to check on the girls, and when she came down the stairs he took her by the hands and pulled her onto his lap and kissed her.

"I love it when you do that."

He held her close and said, "Annie, I'm in love with you."

She was so content with him holding her in his arms. "Maybe there is truth to the old saying, that 'a young man's fancy turns to love in the springtime.' Have you come to accept the fact that Brian will always be part of my life? I know this is a difficult thing for you to deal with."

He thought for a moment and said, "I've been thinking a lot about that and I just hope I can deal with it. I want you in my life, Annie, so I'm going to have to deal with it, if you'll have me." Then he added, "You don't have to answer that now."

"Doug you are such a wonderful man and I love being with you. Your reaction to Brian is my only problem with you. I'm not asking you to like him, but I can't handle the way you react to him. You haven't even met him. I know you think he is horrible for what he did, but if I can forgive him, surely you can tolerate him. He's an outstanding father and wonderful with the children. I was deeply hurt by what he did to me, but I can also see his good qualities. He has asked to take Betsy to Iowa with him for a week at the end of May. You can meet him when he comes to get her. I do wish that you would talk to me when you get upset and not just walk out the door. Perhaps we can resolve something if you'll just talk about it. Walking out just doesn't solve anything."

"I'm sorry, Annie. I'll try to do better. I know that is not the way to solve problems."

Annie was feeling tired all the time and didn't know why. She was getting enough sleep most of the time. She was eating right, and she was exercising when she could, but she had no energy. Her appointment with Dr. Gill for her yearly checkup was scheduled for the last of May and even though that was several weeks away, she thought she would just wait. They would do blood work and if anything was wrong it would show up then.

Betsy had her birthday and Annie took pictures, some to send to Brian and Jon. Betsy started walking when she was ten months old, and she moved so fast it was hard to keep up with her. Annie had weaned her and she was drinking from a cup and doing great. She ate everything and wanted more. She was so different from Katie, who was quiet and reserved. When she was learning to walk, Annie got Katie to turn around and come down the stairs backwards on her stomach. However, Betsy insisted in holding on to the spindles on the banister and came down standing up. She was trying to say lots of words and Katie helped her with that. She sounded like a parrot, repeating everything Katie said.

Two weeks before Brian came to get Betsy, Annie was so tired she just wanted to go to bed and sleep for hours. It was beautiful weather and she usually was outside weeding and planting, but she just didn't have the energy. She had planted tomato plants and the rest of her salad garden, plus a few bedding plants in the front of the house. Usually she had pots filled with geraniums on the patio, but this year she just didn't have the energy to do it.

The morning that Brian and Brett were coming, Annie told Doug that she was always a little tense when Brian was coming because she wanted everything to go well. She also told him that she was really tired and a little concerned that something was wrong with her.

She said, "I just don't feel right."

Doug told her that she tried to do too much and that was probably why she was always so tired.

When Brian and Brett arrived Annie made the introductions and Brian said he would take the children to the park and then out to eat. Brian couldn't wait to pick up Betsy and hold her. She gave him a hug and patted his shoulder. He was so enamored with his daughter that he hardly talked to Doug.

Brett came to hug her when he came in the door and said, "I've missed you, Annie."

Brett and Katie went upstairs to Katie's room and Betsy was crawling up after them. Brian was watching Betsy with adoring eyes.

Annie told him, "You are going to have your hands full with your daughter."

They all talked and Annie fixed iced tea for them. Brian said he was ready to take them to the park and Annie went outside to help him get the children in the car.

Brett came up to Annie and said, "Aren't you coming with us to the park, Annie?"

"No Brett, I'm staying here." She squatted down to tell him that and he grabbed her and hugged her. Tears were running down his cheeks.

"I wish you were still my mom, Annie. I want you to go with us." She was so moved she could hardly hold the tears back.

"I'll be here when you come back, and we can spend some time together." Brian drove away with the children and Annie stood there with tears running down her cheeks.

She slowly walked back into the house, and Doug said, "What happened to you? Why are you so upset?" Annie went to the kitchen to get a Kleenex. Doug followed her and said, "What's the matter with you?"

She was so upset she couldn't talk and just stood there with her head down. She tried to calm herself and said, "Just a minute and I'll tell you," then she started to cry.

Doug was losing his patience and said, "Please tell me what is going on, why are you crying?"

Annie reacted to his impatience and couldn't stop crying. Doug was so annoyed at this point that he said he was leaving. She watched him walk out the door and couldn't say a word. Annie had a good cry and washed her face and sat there thinking that Doug would never return. *I needed him to help me through this, not just walk away.*

When Brian came back with the children he asked if she was okay and she told him that she wasn't and what had happened.

"It just breaks my heart when Brett says he wants me to be his mom." She told Brian that she was not feeling well and she didn't know why. "I do have a doctor's appointment, hopefully I can find out what is wrong."

Brian and Brett stayed in a motel and were back early in the morning for breakfast. Annie made "apple French toast" and while Brian was loading Betsy's things she talked to Brett for a few minutes. He told her about what he had done in kindergarten and that he was going to take swimming lessons in the summer. Annie kissed Brett and Betsy goodbye and then she took Katie inside the house.

Chapter Thirty

Jeff called the following week to say that Emily had delivered a little girl and they named her Megan Louise. Mother and baby were doing fine. Jeff was such a proud father. Annie was thrilled for them. She would go see them tomorrow.

Brian and the children arrived at Annie's on the following Saturday at lunchtime. Annie had lunch waiting and was so glad to see Betsy. She had missed her little darling. Brian said he was glad he had his dad's help to watch Betsy, as she was into everything. At the family reunion everyone was pleased to see her. As soon as lunch was over Brian and Brett left to go back to Florida.

Before he left, Brian said, "Thanks so much for letting me have her for a week. It was a very special time for both of us." Then he asked if Annie was feeling any better, and she said she was about the same. "Let me know what you find out at the appointment with your doctor."

Annie hadn't heard a word from Doug and realized that she probably owed him an explanation, but she was hurt that he had walked out once again without saying anything. At the moment she was too exhausted to even think.

She went up to see Emily and her baby, and Emily was thrilled to have a little girl. She looked like her mother with beautiful blue eyes and black hair. What a joy it was to see them both. Annie told her she would bring dinner to her when she and the baby went home.

Annie had her appointment with Dr. Gill on Tuesday and when he did a breast exam he found a lump in her breast. He said she would need a mammogram. When he did the pelvic exam, he said he felt something on her ovary and said she would have to go have an ultrasound to see what it was. When she got dressed and came back to his office, he had already scheduled her for an ultrasound that afternoon. After the ultrasound, she went back to her office and before she left that afternoon she had a call from Dr. Gill.

On her way to his office she was very apprehensive and tense. As soon as she sat down Dr. Gill said, "Annie, you have a growth the size of a grapefruit on your left ovary and it needs to come out. We have no way of knowing if this is benign or malignant; surgery is the only way we can tell. I've also scheduled a mammogram for you in the morning."

Annie sat there stunned and in disbelief. "What do you think is wrong with me, Dr. Gill?"

"I don't know, but we'll find out."

After her mammogram the next morning she was so nervous she couldn't concentrate. She picked up the girls after work and went home, but that is all she could manage. Dr. Gill called just before 5:00 to tell her he had scheduled her for surgery on Friday morning for a breast biopsy. She called her mom to tell what was happening, and ask if she could come and stay with her after her surgery on Monday. Her mom wanted to come on Friday, but Annie said she would be fine, that they were just going to do a local anesthesia.

After she put the girls to bed, she called Brian and told him what was happening. Before she finished telling him, she became emotional. "Brian I'm so scared; what if I have cancer? I know if something happens to me you will get Betsy, but I want you to have Katie, too. She can't be separated from Betsy and she loves Brett. Please think about this for me. I know this is a lot to ask of you." This opened the flood gates and tears were flowing faster than she could dry them.

Without hesitation he said, "Annie, don't worry another minute about this. I will be happy to have both of the girls. What you need to do is talk to your lawyer and put this in writing before you have your surgery."

"Brian, you are so right. Thank you. I'm sure Tom would not approve of this."

He talked to her for a long time trying to calm her down and then he asked, "Would you like me to come and be with you for the surgery?"

"Brian, you were just here. How could you come again so soon?"

"I'll check with my squadron commander tomorrow and see if it is possible."

Annie had to reschedule appointments as she was supposed to be home for six weeks after the surgery. This was going to be difficult. She talked to Angela and she said she would be happy to help whenever Annie needed her. "Angela, what would I do without you?" She was so apprehensive she wasn't sleeping well at all.

When Brian called again, he said that he and Brett would be there on Sunday afternoon and gave her the flight number and time of arrival. He said he could just stay a week, but that would at least be a help. Annie was so relieved that he was coming. She was very frightened and she felt so alone. Facing the thought of cancer was terrifying. She knew she would have days of waiting and wondered if she could handle it. Not knowing was scary…

Friday morning she took the girls to day care and went to radiology for another mammogram. They placed tiny needles to pinpoint the lump before the surgeon could remove it. She had met with Dr. Bauer earlier, and he was going to do the biopsy. Rick had had great respect for Dr. Bauer and that was a comfort to her. She was so frightened when she was waiting for them to come in to do the biopsy. Her mind was racing with prayers and thoughts of her girls. She wondered what would happen to her if she had cancer. This was a terrifying thought.

When Dr. Bauer came in, he explained what he would be doing. Then they talked about his children she had done babysitting for several years before. After the surgery, he gave her a prescription for pain in case she needed it. He said it would probably be a week before they had the results of the biopsy. She got dressed and went back to work. *Perhaps work will help me think about something other than what might be wrong with me.* She had some files she needed to update and this was the last day she had to do it. As she worked, thoughts kept creeping into her mind about the biopsy and the tumor on her ovary. She was beginning to feel some discomfort when she picked up the girls. Pain medication tended to knock her out, and she thought she would just have to do without it.

She was putting the girls in the car when Katie said, "Mom, you have blood on your blouse, what happened?"

Annie explained to her that she had had a biopsy, and that she would see to it when she got home. "Katie, the doctor made a small cut and took a tiny lump out and sewed it back together. It is bleeding a little right now." She got home and put Betsy in the highchair and strapped her in. She asked Katie to give her some juice, some Cheerios and a banana, and just keep her in the highchair. She went up to see what was happening with the incision and why she was bleeding. After removing the bandage, she realized she had bled through the bandage and her clothes, and it was still bleeding. She cleaned herself and went down to get an ice pack and then went back up and crawled into bed. She used towels so she wouldn't bleed on everything and used pressure on the incision.

The doorbell rang and Katie called up and said she would answer it. Annie heard her say to someone, "Mommy is bleeding and she is upstairs trying to fix it." The next thing she knew there was Doug standing in the doorway of her bedroom.

He looked at her and said, "Why didn't you tell me what was

happening to you? You look like you might need a little assistance."

"How did you find out about this?"

"I was walking down the hall, when John Bauer asked me how you were doing, and I said, fine, as far as I know and asked him why?" He thought we were still seeing each other, and told me he had done a biopsy on you this morning.

Katie came in and said Betsy needed her diaper changed. Doug went to take care of her. "Did you get the bleeding stopped, Mommy?" Katie asked, looking very serious.

"I hope so." Annie dialed Angela's number and explained to her what was going on and asked if she could come and get the girls for a little while. She said she had supper ready in the refrigerator; it just had to be heated. She told Angela that she should be fine in a little while. Within minutes, Angela came over and took the girls to her house.

When Doug came into the bedroom again, he was very serious with her. "I just don't understand you at all. Why do you think you can handle everything by yourself all the time? Why can't you ever ask for help? You really make me angry." Annie didn't answer. She either felt ice melting or blood running and she wasn't sure which.

"Would you please get me another towel from the bathroom, since I can't get one myself?" He walked into the bathroom and there were Annie's clothes and bandage covered with blood on the tub.

He turned around and walked back into the bedroom and said, "Annie, are you still bleeding from your incision?"

"Doug, I don't know. I can't check it because you are here. I wish you would leave, I'll be fine." She was very annoyed with him.

"Annie, you have lost a lot of blood. Will you let me check your incision?"

"No, I think I've stopped bleeding now. Please just leave me alone and go home." She pulled the covers up under her chin and closed her eyes.

"I don't want to leave you here by yourself unless I know you are okay. If you won't let me check you, let me call John and have him come over."

"Just go downstairs and I'll see if I am okay. I don't need you to take care of me. You walk out on me every time things don't suit you, and I don't need that in my life." He turned around and went downstairs. She got up and put a bandage on the incision and got dressed and went downstairs. "I'm going to be fine. Thank you for coming by to check on me. I'm sorry I got so upset with you." Annie winced a little, and Doug asked her if she had pain medication to take.

"Pain medication tends to knock me out, Doug, I just can't take it. I can't be in that state and still be responsible for the girls."

"Would you like me to stay overnight?"

"No, Doug, I will be fine. Thank you."

Feeling weak, Annie sat down on the couch. "Doug, I need to tell you something before you hear it from someone else." She lowered her head and took a deep breath. She was quiet for a moment. She hoped she could say this and not be emotional.

"What is it, Annie?" He could tell she was having a hard time saying what she wanted to.

Her voice was shaky when she started to speak, "They found a tumor on my ovary the size of a grapefruit, and I'm having surgery to remove it on Monday morning." Tears were streaming down her cheeks. "I'm so scared." He sat down beside her and tried to comfort her.

"Oh, Annie, what can I do to help?"

"Brian and my mom are both coming for the surgery."

"Annie, will you please let me know if I can help you in any way. I wish you would have called me, at least I could have come over and we could have talked about this."

"Doug, you were angry with me when you left here the last time. You wouldn't stay and listen to me then, why do you think I would call you when I'm in trouble? I was in trouble then, and you didn't want to hear anything I had to say. I've been telling you for months that I was tired and had no energy and that I didn't feel well. I was crying that day because Brett hugged me and said he wished I was still his mom. That just breaks my heart when he says it and I was just too upset to tell you. I need someone to be there for me all the time, not just when it's convenient. I was really desperate that day, and I could have used a little care and compassion from you. That's why I didn't call you and tell you what was wrong with me. I'm sorry to be so blunt, but you asked." She could see that her words had moved him.

"Annie, I'll be happy to stay here and help you with supper and get the girls ready for bed."

"I'll be fine, Doug, but thank you for offering."

Doug got up to leave, then hesitated. "Annie, I wanted things to work out with us. I'm sorry they didn't."

She got up and stood by the couch and tried to steady herself before she took a step. "I'm sorry it didn't work out, too. You are a wonderful man, Doug. You've brought such happiness into my life. I'll just remember the good times." She started to walk and then sat down on the couch. "I think I do need your help, Doug. I know you are surprised that I would admit it, but I'm really weak." He sat down beside her and took her in his arms and held her as she cried.

"Oh, Doug, I'm so very frightened and I'm not coping very well with this by myself."

He held her and tried to calm her down. Doug explained to her that not all growths were malignant. He told her he would help her through this, if she would just let him. She relaxed in his arms.

"I have a casserole in the refrigerator and a salad already made. Would you put the casserole in the oven at 350, and go get the girls? Thank you from the bottom of my heart." She managed a weak smile.

Doug fed the girls, bathed them and put them to bed while Annie rested in bed. Annie was sorry she had been so unkind to him. He had been good to her and didn't deserve such treatment. She apologized to him again before he left.

Chapter Thirty-One

On Sunday afternoon Annie was feeling stronger and was able to go to the airport to pick up Brian and Brett. Her mom stayed with Betsy while she took a nap, but Katie was so excited that Brett was returning again so soon and she wanted to go and meet him. Brian drove the car home and was very quiet.

That night he knocked on her door and came in and sat on the bed. She had papers for him to sign about keeping the children if something should happen to her. Nervous about the surgery, she was on the verge of tears; Brian held her hand and tried to calm her. He asked, "What time do we need to leave in the morning to go to the hospital?"

"I need to be there by 6:00, so we need to leave here by 5:30 at the latest."

They arrived at the hospital and she was prepped for surgery and Dr. Gill came in and patted her hand.

"I'm going to have to put you out for this, Annie."

She smiled. "That's fine with me. I'm brave, but not that brave. Please don't take anything unless you have to, I don't know what the Lord has planned for me, but I would love to have more children."

The wait was agonizing for Brian. He went to eat breakfast and drank several cups of coffee while he waited in the surgical waiting room. He prayed and couldn't begin to think about what would happen if this was cancer. Dr. Gill came in and sat down beside Brian.

"Annie is in recovery and will be for a while. I removed the tumor and I had to remove her left ovary along with it. There was no way to save it. She will be able to have more children, if she wants. She was concerned about that. You can see her as soon as she is taken to a room. I've sent the tissue to pathology and we should have the report before the end of the week." Brian thanked him and went to find a telephone to call Annie's mom and his dad.

Hours later, Annie smiled at him when he walked in her room. He sat down in a chair beside her bed and held her hand. She was so groggy, her thoughts were very disjointed and she couldn't say what she was thinking. She slept until the nurse came in to check her. When she opened her eyes in the afternoon, Brian was still at her side. He told her he was going home to watch the children, so her mom could come to the hospital and see her. Several doctors came in to check on her, and finally at the end of the day Dr. Gill came in to see her. He explained to her what he had done; Annie thanked him in a soft voice.

She closed her eyes and was just drifting off to sleep again when Tom came in the room. He had a look of concern on his face. Annie knew he didn't like hospitals.

In a very groggy voice, Annie said, "What are you doing here?"

He came over and gave her a hug and said, "Little sister, I've been so worried about you and I came to see how you are doing and tell you I love you. I'm so sorry I have been so judgmental. I just want you to know that I have always wanted the best for you and I don't have to agree with all the decisions you make. I love you because you are the best sister anyone could have. I haven't liked these years that we haven't gotten along and it's my fault for being so critical of you. Can we just be like we were years ago? I have been so frightened that something would happen to you and that I couldn't live with myself if something did. Can you forgive me, Annie?"

She took his hand and tears were streaming down her cheeks. "Sure I can, Tom; thank you for coming to see me. I've missed having you in my life. You have been such a wonderful big brother and there has been a void between us for far too long." She hugged him as best she could.

That night she woke up and thought she was dreaming as she saw a man in a white coat with a stethoscope around his neck sitting by her bed. She was half asleep and for a moment she thought, *This is an angel sitting by my bed.* This thought made her wake up in a hurry, and then she realized it was Doug.

She whispered, "What are you doing here? You're supposed to be home asleep."

He took her hand and held it and said, "Tomorrow is my day off and I just wanted to see how you were doing." Annie drifted off to sleep again and when she woke up again he was still holding her hand.

Dr. Gill came in to see her very early in the morning and told her that her breast biopsy was negative.

She was elated. "With that news I think I'm ready to go home!"

He smiled and said, "Maybe tomorrow or the next day."

When Brian came in she told him the good news. He came over to her and kissed her on the cheek.

"You are looking good this morning, how do you feel?"

She said she had been up walking and she was really sore, but she was eating and she had had a bath—well sort of a bath. It was the best they could do right now.

Brian took her home the next day and Brett and Katie had made welcome home signs for her and get well cards. Annie's mom had lunch ready when they came in the door. Afterwards, Annie went up to her room and Brian put Betsy down for a nap. Brett and Katie went outside to play in the back yard.

The telephone rang and Dr. Gill said, "Annie, I have good

news. The tumor I removed is benign." Overjoyed, Annie told her mom and Brian the good news. Brian stayed in her room and said he wanted to talk to her.

"Annie, I've waited to tell you this, but I have some good news, too. I've been going to therapy for almost a year and the therapist thinks I'm fine now. I started going downtown right after I got the divorce papers from you. I think that shocked me into reality, and made me get my priorities straight." He looked at her with adoring eyes and continued, "Annie, I've never stopped loving you. I'm hoping you can find it in your heart to forgive me for all the things I've done wrong. Will you think about it?" They talked for a long time about the therapy and Annie had lots of questions for him.

Finally she said, "Brian, one thing I have never understood is why you would have a woman spend the night with you in your house with Brett there. Did you think he wouldn't notice?"

Brian looked puzzled and said, "Annie, I've never had a woman spend the night with me, what are you talking about?"

"Well, when Betsy was just a few months old and I had just gone back to work, you called me several times and woke me up. So, I called you early one Saturday morning and a woman answered the phone, she said her name was Bonnie. Please tell me, who was Bonnie?"

Brian smiled and shook his head. "Annie, we were in the middle of an inspection at the base, and Bonnie came to stay with Brett because I had to work all night. I got home early in the morning, and I asked her to wait for me to take a shower and change clothes before I took her home. Bonnie is a sixteen year old girl. She is the granddaughter of my regular babysitter who was sick at the time."

Annie couldn't believe what she was hearing. "Brian, that was the reason I filed for divorce! I thought there was no reason to try to work this out if you were having a woman spend the night with you. I'm so sorry, Brian. I should have talked to you about this." She was horrified at what she had done.

Brian moved up toward her on the bed and opened his arms to her. Annie hugged him and then they kissed. Brian held her for a long time and then he asked her if she could ever forgive him for everything that had gone wrong.

"I can forgive you, Brian, but I don't think I will ever be able to forget."

"I'm so sorry Annie, that I hurt you. I can't begin to imagine what you have gone through."

Then he smiled and said, "Can we try again? I've learned so many things in this year we've been apart. I miss your loving ways most of all. I feel so empty without you in my life. We have a beautiful family and I would be so happy to have us all together again. I will do everything in my power to make you happy. I love you, Annie, with all my heart."

When he kissed her again she said, "I've missed your wonderful kisses, Brian. I'd marry you again in a minute if I knew for sure that you wouldn't stray from me again. That is my only concern. I would love to be able to trust you, but I'm not sure I can. I just know that every time you would call and say you had to work late, I would have doubts creeping in. I love everything else about you. You are a precious man and I could sing your praises for hours because you have so many wonderful qualities. However, I'm not sure I could withstand another of your infidelities."

"I can promise you that will never happen again. Will you think about it, Annie?"

Annie slept for a while. When she woke up she started counting her blessings. *I have so many things to be grateful for.* That night after the children were bathed they all climbed in bed with her and she read to them. They all smelled so sweet and clean and she loved this time with them.

After Brian put them all to bed, he came back in to her and said, "That was a perfect picture of you with the children all around you. The only thing that would be more perfect is if I could be in there with you."

She smiled. "I think we would need a bigger bed."

"That can be arranged."

The next morning she came down for breakfast and Betsy was standing beside her dad holding onto his leg. She had loved to do this ever since she learned to crawl. When they finished breakfast Brian took the children outside and Annie sat with her mom drinking coffee.

"Annie, I can tell by the way he looks at you that he still loves you. It is so evident."

"I know, Mom, and I do still love him. He has hurt me so much and I just can't seem to get over what he did to me." She told her about her conversation with Brian. "I would really love for us to be a family again. We need each other now more than ever." Annie went upstairs to rest. A little later Brian came in and smiled at her.

"I still love your dimples after all these years, you have a beautiful smile."

He asked if she had thought about getting married again.

"Brian, I wish I could tell you I would, but at the moment I just can't. These last years have been worse than a nightmare for me. I just can't make any more mistakes. I love you and even though part of me wants to be with you, I don't feel comfortable saying I will marry you again. I'm sorry; I know this is not what you want to hear." They were both quiet for a few minutes. Annie looked in his eyes and saw such sadness.

The next morning Brian came in to tell her goodbye. "If you change your mind please let me know."

"You know I will. Thank you so much for coming and being with me through this crisis. I'm not sure I could have made it without you. You have been so supportive and wonderful to me. I wish things were different between us. I wish I could love you and trust you all at the same time." He hugged her and said he needed to go. Brett came in to hug her and tell her goodbye.

Annie's mom took them to the airport, and when she returned she said Brian was rather subdued when he left.

"What happened between you, Annie?"

"Mom, I just told him I couldn't marry him. I have already made that mistake and I don't want to repeat it. I don't know if I'll ever be able to trust him again, even if he does say he is fine."

Annie hired a woman to clean every week. Angela would help with the girls, especially with baths and getting them to bed. Annie wasn't supposed to lift anything for six weeks. She just did what she could and ignored the rest. She spent hours reading to the girls and tried to rest while they napped. She was gaining strength every day.

Chapter Thirty-Two

Tom called one evening during Annie's recovery; she was so pleased to hear from him. She couldn't remember the last time he had called her. He seemed very concerned about her and how she was doing. He told funny stories about Paul and Mike. She was so thankful to have him back in her life.

Katie was such a big help to Annie. She entertained Betsy and that was the biggest help of all. Just having an extra set of eyes to watch Betsy was great because she was always in to something. Annie couldn't turn her back on this child or she would have a mess to clean up. Betsy climbed up on everything and even moved chairs so she could climb to higher places. The only time she was still was when Annie read to her.

Brian called to see how Annie was feeling, but he sounded unusually solemn. They talked for a few minutes, and then he told her that he had an assignment to Vietnam for a year. He said he needed to make a will and was filling out forms and had stacks of paper work to do in preparation.

"Who will be keeping Brett?" was her first question.

Brian said his dad would be glad to have him stay with him. He was looking forward to having someone in the house with him. He was still very lonely without Sue. Brian said he had to go to water survival school and then he would be leaving in September. Brett would go to Iowa just before school started.

His dad was looking for someone to come early in the morning to get Brett off to school, so that Jon could leave for the hospital. Brian's mood continued to be somber. Annie knew he was concerned about leaving his son for a year.

Annie tried to cheer him up. "Brian, I would love to have him come here for a while next summer. You know Katie would love that, too. And you can be sure that I'll check on him while you are gone."

Brian thanked her. He was silent for a long time and then he said, "Annie, I need to ask a big favor of you. If something happens to me in Vietnam and I don't come home, would you be willing to raise Brett as your son? I know this is a lot to ask and I'll let you think about it for a while before you decide."

She didn't hesitate. "Brian, you know that I love Brett like he was my own son. I'm honored that you would ask me to do this for you. You were kind enough to offer to do the same thing for me."

Brian thanked her and with more emotion in his voice said, "Oh, Annie, I wish you were here, I really need you right now. I miss you so much." She could only imagine what he was going through...

Though Annie was going back to work; it seemed she was still in recovery. She was trying not to lift Betsy and that took lots of help from Katie. She had been walking with the girls to try to get her strength back, but she still tired easily. Working full time was going to be difficult. Fortunately, the cleaning lady would be able to come for an extra month. She just had to be thankful that she was healing and that she didn't have cancer. *Sometimes you just have to put life in perspective,* she would tell herself.

Meanwhile, Katie was enrolled in morning kindergarten. Annie would have to pick her up during her lunch hour and take her back to day care for the afternoon. It didn't seem possible that Katie was old enough for kindergarten. She was so bright and had a real zest for learning. Perhaps the reason she could recognize a lot of words was because the stories had been read to her so many times that she had memorized them. Annie knew that her daddy would be thrilled with his little girl, she was such a joy.

Annie was overwhelmed when she got back to work. There hadn't been anyone to fill in for her while she was gone. The appointments were scheduled for weeks ahead. She was encouraged; however, when she received a note from Mary Masters saying Bobby was in remission and gaining weight and was looking forward to going back to school and playing soccer. Annie was pleased to hear this. She would write him a note, if she ever got caught up on her work. She added this to her list of things to do.

On Annie's first week back, Mrs. Burton, the head nurse on ward five, asked her to come to the office. She told Annie that there was a cantankerous old man that had been admitted and he didn't like anything that was served to him. She said he wouldn't fill out the menus and the only things that he ate were the desserts.

She said, "Prepare yourself for Mr. Abbott; he was admitted with an infection in his leg and when they started cleaning the wound they were surprised it looked so clean. The reason it looked as good as it did, was because it was full of maggots. This old man lives alone in a log cabin and when a neighbor didn't see smoke coming out of his chimney, he went to check on him. He was in a debilitated state, confused and dehydrated. He has been very difficult to manage. He was in dire need of a bath, but didn't want anyone to bathe him. I'm telling you this so you can be prepared. Good luck. After you've seen him, please come back to see me."

Annie went to Mr. Abbott's room and knocked on the door; she heard a grunt. No one could have prepared her for what she saw. Mr. Abbott had a wild head of hair that looked like it had never been cut and a beard down to his chest. He had several missing teeth and the ones that remained were stained with chewing tobacco.

Annie couldn't help but smile at him. "Mr. Abbott, how are you doing?"

"Well, I ain't doin a hoe lot o nuttin since I bin here. What ya hair fer? Air ya one of em vampires that come and sucks blood outa me?"

Annie introduced herself and assured him that she was not here to take blood. She said she was here to see if she could find out what he would like to eat. "What do you usually have for lunch?"

He told her he ate the squirrels and rabbits he shot and fish he caught in the stream. "I hain't never seen soma at stuff they brings in hair fer me ta eat."

When she asked him about the menu that they brought in every day for him to check and he said, "I cain't read no menu, dearie."

"I'll get a menu for you, Mr. Abbott; tell you what is on it, and you can decide what you would like to eat. I'll be back in just a few minutes." Leaving the room, she saw her friend Paula at the nurse's station.

Paula smiled and said, "Who are you here to see?"

"I've been talking to Mr. Abbott, and I think I've found a challenge." Her eyes were widening and she was smiling.

"We all concur with that. We could write a book about Mr. Abbott, and he has only been here two days. I gave him an enema when he first arrived and it was fine for me to clean him out, but he wouldn't let me clean him up. He refused to let me give him a bath and, believe me, he hadn't had one in a very long time. He told me the last woman to bathe him was his mother. When it came to inserting a catheter in him, he made so much fuss I had to get the doctor to do it. Mr. Abbott has all of us tiptoeing around him."

Annie returned to Mr. Abbott's room with the menu and tried to explain what the foods were and how they were prepared. Since he was familiar with fish, she suggested he have halibut with mashed potatoes for his evening meal. He wasn't familiar with broccoli, which was included. Annie decided she would deal with vegetables at a later time. For dessert she suggested applesauce because of his teeth, or lack of teeth, but he told her, "I luvs em sweets, dearie."

"I will come in every morning and tell you what is on the menu, and then you can decide what you would like." She smiled at him and he gave her a toothless grin.

Annie returned to Mrs. Burton to tell her what progress she had made. She felt Mr. Abbott was definitely an unusual character, but that no one had taken time to understand his problem.

"Well, how did you do with Mr. Abbott?"

"The reason he's having trouble with the menu is because he can't read. I got him a menu for today and I've marked what he would like. I will come by every morning and help him make his selection." She thanked Mrs. Burton for the fair warning about Mr. Abbott.

Annie went every day to Mr. Abbott's room and tried to explain what choices were on the menu. Breakfast seemed fairly easy. He liked bacon and eggs, but he told her, "I'z had enuff of at saar stuff ina glass."

Annie assumed that it was grapefruit juice he was referring to. She asked about apple juice or orange juice, and he said he would try apple juice.

Lunch was a different matter. She explained that the kitchen didn't serve rabbit or squirrel, but they had chicken, pork, beef, and ham. He just stared at her. She tried to describe vegetables, and he understood potatoes and onions and carrots and that was all. He was not familiar with salad. They decided on ham and a sweet potato, and he seemed to be pleased with that.

The next morning he told her, "At sweet tater weren't sweet atal and I'z had enuff of em." The good news was that he was improving.

Katie came in one day and asked if she could take afternoon swimming lessons with Maggie, who lived down the street. After Annie talked to Maggie's mom, and they worked out a carpool, she enrolled Katie in the class. Katie was a bit timid at first, but after the first week she didn't want to get out of the pool. Annie had loved swimming since she was a little girl and was so pleased to see that Katie loved it, too.

Mr. Abbott seemed to look forward to Annie coming to his room every morning. His infection in his leg was improving, but he still was on IV antibiotics. She talked him into trying several different fruits and he said he liked them. He asked her one day if she would help him with the "gadgets" on the bed. He said that when he pushed the call button the bed moved. Annie showed him which control to use to make the bed move and which to use to call the nurse. He was really impressed. She let him try it for himself and he looked at her and said, "Uz jest as handy as uh pocket on uh shirt." She thanked him and was very amused when she left his room. *I'll have to remember that one.*

He asked her one day, "Why air they tryin ta feed me em worms?" She thought for a moment and almost laughed when she realized what he was talking about.

"Mr. Abbott, those aren't worms, that is spaghetti." He had no idea what she was saying. The decision to mark spaghetti on the menu was because she thought it would be easy to chew. Some days she felt like she was talking to someone from another planet who didn't speak the same language. Nothing she studied in school prepared her for Mr. Abbott. What a character.

When Mr. Abbott was going to be released from the hospital, Annie went up to his room to tell him goodbye. She was surprised to see him dressed in a new shirt and pair of pants. She wondered what had happened to his clothes he arrived in, but later learned they had been thrown away. He was not at all pleased that he was going to have to sit in a wheelchair and be wheeled out of the hospital. Social services had arranged for someone to pick him up and take him home.

He smiled at Annie and said, "Thank ye, dearie fur bein sa kind ta me while I'z heer." He offered his very gnarled hand; taking it, she smiled.

"I hope you do really well when you get home, Mr. Abbott."

One day after work she had an appointment with Doug for Katie to get her school physical. She hadn't seen him since her surgery, but had so much respect for him that she didn't want to request another pediatrician. Katie missed having Dr. Campbell read to her, and had asked why he didn't come to the house anymore. Annie was not sure how to answer this question, and just said she and Doug weren't seeing each other anymore.

When he called them into his office, Katie said, "I miss you reading stories to me; that was fun."

"It was fun, Katie; I miss it too." He checked her and then announced she could go to kindergarten. Finally turning to Annie, he said, "How are you doing?"

She said she was fine.

"You have two delightful daughters, Annie."

"Thank you, Doug; I really appreciate you taking such good care of all of us." She lowered her head and thought, *There is so much more, but right now I can't begin to put it into words.*

As she was driving home, she thought about Doug and his love for children. He had treated her girls with such kindness and affection. She had loved watching him with Katie. She hoped he would be a father someday and have children of his own.

Brian called and said he was bringing Brett to Iowa at the end of August, so he could enroll him in school before departing for Vietnam. He said he would like to stop and see Annie and the girls' enroute. Annie said she looked forward to seeing them. Brian seemed like a different person since he had received his assignment orders to Vietnam. Annie had done a lot of thinking about their relationship, and knew she needed to decide if things would ever work out for them. She knew she still loved him, and this is what made it so hard to decide. She wanted so much to trust him...

When she opened the front door, Brian and Brett were standing there; both of them looked beautifully tanned, healthy and handsome. It was a miserably hot day in Kansas and the wind was blowing. The girls came running to greet them and Brian picked up his daughter and hugged her to him. *Bless his heart; I know he is thinking about leaving her for a whole year.* Betsy hugged her daddy and kissed him and hugged him again. Annie asked if they would like to go swimming and everyone got excited and said yes. They all went to the nearby pool and cooled off.

Katie wanted to show everyone what she had learned in swimming lessons. She loved the water and was fearless. She thought swimming under water was such fun and loved jumping off the diving board to Annie. Brian had his hands full watching Betsy in the wading pool. Brett and Katie had a wonderful time together.

They went home and changed clothes and Brian said he would take them out for dinner. It was a fun evening and everyone was weary when they got back to the house. It was time for a bath and a story and then to bed. Brett wasn't sure he needed a bath since he had been swimming. Annie looked at him. "Typical boy! The girls never question taking a bath." He grinned and said he would go take a shower.

When everyone was asleep, Brian and Annie sat down to talk. Brian thanked her again for saying that she would take Brett if something happened to him. This was so difficult for Annie to think about. She didn't want to get emotional, for Brian's sake. She thought she was handling this well, when he added, "Annie, if something does happen to me in Vietnam, I want you to know that I died doing something that I love to do. I've dreamed of being a pilot since I was a little boy." She hugged him and tears fell on his shirt. Looking at his face she knew this was very difficult for him.

"I'm sorry hon, I told myself I wasn't going to cry, but I can't help it." Tears seemed uncontrollable. He offered her his handkerchief, but then he dried her tears.

"I have so much respect for you as a mother and it is only right that he be raised with his sister. He and Katie really get along better than most brothers and sisters ever do. They have always had a most unusual bond."

Annie asked him how he felt about going to the war. He said this is what he had been training to do since he graduated from pilot training, and he was ready to go. His only regret was that his family was fragmented and that was a real concern.

"I love you so much, Annie. Have you thought anymore about our relationship?"

"Brian, I think about it all the time. Your assignment has made me think about 'what if' and I've tried to do some soul searching. I have no need to ask myself if I love you, because I know that I do."

He pulled her toward him and took her hand in his. "I know, it's still a matter of trust," he said.

Brian kissed her. "What can I do to help you trust me? My therapist says that I am fine. I haven't been out with anyone since you left me. All I want is to have you back in my life and be married to you." He kissed her again.

Annie closed her eyes and thought for a moment. "There are times when I really want to get married to you again, and I get this warm wonderful feeling of happiness and then I think of you on the dance floor with that girl and I just turn cold inside. I just haven't been able to get past that. I'm working on it, Brian. I'm still healing from that horrible ordeal. You shattered my whole being when you did that. I see all your wonderful qualities, and I admire so many things about you, but I'm still very conflicted about our relationship. Maybe I should go see a therapist and get some help, since I seem to be the one with the problem. I tell myself that I have forgiven you; that you had a problem, but I guess I can't forget what you did. I'm sorry; I'm not trying to be difficult. I really think we could be happy, if only I could put this behind me. I'll work on it."

He was quiet for a long time. "Are you still seeing Doug?"

"No, I haven't seen Doug since I had surgery, with the exception of taking Katie in to see him for her school physical. Our relationship is over."

"I have another question for you; do you really think that we can get married again, can you see yourself married to me in the future?"

She smiled. "I sure hope so. I really loved being married to you. After Rick died, I wasn't sure I would ever be happy again. You came back into my life and I found so much happiness with you. I was content just to be with you and be part of your life. You made me feel loved and appreciated and cared for, and then it was all over in an instant. I just hope we can try again at some point, and I would never say this unless I really meant it. *My love for him is so strong. I do want to trust him.* "I'll talk to my friend Jerry Nicholson and see if he can help me."

Brian held her and kissed her and said, "Thank you, Annie. I'm more encouraged than I've been in a long time. I love you so much. Maybe when I get back from the war we can start a new life together."

Chapter Thirty-Three

The next morning started with a special request from Katie for poached eggs on toast and bacon. This was her new favorite breakfast and she loved to dip her toast in the egg yolk. Betsy tried to mimic her and did a pretty good job. Annie noticed Brian smiling at her attempt. Brett said he wanted his special request for tomorrow morning: "apple French toast." Annie looked at these three adorable children and was sad to think that Brian would be away from them for a year.

The children went upstairs to play and Annie cleared the table and then picked up her basket and said to Brian, "Come help me pick tomatoes. I have a bumper crop." She went out the door and down to the patio and turned on the soaker hose to water the plants while she picked.

"Good grief, Annie, you have enough tomatoes here to feed the whole block. What do you do with all of them?"

She said she used them in salads and sandwiches and made tomato sauce with fresh onions, garlic and basil which she put it in the freezer. He helped her pick and she said she would make bacon, lettuce and tomato sandwiches for lunch.

"I have steaks for you to grill tonight."

As soon as they got back in the house he put his arms around her. "Annie, thank you for opening your heart to me last night. I feel so much better about our relationship. I have renewed hope, and that is so important to me now." He kissed her and held her for a long time when suddenly a scream came from upstairs.

Unnerved, Annie laughed. "Don't worry. It's just Betsy. When she doesn't get what she wants, she isn't happy. She can make piercing screams and when you check on her you find out she is just annoyed. It is always so loud and urgent that I can't ignore her, but sometimes I wish I could." Brian smiled ruefully, and went to check on her.

It was another very hot August day and they decided they would go swimming again. It was too oppressive to do anything else. Betsy took an early nap and when she woke up they went back to the pool. Annie was able to spend some time with Katie and Brett in the pool. Usually it was spent with Betsy, but her dad had her today. She was pleased at how attentive Brian was with this precious daughter of theirs. She did take time to take some photographs of the children. She knew Brian would cherish them when he was away. Everyone was having such fun and Annie thought to herself, *this is the way life is supposed to be.*

They went home and had a great meal. Brett said steak was his very favorite and he could eat one all by himself...and he did. Annie made a salad with lots of tomatoes, and had enough tomatoes left over to send home with Brian for his dad. There was homemade peach ice cream for dessert. It was churning on the patio while they ate. There was nothing better than peach ice cream right out of the ice cream freezer.

Annie didn't want to be emotional in the morning when Brian and Brett left. She watched Brian put Betsy's nightgown on her and hold her in his arms, and it made tears come in her eyes. *How am I ever going to tell him goodbye without crying?* She read to the children, who were always exhausted from a day at the swimming pool. They were all ready to crawl into their own beds and go to sleep.

When she came downstairs, Brian opened his arms to her. She held him and put her head on his shoulder.

"I love you, Brian. I'm sorry that I haven't been able to get over the past, but I do love you for so many reasons. You still thrill my heart. I just wanted you to know that. I hope you always will. I'll be here for you when you return. Hopefully, I can heal my heart by then. We have wasted so much time." He held her for a long time and then they sat down and she lay in his arms and they talked and kissed.

The next morning, as soon as Annie opened her eyes, she dreaded what was coming. She never liked saying goodbye, but this would be a very difficult one. She prayed for composure and to have control of her emotions. She didn't want to make it difficult for Brian. They ate "apple French toast" and bacon for breakfast and Brett said it was yummy. Brian watched Betsy take every bite; he just couldn't take his eyes off her. *He is such a tender hearted soul.* She was so sensitive about Brian's feelings. They finished breakfast and Brian loaded the car. Katie and Brett were playing in Katie's room and Annie was changing Betsy's diaper when Brian came in and smiled down at her. "She should be potty trained the next time you see her."

Brian grinned at both of them. "We can only hope." He picked up Betsy and carried her downstairs. Annie went to wash her hands and took a deep breath to calm down. Brett and Katie came bounding down the stairs and Brian said it was time to load and go. While everyone was hugging, Katie and Brett were being silly, unwittingly making the whole process easier.

Brian hugged Annie and whispered, "I love you" in her ear. She told him she loved him, too. Betsy kissed him and patted his back and hugged him. Annie and the girls stood at the door and waved as they drove away. Annie swallowed hard to keep the tears from flowing and said a silent prayer for his safe return.

Sitting at her desk one morning, Annie received a call from a nurse asking if she knew a Mr. Abbott. When she said that she did, the nurse explained, "He is asking to see you; he is in Dr. Greenberg's office." When Annie opened the door to Dr.

Greenberg's waiting room, she saw Mr. Abbott sitting in a chair. She started walking toward him and as soon as he saw her he stood up, and when he did his pants fell down around his ankles. There was an audile gasp from the other patients in the waiting room. Mr. Abbott leaned down in his thread bare underwear and pulled up his pants. They were at least two sizes too large for him or he had lost a lot of weight. He was smiling from ear to ear at Annie and shook hands with her. "I'z sa glad tha found ya."

"How is your leg, Mr. Abbott? Has it healed properly?"

"Wall, tha sent ah nurse ta my place an she took reel good care uh me." When they called Mr. Abbott's name, Annie held his arm and helped him down the hall into an examining room. There was only one chair in the examining room and Mr. Abbott wanted Annie to sit in it.

"You need to sit in the chair, Mr. Abbott, you are the patient." He sat down and Annie stayed and talked to him until the doctor arrived. He asked if he could have her write her name down for him, so if he came again he would know who to ask for. She shook his hand and wished him well. She would always remember his toothless grin. *What a dear old man.*

Dr. Livingston called and asked Annie if she and the girls would like to come over and pick fruit. He said they had more than they needed and she was welcome to pick as much as she wanted. They would have a barbeque afterwards, he said, and Mr. Delgato would be there as well. He also wanted Annie to bring her recipe for plum and raspberry jam which they so enjoyed. Annie was delighted.

When they arrived at the estate the Livingston's welcomed Annie and the girls as if they were family. Mrs. Livingston took Betsy, and Katie saw the tricycle she had ridden. They had cleaned it up and brought it out just for Katie. It was almost too small for her, but she got on it anyway. They had already picked apples, pears and plums for Annie, but she went to pick some raspberries. Dr. Livingston walked with her to the raspberry bushes and told her he was so glad to see her looking so well. She told him about her surgery and said she was so thankful to be well again. When she heard Mr. Delgato's distinct voice, they returned back to the house to see him. He welcomed her with open arms. They all gathered for a delicious meal of barbequed chicken, baked beans and an assortment of salads and rolls. Mrs. Livingston had made an apple cobbler and she put a scoop of ice cream on it. This was such a relaxing afternoon for Annie. The girls were well behaved and she was very proud of them. After they loaded all the fruit in the car, Annie thanked them for a most enjoyable afternoon.

On the way home, Katie said she loved that place and wanted to go back. Annie told the girls that she was very pleased with them for being so well behaved.

Annie unloaded the fruit in the garage. The pears weren't quite ripe, so she spread newspapers on a shelf to put them on until they ripened. The plums were ready to eat and so sweet and juicy, the kind you needed to eat over the kitchen sink. She would have to make plum and raspberry jam right away. Some of the apples had bruises and she would make applesauce with them. *Sometimes, there aren't enough hours in the day.*

Chapter Thirty-Four

Katie looked forward to her first day of kindergarten. She would go to Maggie's house and Maggie's mother would take them to the school. Annie would pick them up at noon and bring Maggie home, and then take Katie back to day care. This schedule had worked better than she could have ever imagined.

Brian called to say he had finished water survival school, and he was leaving the U.S. in two days. He gave her his address and told her he loved her. He was using a pay phone and there was a long line of guys waiting to make calls, so their conversation was brief.

Annie sat down and wrote Brian a letter after the girls were asleep. She started thinking about how she would feel if something happened to Brian and she knew she would be devastated. She had an appointment with Jerry Nicholson the next week. She really hoped talking to him would help.

Annie got the pictures that she had taken at the swimming pool developed and put them in an album and wrapped them to send to Brian. She sat down every night and wrote him a letter. She couldn't wait to get home in the afternoon to see if she had a letter from him. She had loved getting his letters when they were in college, but these were different. These were love letters that touched her heart. One letter told her that being away from her "was like night that had no morning." Annie was deeply moved. Brian had become her incurable romantic.

Annie talked to Jon and Brett, who seemed to be adjusting very well. Jon said he didn't have time to be lonely anymore. Brett liked his teacher and was doing well in school. Jon had found a young woman to get Brett off to school, so he could go to the hospital at his usual time. Brett got on the phone excitedly reporting his latest accomplishment. "Grandpa Jon took off my training wheels and I get on my bike by the step and I can ride all the way down the drive by myself."

When Annie got to Jerry Nicholson's office he told her she looked so happy he wasn't sure she needed to see him.

"Jerry I do have some things I need to talk through with you. I originally made this appointment because I was very conflicted about Brian. I know that I love him, but I have never dealt well with his infidelity. I just can't seem to get beyond that. There is still this lack of trust that I can't seem to get past. The fact that he has gone to Vietnam has made me more aware of the fact that I probably love him even more than I thought I did. I have done some serious thinking about us. We have always had a wonderful love for each other, get along really well, and he is a great father. I know he has been through a year of therapy and he says the doctor says he is fine. I really want to trust him. This is what I need help with." Jerry asked her several questions and they talked for the rest of the time about love and trust and their relationship. Jerry gave her two books to read and said he would see her in two weeks. Annie was encouraged when she left and hoped her heart would heal. She wanted so much to trust this man that had touched her so deeply.

On Katie's fifth birthday, Annie invited six of her friends from the neighborhood and kindergarten class for ice cream and birthday cake. Katie was pleased to open her presents. The best was all the Barbie doll clothes. Annie's mom came down to spend the weekend with them and help celebrate. Having their grandma come was always a special occasion.

Annie read the books Jerry Nicholson had given her. The first one was about forgiveness, which Annie found very helpful. The other one was about relationships, but most of them didn't pertain to her situation. When she returned to see him she told him, "If Brian asked me to marry him tomorrow, I would say yes. I put myself in all sorts of hypothetical situations and think what if Brian wanted to marry someone else, what would I do? I just can't bear the thought of it. I have just tried to think positive thoughts and let that horrible night go away. I think I'm making progress. Part of the progress may be that I miss him so very much and he hasn't even been gone three months." The doctor encouraged her to forgive Brian, and said he thought she would be able to work through the problem. He told her he thought she was making real progress and seemed optimistic.

"Trust will come, Annie; you just need to let it happen."

Annie and the girls went home for Thanksgiving and had a most enjoyable four days. The girls played with their cousins and had a great time. Julie came by to see her and said she and Ben were getting married in June. She asked Annie to be her matron of honor. Annie and Julie talked for hours one evening. It was impossible to get caught up on everything that had happened.

Chapter Thirty-Five

The Christmas tree was up and decorated, and Betsy was being very good about leaving the ornaments on the tree. She would stand and look at it, but not touch. Maybe they were making progress.

Jon and Brett were having a great time. Jon sounded young again. He had so much energy and Brett was enjoying all the attention. Brian was pleased to hear this news. Jon had asked if he and Brett could come for the weekend after Christmas, and Annie said she would be thrilled to have them. She thought they were starting a tradition.

After spending Christmas at the farm, Annie returned to get ready for Jon and Brett's visit. She prepared food and put it in the freezer. Hopefully this would allow her more time to visit and not spend all her time in the kitchen.

The weekend with Jon and Brett was such fun, even though it made her miss Brian even more. When Annie told Jon this, he smiled and said, "I hope that is a good sign." She told him it was.

One evening at the end of January she turned on the news just when the broadcaster announced, "A cease-fire accord ending the Vietnam conflict has been signed in Paris. The agreement calls for withdrawal of U.S. troops from South Vietnam, release of U.S. prisoners held in North Vietnam, and a four-nation commission to supervise the truce." This sounded too good to be true. Would Brian be coming home? She sat there stunned and could hardly believe what she had heard. She called Jon to see if he had heard the same thing. She wanted to know more. Jon said they would just have to wait and pray that Brian would be coming home very soon. Annie was filled with so much hope and excitement that she couldn't sleep very well that night. She prayed for his safe return.

Emily came over for a short visit on the weekend and Annie talked to her about Brian. "I want so much to trust him. I'm in a real turmoil over the decision to try again. It isn't a question of love." Annie told her she had gone to see Jerry Nicholson and that had helped, but nothing was resolved. "I'm to the point now that I love him so much that I can't imagine being without him, so I have to trust him."

Emily broke out in a smile and said, "I think you have the answer to your problem with that statement."

"Oh! I hope so, Emily. We've wasted so much time."

A week went by and all the letters Annie got from Brian were written before the cease-fire announcement. Then one night after she had just gone to bed the phone rang and it was Brian. He told her that he had just landed at Hickam Air Force Base in Hawaii and that he was going to be in California the next day.

"I want to come and see you, Annie. Is that okay?"

"Brian nothing would please me more! I miss you so much." This was an answer to her prayers.

Brian told her he didn't have reservations to Kansas City, but he would get them the next day and give her a call. She was so thankful that he was on his way home and that he would be with her in a day or two.

Annie could hardly keep her mind on her work. She picked up the girls from day care and went to the grocery store and then went home and cleaned the upstairs. She could clean the downstairs after the girls went to bed. Brian called while she was mopping the kitchen floor and said he would be in at 9:45 the next evening. He had talked to Jon and Brett.

The next day she called Angela to arrange for her to keep the girls while Annie went to the airport. The whole day seemed to drag. Annie picked up the girls and told them that Brian was coming that night, and she would go and get him while they were asleep. When they woke up in the morning he would be there. They were both excited.

When Annie arrived at the airport, the flight had been delayed because of weather. Sitting down on a bench, she started thinking about Brian and all they had been through. She had endured a rollercoaster of emotions because of him. There was a magic between them that had thrilled her heart, but he had also hurt her beyond belief. Since that time, her painful memories had faded and her love for him had grown even more profound. He had such wonderful qualities that she loved about him, especially the gentleness and compassion he had for the children. When he looked at her and smiled, it moved her beyond words, she hoped that feeling would never go away.

Finally, the plane was coming into the gate. As each person came out of the gate she looked to see if Brian was behind them. When Annie first caught a glimpse of him, she seemed frozen in place. He was wearing civilian clothes and looked incredibly handsome. She wanted to run toward him, but just stared at him as he walked toward her. He grabbed her and kissed her and kissed her again. She felt as weak as a newborn kitten. They walked hand in hand down to the baggage area; she just wanted to look at his face. He looked weary to her, but wonderful.

"How long can you stay?"

"I have two weeks of leave" he replied. The luggage finally arrived and they went to the car.

When they got in the car, Brian started the engine and then said, "We need to catch up on kisses, Annie." He smiled at her with those beautiful dimples and pulled her next to him.

"I'll never get caught up on your kisses," she told him. They got home and he asked if she was too tired to talk. She looked up at him and said, "After being away from you for six months, I could stay up all night if that's what you want." He pulled her into his arms. She fixed them hot chocolate while Brian ate some cookies. They sat down and he asked her if she had made a decision about trusting him. He took a deep breath, and his eyes were on her with anticipation,

"Brian, I love you so much and I don't want to live without you, so I'm just going to have to trust you. I have had plenty of time to think about this, and that is my decision."

"My next question is will you marry me?"

She was glowing when she said, "And my answer is, yes I will!"

They kissed for a long time; catching his breath, Brian said, "Annie, you couldn't have made me any happier if you had tried. I love you."

"I want to grow old with you, Brian."

"That is a really nice thing to say, I'm glad you feel that way. Forgiveness is a wonderful thing; I want to thank you again for having it in your heart to forgive me for everything I have done to hurt you. There were times when I wasn't sure this would ever happen."

She was quiet for a long time and Brian said, "What's on your mind, Annie?"

"I'm going to have to call Tom and tell him that we are getting married. I really dread doing it."

"I'm sorry I've caused this problem between you and your brother."

"This is not going to be an easy phone call to make." She suddenly felt exhausted.

"I'm sorry, hon."

"I'll call him tomorrow; it will give me time to think of what to say." She yawned and stood up. "We need to get to bed, it is late. In the morning you can sleep in. I'll come and get you when

I pick up Katie from kindergarten. We can go get our blood test."

When they went upstairs, Brian stood outside her bedroom door and asked, "May I sleep in your bed?"

"Just as soon as we are married."

He held her and kissed her and told her he loved her. "How can you resist the temptation?"

"Believe me, it is not easy."

The next day Brian talked to his dad and Brett to give them the big news. Jon said they would come down on Friday night. Annie called Reverend Habersham to arrange for the wedding on Saturday morning. Annie told him that it would be a very small wedding with three children and perhaps a few family members.

When Annie sat down to call her mom she was almost giddy with excitement. "Mom, I have some wonderful news for you, Brian flew in last night from the west coast; he asked me to marry him and needless to say, I said yes. He has two weeks of leave, and Reverend Habersham will marry us on Saturday at 10:00. I hope you can come. I know I am babbling, but I'm thrilled to pieces."

"You sound so happy, Annie. I'll be there. Have you talked to Tom?"

"No, I haven't. I know he won't be pleased, but I will call and talk to him. Do you think he will come?"

"Paul has a basketball tournament this weekend. His team has won all of their games and this is the championship. I doubt if they will be able to come. You know how involved he is with his boys." They talked for a long time. Finally, her mom said, "It is wonderful to hear you sound so happy, honey."

When Tom answered the phone, she took a deep breath. He was pleased to hear from her and asked how she was. "Oh Tom, I'm happier than I've been in a long time." She couldn't control her emotions and then added, "Brian and I are getting married on Saturday morning at 10:00. He just returned from Vietnam and asked me to marry him. I love him very much. I'm not asking for your blessing, I just wanted you to know. Mom told me that Paul has a basketball tournament. I didn't realize that they were undefeated. That is great. I know you are proud of him."

Tom sounded kinder than Annie had expected. Perhaps the talk of the basketball tournament had helped soften the tone of the conversation.

"Annie, I want you to be happy. Brian is very lucky to have you. I just hope that you have made the right decision."

Annie was so thankful that Tom had been kind to her; she seemed to relax as he was talking to her. He told her all about the basketball games leading up the championship. She ended the conversation with, "I love you, Tom. Please let us know who wins and give everyone a hug for me."

Annie had talked to Dr. Gaston and told him she would be leaving and that she was getting married. Brian didn't have an assignment yet, but expected to hear where he would be going very soon. She said she would be happy to work as long as she could. She thanked Dr. Gaston for being so supportive of her and helping her through so many difficulties in her life. She told him that she really appreciated all his help and understanding. She also called the realtor she had used before and said she needed to put the house on the market.

When they went to get the girls at the day-care center, Betsy saw her daddy and squealed and ran toward him. He had peeked in on her the night he got there, but he hadn't held her yet. She was talking up a storm, amazing her father, who held her tight.

The girls had darling dresses that they had received for Christmas from their grandma; they would be perfect for the wedding. Annie wasn't sure what she was wearing. She never had enough money to buy clothes for herself; she just wore what she had. Brian didn't have to worry, he would wear his uniform.

They went shopping after Annie finished work and Brian kept up with the girls while Annie tried on dresses and suits. She finally found a wool dress with a jacket in royal blue. Brian thought she looked gorgeous. They needed to get Betsy a pair of shoes. Her feet were growing faster than she was. She loved everything she tried on and wanted them all. When they stopped at a restaurant before they went home, Annie declared she was going to be spoiled, but she would try really hard to get used to it.

Annie worked on Friday and when she got home Brian was preparing supper.

"What would I do without you?"

He held her close and said, "I don't ever want you to find out."

Annie was getting the girls ready for bed when Jon and Brett arrived. His reunion with his dad was so moving. Jon seemed so relieved to have Brian home. Brian was like the pied piper with all three children following him everywhere, watching his every move.

Jon was concerned, as there was a snowstorm predicted for Saturday evening. After the wedding, they would all go to lunch together, and then he needed to leave right after lunch to get back to Iowa. Brett would return with him and go back to school until Brian got an assignment.

Brian sat down with Annie and said, "Honey, we will have a proper honeymoon, I promise you. I just don't know when it will be."

She kissed him. "Brian, the main thing is that we're getting married and I'm so happy to have that decision made and feel it is the right thing to do. I'm content to have you here and very thankful that you returned safely from the war. We are very blessed."

When Elizabeth arrived the next morning, she looked lovely in a new burgundy wool suit. Annie was combing Katie's hair and Grandma helped Betsy get into her dress. The girls were precious in their dresses and acted very grown up. They drove to the church where Reverend Habersham was waiting for them. Katie stood beside her mom, Brett stood beside his dad and Betsy hung on to her daddy's leg. After they said their vows they turned, and Jon took a picture of the whole family.

They went to an Italian restaurant for lunch. The children loved it when the waiter came around and put red checked bibs on everyone. This amused Katie, to think that adults had to wear bibs. The waiter definitely had an Italian accent. He was joyful and very playful with the children. They loved all the attention. Jon took numerous pictures of this, also. Jon and Brett said their goodbyes and returned to Iowa, hoping they would beat the snowstorm. Annie hugged her mom and walked her out to the car, then returned to the house with a smile on her face.

When she started to put Betsy down for a nap, she didn't want to take off her pretty dress. This took gentle persuasion. Her behavior was improving, but Annie wasn't sure it would last with "the terrible twos" fast approaching. She asked Brian if he was a well behaved child and he just grinned at her and said he didn't remember.

"I'll have to remember to ask your dad the next time I see him and get the real story about you." There were so many things to do if they were moving, but Annie decided she would worry about that tomorrow and sat down beside Brian and snuggled with him on the couch.

When Betsy woke up she told her daddy, "Come see what I can do in the potty." Annie said they were making great progress, and she was sure that with daddy's praise she would do even better.

Annie was putting Betsy's shoes on when she saw Brian coming down the hall with his clothes. He gave her one of his sweet smiles with a bit of devilment in his eyes and said, "I'm not sleeping in the guest room anymore. I'm moving into your bedroom."

He had the cutest expression on his face and she told him, "I'm happy that you are."

Brian went to get pizza and buy milk before the storm hit. Annie cut up a salad and they sat down to eat as soon as Brian returned. He had gotten one pizza with everything including anchovies, and when Betsy got one of these in her mouth she shuddered and closed her eyes tightly and said, "Mommy, I can't like it." Brian was having a hard time not laughing out loud at her. Annie picked the anchovies off the pizza and Betsy continued to say, "I can't like it."

Katie asked, while making a horrible face, "What are these things, Mom?" Annie explained that they were tiny fish and Katie's response was, "I'm glad they don't get big, these are awful."

When they had finished eating and the girls left the table, Annie said to Brian, "See what you have been missing." He took her in his arms and kissed her and told her the main thing he had been missing was her.

Then he whispered in her ear, "How soon can the girls go to bed?" She loved him so much. His impishness had always amused her.

The snow was coming down and the wind was blowing. The weatherman had predicted over a foot of snow. Annie was just glad the storm had waited until that night. She bathed Betsy, and Katie took her shower and they crawled in her bed to have a story read to them. This was their routine and they all looked forward to it. Brian sat on the bed and listened to the story and looked lovingly at Annie as she read to the girls. Annie put the girls to bed and came back to her bedroom. Brian had his arms outstretched to hold her. She kissed him and said, "Thanks for being so understanding, I love you so much." *Sometimes you need to stop and do something that purely delights you!*

Chapter Thirty-Six

The next morning was bitterly cold, but it was a beautiful winter wonderland. The temperature was below zero, and until it warmed up there would be no playing outside. Annie cuddled next to Brian; it was so cold she didn't even want to get up and turn up the heat. The girls were still asleep and she told Brian to enjoy the quiet because it wouldn't last long. It felt so wonderful to be snuggling next to him again. "I missed so many things about you and this is definitely one of them."

When Betsy woke up it was time to start the day. Annie went to get her and turn up the heat, and then they came back to snuggle with Daddy. When Katie came in to get in bed with them Brian said they had a whole family of snugglers.

Annie fixed scrambled eggs and bacon and they all ate and watched the snow blow by the window.

Annie said, "I'm just glad I don't have to go to work today." Betsy got down from the table and told her daddy she wanted him to take her to the potty. He was praising her all the way. They spent a quiet morning of drinking coffee and reading the paper while snuggling under a blanket.

Brian said, "I had almost forgotten how nice it is to do nothing and just relax."

Annie thought how wonderful it was just to be with him. "I'm sure this is exactly what you needed. Maybe the snowstorm was a blessing."

Later that afternoon the sun came out and the wind stopped blowing. Brian got the snow shovel out of the garage and cleaned the driveway and the steps.

"You don't know how much I appreciate your help. I've had to do this so many times. I know it is grueling work."

They watched TV coverage of the storm and it looked like Monday was going to be a "snow day." The drifts were so high that it was taking the snowplows a long time to clear the main roads. They hadn't even started to clear the residential areas. Annie looked at Brian teasingly and said, "I think I can handle another day with you. This has worked out better than I could have ever planned."

Tuesday morning, Annie went back to work. Brian was up early and had backed her car out of the garage and was warming it up for her. Betsy wanted to stay home with her daddy. Annie called the day-care center to see if that would be okay and they said that some of the caregivers were unable to get to work because of the snow, so that wasn't a problem. Brian said he would fix lunch when she brought Katie home from kindergarten, so they could all eat together. Annie wished she didn't have to go back to work. It would be great just to stay here with the family. As she was putting on her coat, Brian came over and kissed her.

Katie and Maggie were waiting to be picked up in front of the school after kindergarten. The high, imposing drifts of snow made it difficult to maneuver the cars to get the children.

As they opened the door to the house, a rush of cold air came in with them. This made the hot lunch that Brian had fixed even more inviting. Katie hurried up to her room to change her clothes, suddenly they heard a shriek. She came running down the stairs, extremely upset. "Mom, you won't believe what Betsy has done in my room. She has gotten into my Barbie things and dumped everything out on the floor. It is a horrible mess." She then turned to Betsy and said, "You know you aren't supposed to play in my room when I'm not home. Why did you do it?"

Betsy was sitting still in her highchair looking very somber. She narrowed her eyes and lowered her head and said, "I wanted to."

Brian was looking concerned and a little sheepish. "I asked her when she went in there if she was supposed to play in Katie's room and she said it was okay." All three were staring at Betsy. Betsy knew she had done something very wrong and started crying.

"Sorry, Katie," she whimpered.

They ate lunch, and when Brian was washing Betsy's hands she dissolved in tears. Annie looked at her watch and said she needed to get back to work.

"You will have to deal with your daughter. She knows what she has done wrong." Katie was distressed because Betsy was crying and also that her room had been trashed. Annie kissed her and said she would help straighten up the mess when she got home. "Betsy will help too, since she is the one who made the mess." That said, Annie kissed Betsy and Brian, who looked like he wished *he* could go back to work.

Pulling into the driveway after work, Annie saw Brian and the girls playing in the snow. The sun was out, but it was still cold. There were three snowmen in the yard and they had been sledding, she could see the tracks of the sled runners in the snow.

The house was warm and inviting and Annie was ready for a cup of tea. The girls and Brian wanted hot chocolate. They sat around the table and talked. Katie informed them in a very matter of fact voice, "I have already started picking up some of the mess in my room while Betsy took her nap."

When they all went up to view the catastrophe, Betsy was extremely timid with everyone looking at the mess she had made. She put her head down and put her arms up for her mother to take her. She was on the verge of tears. She put her head on Annie's shoulder and was silent. Annie whispered to her, "I think you need to sit down here beside me and help pick up this mess."

There was a tiny whisper in her ear from Betsy, "Okay."

All four of them sat down and Katie started to tell everyone where things went. Brian couldn't believe all the tiny things that Barbie had. Betsy was very subdued; she helped, but she knew she was in a heap of trouble.

That night when Annie was getting Betsy ready for bed, she asked her if she had learned her lesson. She was very quiet, but nodded her head. "You know now that you aren't supposed to go in Katie's room and play when she is not here?" She nodded again. "And when your daddy asks you if it is okay for you to play in Katie's room, what do you say?"

Her eyes got big and she said, "I'll tell him no." Annie hugged her.

Brian looked exhausted when Annie came downstairs. She sat down beside him, and he put his arm around her. "I don't think I did very well on my first day at home with Betsy."

"You did fine; she can be a real handful at times. I talked to her tonight, and she knows what she did wrong. She gets very upset when she realizes she is in trouble."

"I noticed that."

"She is doing so much better than she did when she was younger. Progress is wonderful, and this little one isn't even two, yet." She moved closer to Brian. "It is wonderful to have you here with me. You don't know the many nights I wished you were here. You make me feel that all is right with the world when I am next to you."

The next morning while they were still sitting at the breakfast table the phone rang and it was for Brian. He talked for a few minutes, asked several questions, and wrote everything down on a piece of paper. When he finished, he smiled at Annie and said, "Annie, how would you like to live in England for the next three years?"

"That sounds wonderful! I've always wanted to go to England. When do we leave?"

Katie had never seen her mother so excited. "Can we come, too?" It seemed a fair question.

Printed in the United States
85867LV00004B/37/A